The Calamity Café

A Down South Café Mystery

GAYLE LEESON

AN OBSIDIAN MYSTERY

OBSIDIAN
Published by New American Library,
an imprint of Penguin Random House LLC
375 Hudson Street, New York, New York 10014

This book is an original publication of New American Library.

First Printing, June 2016

For more information about Penguin Random House, visit penguin.com.

ISBN 978-1-101-99078-0

Printed in the United States of America
10 9 8 7 6 5 4 3 2 1

Designed by Kelly Lipovich.

Penguin
Random
House

To Tim, Lianna, and Nicholas

Chapter 1

&I took a deep breath, tightened my ponytail, and got out of my yellow Volkswagen Beetle. I knew from experience that the morning rush at Lou's Joint had passed and that the lunch crowd wouldn't be there yet. I put my letter of resignation in my purse and headed inside. Homer Pickens was seated at the counter with a cup of coffee. He was a regular . . . and when I say *regular*, I mean it. The man came to the café every morning at ten o'clock, lingered over a sausage biscuit and a cup of coffee, and left at ten forty. It was ten fifteen a.m.

"Good morning, Homer," I said. "Who's your hero today?"

"Shel Silverstein," he said.

"Good choice." I smiled and patted his shoulder. Homer was a retiree in his late sixties, and he chose a new hero every day.

You see, when Homer was a little boy, he noticed his

daddy wasn't around like other kids' daddies. So he asked his mom about him. She told him that his dad had died but that he'd been a great baseball player, which is why she'd named him Homer. When Homer was a teenager, she'd finally leveled with him and said his father hadn't been a baseball player . . . that he'd basically been a bum . . . but that Homer didn't need a father to inspire him. Heroes were everywhere. Since then, Homer had chosen a new hero every day. It was like his inspiration. I looked forward to hearing Homer's answer to my question every day I worked. When I was off from work, he told me who his hero was the day I asked plus the day I'd missed.

I could sympathize with Homer's desire for a heroic father figure. My dad left Mom and me when I was four. I don't really remember him at all.

"That apple tree? The one he wrote about? I have one like it in my backyard," Homer said. "I cherish it. I'd never cut it down."

"I'm sure the rain we've had the past couple of days has helped it grow. You bring me some apples off that tree this fall, and I'll make you a pie," I told him.

My cousin Jackie came from the back with a washcloth and a spray bottle of cleaner. She and I had waitressed together at the café for over a year. Jackie had been there for two years, and in fact, it was she who'd helped me get the job.

My mind drifted to when I'd come back home to work for Lou Lou. I'd just finished up culinary school in Kentucky. Nana's health had been declining for the past two or three years, but it had picked up speed. As soon as I'd graduated, I'd come home and started working at Lou's Joint so I could be at Nana's house within ten minutes if I was needed. I was only biding my time at first, waiting for a chef's position to come open somewhere. But then Nana had died. And, although I knew I could've asked her for a loan to open a café at any time, I wouldn't have. I guess I got my streak of pride from my mother. But the money Nana had left me had made my dream a reality—I could open my café and stay right here at home.

"Morning, Amy!" said Jackie. "Guess what—Granny says she has a new Pinterest board. It's called *Things I'd Love to Eat but Won't Fix Because What's the Point Anyway Since I Don't Like to Cook Anymore.*"

I laughed. "I don't think they'd let her have a name that long."

"That's what I figured. It's probably called *Things I'd Love to Eat*, but she threw that last bit in there hoping we'll make some of this stuff for her."

"And we probably will."

Jackie's granny was my great-aunt Elizabeth, but Mom and I had always just called her "Aunt Bess." Aunt Bess was eighty-two and had recently discovered the wonders of the Internet. She had a number of Pinterest boards, had a Facebook page with a 1940s pinup for a profile pic, and trolled the dating sites whenever they offered a free weekend.

Lou Lou heard us talking and waddled to the window separating the kitchen from the dining room. She had a cigarette hanging from her bottom lip. She tucked it into the corner of her mouth while she spoke. "Thought I heard your voice, Amy. You ain't here for your paycheck, are you? Because that won't be ready until tomorrow, and you ain't picking it up until after your shift."

"That's not why I'm here," I said. "Could we talk privately, please?"

"Fine, but if you're just wanting to complain about me taking half the waitresses' tips again, you might as well not waste your breath. If it wasn't for me, y'all wouldn't have jobs here, so I deserve half of what you get."

Jackie rolled her eyes at me and then got to cleaning tables before Lou Lou bawled her out.

We deserved *all* of our tips and then some, especially since Lou Lou didn't pay minimum wage and gave us more grief than some of the waitresses could bear. That's why I was here. Lou Lou Holman was a bully, and I aimed to put her out of business.

Speaking of daddies, Lou Lou had been named after hers—hence the Lou Lou, rather than Lulu—and according to my late grandmother, she looked just like him. He'd kept his hair dyed jet-black until he was put into the Winter Garden Nursing Home, and afterward, he put shoe polish on his head. According to Nana, he ruined many a pillowcase before the staff found his stash of shoe polish and did away with it.

Lou Lou wore her black hair in a tall beehive with pin curls on either side of her large round face. Her eyes were blue, a fact that was overpowered by the cobalt eye shadow she wore. She shaved her eyebrows, drew thin black upside-down Vs where they should have been, and added false eyelashes to complete the look.

Today Lou Lou wore a floor-length blue-and-white

floral-print muumuu, and she had a white plastic hibiscus in her hair just above the pin curl on the left. She shuffled into the office, let me go in ahead of her, and then closed the door. I could smell her perfume—a cloying jasmine—mixed with this morning's bacon and the cigarette, and I was more anxious than ever to get our business over with. She sat down behind her desk and looked at me.

I perched on the chair in front of the desk, reached into my purse, and took out the letter. As I handed it to her, I said, "I'm turning in my two-week notice."

"Well, I ain't surprised," she said, stubbing the cigarette into the ashtray. "I heard your granny left you some money when she passed last year. I reckon you've decided to take it easy."

"No. Actually, I'd like to buy your café."

Her eyes got so wide that her false eyelashes brushed against the tops of her inverted *V* eyebrows. "Is that a fact, Amy?"

"Yes, ma'am, it is." I lifted my chin. "I'm a good cook—better than good, as a matter of fact—and I want to put my skills . . . my passion . . . to work for me."

"If you think you can just waltz in here all high and mighty and take my daddy's business away from me, you've got another think coming," said Lou Lou.

"If you don't sell to me, I'm going to open up my own café. I just thought I should give you fair warning before I do."

Lou Lou scoffed. "You've got some nerve thinking you can run me out of business. You bring on the competition, girlie! We'll see who comes out ahead."

"All right." I stood. "Thank you for your time. I'll be here tomorrow for my shift."

"Don't bother. I'll mail you your final check."

"I'll be here," I said. "I don't want any of the other waitresses to have to work a double on my account."

"Suit yourself. But don't be surprised if I take the cost of putting an ad in the paper for a new waitress out of your salary."

I simply turned and walked out of the office. I knew that legally Lou Lou couldn't take her ad cost out of my pay. But Lou Lou did a lot of things that weren't right. I figured whatever she did to me in retaliation for my leaving wasn't worth putting up a fight over . . . not now. I'd pick my battles.

I'd also pick my wallpaper, my curtains, my flooring, my chairs, stools, and tables, my logo . . . My lips curled into a smile before I'd even realized it.

"Bye, Homer! Bye, Jackie!" I called over my shoulder on the way out.

"Bye, Amy!" They called in unison.

I went to the parking lot and got into my car. I glanced up at the sign—LOU'S JOINT—as I backed out into the road. The sign was as sad and faded as everything else about this place. If I could convince Lou Lou to change her mind, I'd start with a brand-new sign . . . a big yellow sign with DOWN SOUTH CAFÉ in blue cursive letters. I wanted everybody to know what to expect when they walked into my café—Southern food and hospitality.

I could do so much with this little place. Sure, I could also build a new café, but if I did, I'd also have to buy all-new equipment, get the building wired and up to code, and basically spend a lot of extra money I'd rather save if at all possible. Besides, Lou's Joint was one of only two restaurants in town, and it was really close to my house—a definite plus once winter rolled in.

When I got home, I went straight to the kitchen. Rory, my little brown wirehaired terrier, met me at the door and followed me. Princess Eloise, the white Persian cat, barely looked up from her post in the living room picture-window sill. I bent and gave Rory kisses and then I got his box of dog treats. We play hide-and-seek with the treats before he eats them. Of course, they're in plain sight, but we act like they're hidden.

I scattered the treats in the foyer, hallway, and living room, repeating the word "Hide" each time I dropped one. When I placed the last treat on the marble hearth in the living room, I called, "Seek!" Rory sprang into action, backtracking to find all the treats.

This bought me a good five minutes to wash my hands and get started on an oatmeal pie. Oatmeal pies took a while to make—even when I had a frozen pie crust like the one I was using today—but they were worth it. Nana used to make them. Especially if I was feeling down, I could walk into her house, smell that oatmeal pie baking, and know that everything was gonna be all right.

I took my pie crust out of the freezer and preheated the oven. I got a small mixing bowl, put four eggs in it, and set it on the counter while I gathered the rest of my ingredients.

Lou Lou was right about my nana leaving me some money. The estate had been settled for quite a while, but I didn't want to rush to spend my inheritance. I'd wanted to wait until I was absolutely sure I knew what I wanted to do.

Nana had a fairly sizable estate, or at least, sizable by Winter Garden, Virginia, standards. I'd always known my grandparents had money, but I hadn't realized how much Nana *did* have until she was gone. Of course, she'd bought me my car when I'd graduated high school, and it was brand-new then. I'd been impressed, but I'd thought maybe she'd been saving up for that for a long time. I'd been driving that little car for ten years now, and it was still going strong.

I smiled to myself, remembering the day she'd taken me to buy that car. We'd had to go all the way to Johnson City, Tennessee, but the dealership had given us Virginia sales tax on the vehicle. And the salesman had nearly fainted when Nana had paid cash!

I cracked the four eggs into the bowl and beat them until they were frothy. In a larger bowl, I mixed together sugar, cinnamon, flour, and salt. I then added the eggs. As I was pouring in the corn syrup, my phone rang. I'd placed the phone on the counter and could see that it was Sarah calling. She was one of my best friends. I hesitated, but when the oven clicked, indicating that it had reached 350 degrees, I let the call go to voice mail. I'd get back to Sarah as soon as I got the pie into the oven.

Sarah and I had become close when we were in elementary school, and we'd stayed that way. Her family was like one of those perfect television families. I used to wish I had a big family like hers, and whenever I said something along those lines, she'd assure me that I did—I had her family.

And I had Mom and Nana. They were wonderful.

Mom and I had lived in a smaller house on Nana and Pop's property. Despite her parents' abundance, Mom had taken as little from anybody as possible. She'd wanted to earn her own way, and she certainly had done that. And of course, Jackie and I had always been more like sisters than cousins, especially since Jackie had never known her dad and her mother had left her with Aunt Bess when Jackie was sixteen.

I poured the oatmeal mixture into the pie shell and slid it into the oven. Then I called Sarah.

"Hey, girl," she answered. "Did you throw down on the Big Bad Boss yet?"

"Yeah." I groaned. "Lou Lou was *not* happy when I offered to buy her café."

"I'd have loved to have seen the expression on her face!" Sarah laughed. "So . . . plan B?"

"I guess so. I'm nervous about it. It'll take longer than having a place that I only have to redecorate," I said.

"But starting from the ground up, you can get exactly what you want."

"That's true . . . but it's kinda scary."

"I'm sure it is, Amy, but you'll know what you're getting every step of the way," she said. "And you can afford to go with all-new stuff . . . good stuff!"

I laughed. "That's true. But I have to be smart. I won't have my salary to live on while the new place is being built. I gave Lou Lou my two weeks' notice. She didn't want me to come back at all, but I said I wouldn't do that to the other waitresses."

"Well, honey, it's not like you were making a fortune in that place."

"I know . . . but what will I *do* to keep from being

bored out of my mind while I'm waiting for my café to be built?"

"You'll help build it," Sarah said. "I've known you all your life. I can see you jumping right in there with your hammer and nails."

"You've got a point there. Plus, I'll be getting my permits and all that. Do you think we can get the construction done before winter?" I asked. "How long does something like that take?"

"I'd say it'll take four to six months . . . and it's June . . . so, yeah, you can be ready by winter."

I sighed. "Will people wait that long? I so wanted to go in, take over Lou Lou's place, shut down for a week or two for redecorating, and then have a grand opening on Independence Day."

"People won't wait," she said, "but they'll gladly leave Lou's Joint for something better as soon as that option becomes available to them."

"You're right," I said. "Come over after work and have some oatmeal pie with me."

"Is that what I smell?" she teased.

"Mmm-hmm."

She giggled. "I'll be there!"

"Want some fried chicken, biscuits, and mashed potatoes with gravy to go with it?" I asked.

"I'd be satisfied with just the pie . . . but I wouldn't hurt your feelings by not eating chicken and biscuits."

"Good. I'll see you after work, then."

Sarah was Billy Hancock's administrative assistant. In Winter Garden, that meant she was the secretary, bookkeeper, and paralegal to the town's only attorney-at-law. Billy was about fifty-five years old and had taken over the business from his father, William. Being the only lawyer in town, Billy had plenty to keep him busy, but not so busy that he couldn't play golf in Abingdon with his friends two afternoons a week. He handled just about everybody's wills, estates, divorces, and misdemeanor charges. Not that everybody got divorced or had misdemeanors in Winter Garden, for goodness' sake . . . but there were enough to earn Billy a darned good living, and by extension Sarah too.

I closed my eyes and inhaled deeply. The aromas of the vanilla, cinnamon, and oatmeal were divine. I remembered standing on a chair at Nana's side watching her make her oatmeal pie at our house one Thanksgiving morning. Nana was strong and sturdily built, and I must've been only around five years old, because I felt tiny at her side. She was patiently explaining the pie making step by step. At the time, all I cared about was "Can I lick the spoon?" Now I'd love to have the opportunity to live that day over . . . to take in every detail, every loving nuance of her oatmeal pie preparation. But as the author of *Our Town* warned, reliving a day gone by might prove to be too painful.

I opened my eyes and wondered briefly if Thornton Wilder had ever been Homer's hero. I'd have to try to remember to ask Homer.

The pie still had a good thirty minutes to bake, so I went into my fancy room. My fancy room had once been my mother's bedroom. After Pop died, Aunt Bess moved in with Nana. After Nana died, Mom moved in with Aunt Bess. And then when Aunt Bess started getting forgetful— as in, accidentally leaving the stove on—Mom left her job as a sales associate for a retailer in Bristol to look after Aunt Bess full-time.

Nana's house was the biggest house in town, which wasn't saying a lot for the rural community. There were houses in Abingdon and Bristol that would make Nana's house look small in comparison. Most people in Winter Garden lived in farmhouses or small ranch houses. The people of Winter Garden were generally hardworking and proud. The majority thought it was beneath them to take handouts of any kind, and some lived a meager existence because of that.

Nana's house was situated on a hill so that a person could sit on the wraparound front porch and see the entire town of Winter Garden. The house hadn't been built until the early 1980s, when my grandpa had quit working in the coal mines and he and Nana moved here from Pocahontas.

After Mom had moved in with Aunt Bess, I'd remodeled her bedroom. Two of the walls were lined with oak bookshelves—not plasterboard, but real oak. My friend Roger was a construction worker, and he'd built them. There had always been the understanding that Roger would build my café if and when I decided to build. Before I'd given my notice to Lou Lou, I'd spoken with Roger to make sure he could work me in.

Roger had been friends with Sarah, Jackie, and me since we were children. In fact, I'd always thought he and Jackie would make a good couple.

In the center of the fancy room floor was a white velvet fainting couch, and I grinned every time I looked at it. The piece was just so girly and luxurious, and I loved it. I kept the door closed and didn't let Princess Eloise into this room at all for fear that she'd sharpen her claws on the legs of the couch. It was hard to slip off from Rory, though, so I'd wound up putting a doggie bed beneath one of the windows so he could visit if he missed me when I was in the room. He generally liked to be by my side always. Princess Eloise could take me or leave me. She was Mom's cat, but Mom couldn't take her to live with Aunt Bess because Aunt Bess was allergic. So Princess Eloise tolerated me. When Mom came over, she was like a different Persian.

Off to the side of the fainting couch, I had an over-stuffed peacock blue chair with a matching ottoman. There was a floor lamp beside the chair, and when I'd curl up on the chair to read, it was like its big old arms just wrapped around me. I kept a pink-and-blue paisley throw on the ottoman. I had one of those old-fashioned rolltop desks at the window looking out onto the side yard. It too was oak, and I kept stationery supplies in it. I particularly liked personalized stationery, and Nana had made it a point to get me some every Christmas. Ever since seeing the old black-and-white movie *Rebecca*, I'd thought personalized stationery was the pinnacle of class. So what if the title character had turned out to be less than classy? She still had nice stationery.

Rory had long since found all his treats and was in a blissful sleep in front of the living room sofa, so I closed the door behind me when I went into the fancy room. I slipped my sandals off and stretched out on the fainting couch with my laptop. I checked Aunt Bess's Pinterest boards. One of my favorites was *Lord Have Mercy*. On that board, Aunt Bess pinned things that were, in her opinion, in need of grace: weird photos of celebrities, crime stories, strange phenomena, and multiple body piercings.

I'd been surfing the Web for several minutes when the phone rang. I didn't recognize the number that came up on my screen.

"Hello?"

"Yeah, Amy, hi. It's Pete Holman. How you doing?"

Pete was Lou Lou's son. He was several years older than I was, so I hadn't known him until I started working at Lou's Joint. Pete was nice enough, but he tended to be on the lazy side—did just enough to get by and didn't take much pride in his work. He'd always kinda struck me as an overgrown kid. Pete was a skinny balding man of forty who still lived with his momma and tried to pretend to her that he didn't have a girlfriend . . . because Lou Lou would definitely not have approved of the thirty-year-old woman Pete had been seeing. In fact, I doubted she would have approved of anyone Pete dated. Lou Lou liked keeping Pete under her thumb.

"I'm fine, Pete. How are you?"

"I'm all right. Momma told me that you offered to buy the Joint."

"I did. I imagine she also told you that she flat-out refused to sell it to me," I said.

"She did say that, but I believe I've got her talked into changing her mind."

"Really." It wasn't a question. It more like a nicer way of saying, *Fat chance*.

"Yeah. You see, she ain't as young as she used to be . . . and, well, I ain't either, for that matter. I never did want to spend my life slinging hash. Uh, not that you wouldn't enjoy it and all—that ain't what I'm saying," he said. "It's just, I'm saying I'd prefer a life on the open road. I want to drive a truck."

"Well, good for you, Pete. I hope that works out for you." I had a hard time buying what he was saying, much as I would have liked to.

"Thank you. I appreciate that, Amy. I really do. But, of course, for everybody to get what they want, Momma has to sell the Joint, right?"

"Um . . . okay."

"So I reminded her of how she's always wanted to go to Hawaii," Pete said. "She could take some of that money you're paying her and take right off, couldn't she?"

"I think that would be wonderful," I said. *For her and for everybody in Winter Garden . . . especially if Lou Lou decided to stay in the islands.* I had a vision of Lou Lou eating pupu, and I had to stifle a giggle.

"So you come on to the Joint right after closing tonight. I'll have Momma there, and the three of us will work out all the details. I'll even try to have Billy Hancock there to draw up the contract."

"Tonight at closing?" I asked, feeling my hopes rise, even though I knew better. "Can't we discuss the sale tomorrow morning?"

"No, Amy. We don't want Momma to have the chance to change her mind."

"I understand that, but—" The oven timer went off. "I have to go get my pie before it burns."

"See you tonight, then?" he asked.

"See you then."

It was a balmy night and, since it had stopped raining, I had my windows down as I drove to Lou's Joint. I'd had my fill of good food and fun conversation, and I was feeling content. Sarah had stayed until just about an hour ago. We'd played a game of Yahtzee and had gone back to the drawing board on the existing café renovations, and we'd also dreamed about where I could buy land to build a new café and how it would look if tonight's deal fell through.

Sarah and I both felt as if this deal was more about Pete's hope that he could talk his momma into selling than any actual budging on Lou Lou's part. I'd worked for Lou Lou Holman for just over a year. She didn't budge. On anything. So I wasn't particularly optimistic about Lou Lou selling to me, but I had a plan B.

I pulled into the parking lot. The only other vehicle there was Lou Lou's old silver van. I wondered why she didn't get a nicer, more reliable car. The van seemed to be in the repair shop more than it was out. Despite having money, Lou Lou was stingy. Nana had once said that if you were really quiet, you could hear all the little Lincolns screaming in Lou Lou's pocket because the woman pinched her pennies so tightly.

I got out, locked the car, and walked up to the door. It was a cloudless night, and the moon was a waxing crescent. Nana used to tell me that when the moon looked like that, it was pouring out water . . . meaning it was going to rain again soon. A warm breeze blew, rustling the leaves of the sugar maples grouped on both sides of the café. I heard wings flap overhead. I shivered, wondering if it was a bat or a great horned owl. Either would scare the dickens out of me.

I quickly tried the door. The CLOSED sign had been turned toward the glass, but the door was unlocked.

Grateful, I slipped inside. All the lights were off except the one in the back.

"Lou Lou! Pete! It's me, Amy!"

I waited for one of them to come out and wave me on back into the office. I actually hoped that they'd come out, flip on a light, and we could meet in here either at the lunch counter or at a table. I didn't relish the thought of being confined in the stuffy, smoky office with Pete and Lou Lou.

No one answered, and no one emerged from the office. "Hello!" I headed toward the back. I'd simply suggest that we move into the dining area to give us all a bit more space. Come to think of it, I hadn't seen Pete's truck parked outside. Maybe Lou Lou had called off the deal, and he hadn't even bothered to come.

When I reached the office, I saw that Lou Lou was slumped over the desk. "Lou Lou, are you all right?"

She didn't look up.

I stepped closer and patted her arm. "Lou Lou?"

That's when I noticed the blood dripping from the desk pad onto the floor.

Chapter 2

I hurried over to my boss. "Lou Lou, you're bleeding!" I eased over to the desk and put an arm around her. "Here, sit up."

She was nonresponsive, and I wasn't strong enough to move her by myself. I gave her a little shake. "Lou Lou, come on."

I placed my index and middle fingers on her left wrist, but I was unable to find a pulse. I thought it was probably weak because she was unconscious.

I took out my phone and dialed the sheriff's office. It occurred to me that if someone had come into the café with the intention of robbing the place and had knocked Lou Lou out, he might still be here.

"Sheriff Billings's office," answered a woman's voice.

"Hi. I'm Amy Flowers. I'm at Lou's Joint, and something has happened to Lou Lou, the owner. I need for you to send somebody over here right away."

"Okay. You stay put until they get there."

"I will. Please hurry!" As I ended the call, I wondered where Pete and Billy Hancock were. One or both of them should've been here by now. I heard a hoot coming from the large maple tree at the corner of the parking lot, and it sent a shiver down my spine.

It didn't take Sheriff Billings long to get to Lou's Joint. He'd been sheriff here in Winter Garden for the past ten years. When he and his deputy got out of their car, I hurried to the front door to meet them.

"I don't know if somebody broke in and hurt Lou Lou or what," I said. "She's in her office."

He nodded toward the kitchen. "Down that back hallway there?"

"Yes, sir."

"I'm going to go on to the office and have and look around. You stay here with Deputy Hall."

I turned from the tall, lanky sheriff to his deputy—a younger man with an athletic build. He had dark brown hair and brown eyes, and his muscles strained the fabric of his tan shirt. I hadn't seen him before.

"Could we please step outside?" I was shaking and on the verge of hyperventilating.

"Sure." Deputy Hall—R. Hall, according to his nameplate—took out a notebook and pen as we stepped just outside the door. "Could you please give me your name and your account of what happened here from the time you arrived until the time you called the sheriff's office?"

I was surprised his voice rivaled the timbre and depth of that of Sam Elliott.

"I'm Amy Flowers. Lou Lou's son Pete called me this afternoon and asked if I could be here tonight to meet with

him, his mother, and their attorney—Billy Hancock—
about buying the café."

He looked around the parking lot, obviously noting
that the only cars around were mine, Lou Lou's van, and
the police cruiser. "Was Ms. Holman the only person here
when you arrived?"

"As far as I know."

"Was she the only person inside?"

"She's the only one I saw."

"All right," he said. "Walk me through your arrival."

I told him how I'd gotten here and been surprised that
no one except Lou Lou seemed to be at the café. "And
then I walked through the café to the office and found
Lou Lou slumped over her desk."

"Did you call out to her?"

"Of course. When she didn't answer, I asked if she was
okay, and then I noticed the blood. I went over and tried
to get her to sit up, but she didn't answer me, so I called
you guys."

"All right. That's all the questions I have for the moment,
but I'd like for you to wait here with me until the sheriff
comes out."

The owl hooted again, and Deputy Hall glanced up
at the tree.

"That owl make you nervous too?" I asked with a
shaky grin.

"No, Ms. Flowers. I'd like to wait until we get an assess-
ment of Ms. Holman's condition before you leave."

"I was just kidding."

The ambulance—siren blaring and lights flashing—
pulled up beside the police car. The driver hopped out and
addressed Deputy Hall.

"Where's the patient?"

Deputy Hall held open the door. "Straight back and down the hall to the . . ." He looked at me.

"Left," I supplied.

"The sheriff is with her. I'll let him know you're here." He called Sheriff Billings on the radio clipped to his belt and told him the EMTs were there.

I heard the sheriff's reply. "No need to send them in. I'll be out in a minute. I've called Ivy Donaldson. She's on her way."

Deputy Hall relayed the information to the ambulance driver. "I think Sheriff Billings would appreciate it if y'all would hang around until he talks with you."

A black Buick sedan sped into the lot and stopped nearby without bothering with a parking space. Billy Hancock stepped out. Billy had looked the same for as long as I could remember—steel gray hair, light blue eyes, and black-framed glasses that were always sliding down on his long nose.

"I'm Billy Hancock. What's happening here?" he asked Deputy Hall.

"May I ask why you're here, sir?"

Deputy Hall already knew why Billy was here. He was confirming either Billy's story or mine—I wasn't sure which.

"Pete Holman called me and asked me to meet him, his mother, and Ms. Flowers—hello, Amy—at Lou's Joint for a meeting. I had a flat tire and was delayed. First of all, it took the tow truck a good twenty minutes to get to me, and then Wilma had to come and get me, and I had to take her home and then bring her car here."

"Where's Mr. Holman now?" Deputy Hall asked.

"I don't know. Isn't he here? What's going on?"

"No, Mr. Holman's not here, and something has happened inside the café."

"Oh, well . . . I'll call him." As Billy fished his phone out of his pocket, he said, "Congratulations on your decision to open your own café, Amy. I hope you know that I'll help you with the legalities. I won't even ask you to pay a retainer first . . . but, of course, you can if you'd like."

"The phone call?" Deputy Hall reminded.

"Yes, sure." Billy pulled up his contacts and called Pete Holman. "Pete, it's Billy. Where in blazes are you?"

Deputy Hall whispered, "Don't tell him anything's wrong. We don't want him alarmed while he's driving."

"All right," said Billy to Pete. "See you when you get here." He frowned at Deputy Hall. "He misplaced his car keys. Now would you please tell me what's going on?"

"When Ms. Flowers arrived, she found Ms. Holman slumped over her desk. Ms. Holman was bleeding."

Billy gasped. "That's awful. Is she going to be all right?"

"I don't think so."

The sheriff joined us then and confirmed Deputy Hall's suspicion. Lou Lou Holman was dead.

"What?" I asked. "Are you sure?" My head was spinning, and I staggered.

Deputy Hall put a hand on my back. "Are you all right?"

"Are you sure?" I repeated to the sheriff.

"Positive," he said.

The sheriff had turned to go talk with the EMTs when Pete arrived in his souped-up 1992 brown Ford Ranger. Why would anyone soup up a 1992 Ford Ranger, you ask? Who knows? Who knows why Pete Holman did anything he did?

Like Billy, Pete didn't park. He simply stopped the truck and got out.

Sheriff Billings had turned back around when Pete pulled into the parking lot. Now he met Pete halfway. "Pete, I need you to stay calm."

Pete looked at me, his eyes already wild. "Amy?"

I shook my head. I didn't want to be the one to tell him something had happened to his mother. I closed my eyes momentarily, fighting a wave of nausea.

Sheriff Billings took Pete gently but firmly by the shoulders. "I'm sorry to tell you this, but your mother is dead."

Pete looked stunned. "What? She's dead? What happened? Did she have a heart attack or something? I've told her she needs to take better care of herself."

"We don't know what happened yet," said Sheriff Billings. "But we aim to find out exactly what happened to her."

"What do you mean, you aim to find out what happened?"

"Because your mother didn't die of natural causes."

"Then what kind of causes *did* she die of?" He looked from the sheriff to the deputy to me and then to Billy. Poor Pete. He was grappling for answers, and no one really had any.

"I'm sorry, Pete, but it appears that somebody killed

your mother. That makes Lou's Joint a crime scene, Pete, and we're going to have to shut the café and its perimeter down for a day or so to be able to go over it thoroughly. Were you a joint owner of the café?"

"I guess," said Pete. "I don't know if my name was on anything or not, but I helped run the place." He looked dazed.

"Well, then, when you're permitted to return to the café, I want you to see if anything's missing. If there is, then please call us first so we can see whether or not we have the item in evidence. If not, then your mother's attacker likely took it."

Pete's brows drew together. "What do you mean, when I'm *permitted* to go back in? I want to go in now. I wanna see Momma."

"I'm afraid you can't go see her yet, son. The only person we can allow into the café at this time is Ivy Donaldson, our CST. I could have Ivy take a photo of your mother and bring it back outside so you can confirm that it *is* your mother in there. Would that be all right?"

"Y-yes, sir." He wobbled, and if Sheriff Billings hadn't been holding to Pete's shoulders, I think he would've fallen.

"Let's have a seat in my car and have a talk," said Sheriff Billings. "It doesn't look like your mother had either the front or the back door locked. Did she usually leave them unlocked?"

I didn't hear Pete's reply, since they'd opened the door and sat down in the police cruiser by then.

A blue convertible pulled into the lot and parked neatly beside my yellow Bug. Someone had a clear head even in the midst of a crisis—it was bound to be Ivy. I knew Ivy from her visits to the café. She didn't come in often, but when she did, she typically ordered a burger—no mayo, extra pickles—and fries.

In her mid-thirties with shoulder-length auburn hair and gray eyes, Ivy was a no-nonsense kind of person. She got out of her car, nodded toward Ryan, Billy, and me, and then went to the driver's-side window of the sheriff's car. She leaned down and talked with Sheriff Billings for a moment, returned to her car, and opened her trunk. She pulled on white coveralls with a hood and took what looked to me like a toolbox out of the car. I supposed it was some sort of medical kit.

Ivy came over to the door of the café. "Hey, guys. How're you doing? You found the victim, right?"

I nodded.

She placed the back of her hand against my cheek. "Your skin isn't clammy. Do you feel dizzy or anything?"

"Not anymore. If anyone is in shock, it's Pete," I said.

She nodded. "Hopefully, Sheriff Billings can prevent that." She took a pair of surgical booties out of her pocket and put them over her shoes before going inside.

I looked at Deputy Hall. "May I please go home now?"

"The sheriff or I might have a couple more things to discuss with you," he said.

"What about me?" Billy asked. "Unless you think you might need an attorney, Amy."

"No, Billy, I'm fine."

"You may go, Mr. Hancock," said Deputy Hall. "But please make yourself available if the sheriff and I have any questions for you in the next couple of days."

"Will do." Without a backward glance, Billy hurried to his car—or, rather, his wife's car—and left.

"So what else do you want to know?" I asked Deputy Hall.

"You said Pete called you this afternoon to set up this meeting. Why didn't Ms. Holman call you herself if she was interested in selling?"

"I don't know. I thought the idea of selling was more Pete's idea and that he was trying to talk her into it. As a matter of fact, I figured my coming here tonight was a waste of my time. I'd talked with Lou Lou about selling me the Joint earlier today, and she'd made it clear she had no intention of doing so. I told her that I'd open my own café somewhere else."

Deputy Hall scribbled in his notebook. "And you don't think her son could've made her reconsider?"

"It's possible—he said he'd played the Hawaii angle . . . Lou Lou always wanted to go there—but even if he'd convinced her to sell, I can't imagine her selling to me."

"Why's that?"

"Because she knew I wanted the café. She'd rather have had someone buy it and bulldoze it than sell to me. That's why I thought I was wasting my time with the meeting. But I was trying to be optimistic."

"Didn't Ms. Holman like you?" he asked.

"She thought I was an upstart . . . that I was trying to get above my raising."

"Care to explain that?"

I winced and tried to choose my words carefully. I didn't want Deputy Hall to agree with Lou Lou. "I went away to school because I wanted to become a professional chef. When my nana got sick, I came back home and took a job here to be closer to her. My house is only about ten minutes away from this place. Anyway, I took a job as a waitress. I made what I thought were helpful comments about the food and things I thought would help the café be more successful, but . . ."

"But Ms. Holman thought that you were trying to get above your raising," Deputy Hall finished after I'd trailed off. "Got it."

"Right. Plus, she thought the only people who needed to be cooking were her and Pete. And I knew I could do a better job. I didn't come right out and tell Lou Lou that, but I offered time and again to take a shift in the kitchen."

"When you threatened to open a café somewhere else—"

"It wasn't a threat, Deputy Hall. I *am* going to open my own café."

"Okay. But Ms. Holman saw that as competition."

"I guess. So what? Is there anything wrong with good, friendly competition?"

"Not so long as it's friendly," he said.

"If you're asking me if I came in here and knocked Lou Lou in the head—or whatever it was that happened to her—I can assure you I did not. I found her slumped over her desk and called the sheriff's office immediately."

"Duly noted." Deputy Hall held up his notebook to indicate that he had my statement written down.

"Is there anything else?" I asked.

"Not for now." He took a card from his back pocket. "Please call me if you think of anything else you think we should know."

I took the card. "Thank you. I will."

"And be careful going home. That owl could still be lingering around, you know."

I ignored his feeble attempt at humor and left.

When I got home, I was exhausted. It wasn't all that late, but the only thing I wanted to do was get into bed and read until I fell asleep. The trouble was that as I tried to read, I kept playing the evening over and over in my head.

I remembered walking into the office and seeing Lou Lou . . . her colossal beehive almost all the way to the other side of her cluttered desk.

Had she *really* changed her mind about selling to me? I found that hard to believe . . . unless the café was in financial trouble and Pete had been able to convince Lou Lou that he didn't want to work in the café for the rest of his life.

The café *could* be in financial trouble. Neither Lou Lou nor Pete had given much thought or care to their preparation of the food. And Lou Lou almost always had that cigarette hanging on her lip, even while she cooked. I never ate at the Joint, and neither did my friends. It was never terribly crowded. Let's face it—the place was a dive. Had I been able to buy the place, I'd have had to do a lot of PR work to raise the café's reputation to the point where most people—other than the regulars who had eaten there out of habit for so long—would even give me a chance. Maybe it was best that I start from scratch. Like Sarah had pointed out, I could choose everything from the ground up and know exactly what I was getting that way.

*   *   *

I awoke the next morning to Rory licking my face. I groaned. Couldn't he go out the doggie door? It opened onto a fenced yard where he could play and do his business without making me get up.

I reluctantly opened my eyes. "Rory, please. Not this morning. I got almost no sleep last night. Please just let me stay here for a few more minutes."

He whimpered.

I rose up onto my elbows, finally realizing what was wrong with the dog. Someone was at my door. I got up and went to the window. I didn't recognize the car that was in the driveway. Of course, that could possibly be attributed to brain fog.

"Coming!" I called, as I slipped on a robe and hurried to the door.

When I opened it, I saw Homer Pickens standing on my front porch.

"Morning, Homer." I'd known Homer pretty much all my life. He'd always worked odd jobs, and he did some interior painting for Nana the summers after Pop had died. But I'd never known him to just make a social call.

"Morning, Amy. I went by the Joint, but there was crime scene tape all over the place. I couldn't even get into the parking lot."

Last night came rushing back. "Yeah . . . something happened there last night, and they're having to close for a day or two."

"It's ten after ten," said Homer.

"Okay."

"Would you please make me my sausage biscuit?"

"Sure." I moved back so Homer could come on inside. Dealing with Homer's breakfast was a lot easier than coping with what had happened at the café last night. I felt a wave of sympathy for Pete and wondered if Ivy had found anything to tell the police who Lou Lou's killer might be. "Lucky for you, I went to the grocery store day before yesterday and stocked up. So, who's your hero today?"

"Winston Churchill. One of his quotes reminded me just this morning that 'A pessimist sees the difficulty in every opportunity; an optimist sees the opportunity in every difficulty.' It was a good thing I saw that."

"Yeah, I guess it was. I'm going to preheat the oven for the biscuits, and then I'm going to get dressed. You can make yourself at home here in the living room until I get back."

"Thank you, ma'am."

Chapter 3

I quickly dressed and hurried back out to the kitchen. I started a pot of coffee and got to work making the biscuits. By the time the oven light went off to let me know it had finished preheating, I had the biscuits ready to go in. I also had some sausage patties on hand.

"Homer, come on in here to the kitchen, and I'll pour you a cup of coffee." I was still surprised he'd come to my house, but I was also a little glad. Cooking always helped take my mind off my worries, and I sure had a bushel of them this morning.

"Thank you." He ambled into the kitchen. "May I wash my hands, please?"

"Sure." I nodded toward the sink before getting two cups out of the cabinet. "The soap's right there beside the sink, and you can dry your hands on a paper towel." I poured coffee into the two cups. I put Homer's cup on the table along with sugar and creamer. I added fat-free

vanilla creamer to mine and a packet of natural sweet-
ener. That's one thing I wanted to do with my café—offer
most of the items as usual but have some healthier choices
on hand too.

Homer washed his hands and sat down at the table while
I fried the sausage patties. "I see you have some coffee too.
Are you going to have breakfast with me?"

"I thought I would, if that's okay with you."

"That's plenty okay," he said. "I like having breakfast
at your house. The dog is sweet, your kitchen is clean, and
you're even going to eat with me."

I didn't want Homer to think this was our new every-
day routine. "The café should be open and things should
be back to normal tomorrow."

"Oh." He looked crestfallen as he added two heaping
spoonfuls of sugar to his coffee.

I went to the stove and flipped the sausage patties
before turning back to Homer. "May I share a secret with
you?"

"Of course. And it will go no further. My mother
always taught me to be trustworthy."

"I'm going to open my own café. I wanted to buy Lou's
Joint." I sighed. "It looks like that's not going to happen
now. But I'm going to build a new café somewhere nearby."

"That's wonderful news! One of Churchill's famous
sayings dealt with the fact that not enough people see
private enterprise as a healthy horse pulling a sturdy
wagon."

"Okay." I wasn't quite sure what Homer meant by that,
but I supposed it was a good thing. I returned to the stove
and saw that the sausage patties were ready. I put them on

a plate and set them aside. Then I got the biscuits out of the oven. I put one of the patties on a biscuit, put the biscuit on a small plate, and set the plate in front of Homer. "Is there anything else I can get you?"

"No, thanks." He bit into the biscuit and then closed his eyes.

I placed the rest of the biscuits on a platter and brought it and the plate of sausage patties to the table.

"These are the most wonderful biscuits I've ever had in my life," said Homer. "They're so much better than Lou Lou's."

"Thanks. There's plenty. Eat all you want."

"I just need my one morning biscuit, but could I maybe take one with me for lunch? I'll pay you the extra."

"Now, Homer, you aren't paying for anything this morning. You aren't at the café. We're just two friends having breakfast together."

"You mean it?"

"I mean it." I smiled. "Just remember me when I open up my own café."

"I certainly will. And I'll tell everyone in town to do the same."

Homer left, and after I cleaned up the kitchen, I wasn't quite sure what to do with myself. I didn't want to spend the day being lazy, though, and I knew it was always best to be prepared. So I went online and searched for some small-business sites that would help me with getting my business off the ground. I knew how to cook—that wouldn't be a problem. It was the advertising, marketing, accounting, payroll, and tax side of the business that had me concerned.

I hadn't been working long when the doorbell rang. I closed my laptop and went to see who was there. It was Dilly Boyd, another regular from Lou's Joint. Dilly was a wizened little creature who looked half sweet old lady and half impish gnome.

"Hey, Dilly."

"Hi, darlin'. I ran into Homer Pickens, and he said that you made him breakfast this morning. I don't reckon you're making lunch, are you?"

"Well, I wasn't planning on it."

"Shoot. Do you at least have any biscuits left over from this morning? You know, I have that little old raccoon that comes to my back porch every evening about dark, and he won't go away unless I give him a biscuit. Then he scampers on back up into the woods."

"I do have some leftover biscuits," I said. "Come on in."

Dilly followed me into the house and complimented me on my pretty place. "No wonder Homer liked it so good. And he said you sat right down with him and had breakfast with him. That must've been really nice. Shame the café's not open today."

"Give me just a second." I went into the kitchen and put the biscuits into a plastic bag. I was probably getting ready to make a big mistake, but Dilly had thrown such a guilt trip on me with that wistful "must've been really nice" comment. I checked my pantry, freezer, and refrigerator, and then I took her the biscuits.

"Thanks, hon. I appreciate this."

I hated to just send her off with a bag of leftover biscuits, even if the biscuits were for a raccoon. Besides, it would be good practice for me to cook for someone other than my family.

"Dilly, do you think Homer and maybe one or two other people might like some lunch today?"

Her blue eyes sparkled to life, and her face became wreathed in smile wrinkles. "I believe I could round up a friend or two. What do you have in mind?"

"I'll make one meal out of what I have. People will have to eat what I make—they can't come in and ask for whatever they want. All right?"

She nodded. "What is it that we're having?"

"Meat loaf, macaroni salad, scalloped potatoes, creamed corn, collard greens, rolls, and preacher cookies." The no-bake cookies had gotten their name from being something simple to throw together if the preacher came to visit. I didn't mention the oatmeal pie I had left over from last night because I was afraid I wouldn't have enough.

"Oh boy!" She clutched her bag full of biscuits to her chest. "Won't this be fun?"

"Well, I hope it will. Be back in about an hour, all right?"

"See you then!"

When Dilly left, I called Jackie.

"Hi. So what's going on at the Joint?" she asked.

"I'll tell you all about it when you get to my house . . . that is, if you'll come to my house." I told her about Homer and then Dilly coming for food.

"Amy, these people can't expect you to feed them just because the café is closed today. And you can't let them guilt you into it."

"I didn't mean to. At first, it was just Homer wondering where he was going to get his morning sausage biscuit, and then Dilly came by and asked about lunch. I told her I didn't intend to make lunch. . . ."

"But she guilted you into it, didn't she?"

"A little."

"And are these people paying you?"

"Of course, not! That wouldn't be right."

Jackie made a little growly noise, and I could imagine her rubbing her forehead. Even though she was only a year older than me, she saw herself as the more logical and rational of the two of us and sometimes acted as if she were a decade older than I.

"You can't give people free food when you open your own place," she said.

"I won't." Probably. "But I can do this one meal. Maybe it could count as a promotional business expense. And, if you'll come and help me, I'll pay you."

"How could I possibly accept your money, knowing you aren't getting paid for this meal?"

"I'll make you accept it. Now would you please come give me a hand?"

I used Nana's recipe to make the meat loaf, and I was just getting it out of the oven when Dilly arrived.

"I wish I'd thought to make some deviled eggs," I said to Jackie.

"We've got plenty of food."

There wasn't enough room at my kitchen table—and I didn't have a dining room—so since it had turned out to be a beautiful sunny day, I escorted our guests out to the picnic table in the backyard. There was an umbrella in the middle of the table, and it provided them some shade.

"Well, ain't this nice?" Dilly looked around like she was six years old and I'd thrown her a surprise birthday party.

She'd brought two other ladies who were regulars at the café.

"Just sit wherever you'd like, and Jackie and I will bring your plates out to you," I said. "Would everybody prefer sweet tea?"

One of the ladies requested ice water, but Dilly and the other one said tea would be fine.

When I went back into the kitchen, Jackie was busy buttering the rolls. I took our guests their drinks, and then I came back and started slicing the meat loaf.

"This would slice better if it was cold," I said. "It'll make a good sandwich tonight for dinner if there's any left over."

"That does sound good," said Jackie. "I'd like a couple of slices to take home too . . . if there is enough."

Nana's recipe made a big meat loaf, but I wasn't holding my breath.

We had no more than gotten our guests' plates out to them when someone rang the front doorbell.

"There go our sandwiches," Jackie told me.

I gave her an apologetic shrug and went to answer the door. I was surprised to see the more-gorgeous-than-I'd-remembered Deputy Hall standing on my porch. Maybe I'd been too traumatized to notice last night.

"Deputy Hall, what can I help you with?"

Before he could answer me, Homer came up onto the porch. "Hello, Amy. I hate to be a bother, but Dilly said you were serving lunch."

I nodded. "Go on through to the kitchen, and Jackie will fix you a plate." I stood aside to let Homer pass and then stepped out onto the porch. "Are you hungry, Deputy?"

"You know you can't be doing this," he said. "You don't have the proper permits to operate a café out of your home."

"I'm not operating a café out of my home. I've giving a few people a free meal. You want one or not?"

"I . . . uh. . . ."

"I promise it's clean. You can do an on-the-spot inspection if it'll make you feel better."

He hesitated.

"You like meat loaf?" I asked.

"Yeah, but I've had lunch already. I need to talk with you about the incident that occurred at Lou's Joint last night."

"Come on in." I walked back through the house, assuming he'd follow.

"Thank you." He looked around the kitchen. "Why are you doing all this?"

"I hadn't planned on it. Homer came to my door this morning at a little past ten. Not being able to go to Lou's Joint for his morning sausage biscuit threw him for a loop. He has a strict routine. I felt sorry for him and made him his breakfast. Dilly heard about it and wanted lunch. So here we are."

He grinned. "That little brown scruffy dog running around out there . . . was he a stray?"

"As a matter of fact, he was. His name is Rory, and he was at Lou's Joint one morning when I went in to work. I sneaked him some bacon—Lou Lou would've had my head had she known—and I looked for him when my shift was over. I was disappointed that he wasn't around. I guessed somebody had run him off. But when I started home, I saw him walking in the road. I called him, he came and got into the car, and he's been here ever since."

"I figured. It seems you have a thing for strays."

"I guess so." I nodded toward the table. "Have a seat."

His eyes flicked toward Jackie. "Maybe we could talk out on the porch. It's such a nice day and all."

Little did he know, I'd already told Jackie everything about last night . . . everything I knew anyway. "Sure. That'll be fine. Would you like a glass of water or tea?"

"A glass of tea would be nice. Thank you."

He was walking through to the front door when Jackie came back into kitchen from attending to our guests. She looked at me and then at Deputy Hall's retreating backside.

"Mercy, mercy, mercy," she said under her breath.

"Don't you 'mercy' me."

"Oh, don't worry. I'm not going to step on your toes. It's obviously not me he's interested in anyway."

I scoffed. "The only reason he's here is because of what I told you happened last night. He probably thinks I knocked Lou Lou over the head because she wouldn't sell me the café."

"I don't think that's the *only* reason he's here."

"Well, it's the main reason." I poured two glasses of tea.

"Do you know for sure that's what happened? That somebody hit her over the head?"

"I'm not sure exactly what happened. When I realized she was unconscious, I immediately called the police. I was afraid that whoever had knocked her out was still in the café."

"Still, nobody in his right mind would think you could knock out Lou Lou," Jackie said. "She was a huge woman. Not that you're a weakling or anything, but I'd imagine it would take a lot to fell Lou Lou Holman."

"I'd say you're right." I picked up the glasses. "Wish me luck."

Jackie held up her crossed fingers.

I pushed the screen door open and stepped out onto the porch. Deputy Hall was sitting on one of the white rockers. I handed him his drink.

I sat down on the other rocker. It felt good to relax for a moment. But then it felt good to have been able to provide a meal for some of Lou's Joint's regular customers too. "Am I a suspect in the . . . assault . . . or . . . whatever . . . of Lou Lou?" I asked quietly.

Instead of answering, the deputy took a sip of tea.

"Please be up-front with me. I'm being straight with you."

"I know you are," he said. "I guess we'd call you a person of interest because you found Ms. Holman"—he looked around to make sure none of the guests were coming around from the backyard—"and because you'd had a conflict with her. Of course, Sheriff Billings and I have been asking around, and a lot of people had some sort of conflict with Ms. Holman. She didn't appear to have been a very nice person."

I blew out a breath as I tried to decide what to say and what to hold back. I didn't want to come across as being mean, but I didn't want to paint an inaccurate picture of Lou Lou either.

"She was as tight as the skin on a sausage," I said. "She made us waitresses give her half our tips even though she paid the bare minimum she could get away with, so I doubt any of us would write to Santa on her behalf. She was nice enough when it came to the customers the biggest part of the time, but they could hear her yelling at us over every little thing, and I imagine most of them knew she was just flattering them to keep them coming around."

"You said you didn't work yesterday."

"Right. I only went in to give my notice and to talk with Lou Lou about buying the café."

"Did you notice anyone out of the ordinary—anyone who looked suspicious—while you were there?" he asked.

"No."

"Was Ms. Holman having any work done to the café that you know of?"

I shook my head. "Like I told you, she was stingy. Something would have to literally be falling down before she'd spend money to have it fixed."

"Did you happen to meet any cars coming from the café as you were driving toward it last night?"

"There was very little traffic. Come to think of it, I only met one car that I can recall. It was an SUV of some kind . . . red, I believe. I just remember it because one of the headlights was out."

He nodded and took another drink. "I'll make a note of that."

"What exactly happened to Lou Lou?" I asked. "I mean, I didn't look. I tried to get her to sit up, but I didn't lift up her head or anything. I saw the blood, and when I couldn't get a response, I called the sheriff's department."

"It was probably a good thing you didn't look. She'd been hit in the forehead with a blunt object."

"You mean, like a baseball bat or a golf club?"

"Likely something smaller—maybe a hammer or a crowbar."

I shuddered. "That's awful!" A hammer or a crowbar? I involuntarily shuddered at the thought of either of those weapons cracking open Lou Lou's skull. And why would someone bring something like that into her office anyway unless they were intending to harm her? "Is there anything I could've done for her?"

"No. Ivy said Ms. Holman likely died almost immediately upon suffering the blow."

I closed my eyes. "Oh my goodness. She must've been hit so hard." Then I thought about Lou Lou's son and my eyes flew open. "What about Pete? Does he know? I mean, you didn't let him go into the café last night, but did he see her like that, Deputy Hall?"

"Please call me Ryan. And, yeah, I'm afraid he did. The sheriff showed him the photo, remember?"

"That's right. And Pete had nearly fainted even before that."

"Yeah, he was in pretty bad shape last night."

"I should check on him . . . take him some food."

"That'd be nice." Ryan stood. "I have to get going. Thank you for your time."

"You're welcome."

I returned the glasses to the kitchen and put them in the dishwater.

"So he was here about the case?" Jackie asked.

"Yeah." I glanced out the window and saw that our little group was starting to disperse. "I'll tell you everything once they're gone."

Chapter 4

ℰAfter everybody had gone and Jackie and I had cleaned up the kitchen, we went into the living room for a well-deserved break.

"I'm tired," I said. "But it's a good tired. We did a nice thing today."

"Yeah, we did. I'm proud of us . . . of you, in particular, because I wouldn't have dreamed of inviting those people to lunch . . . except maybe the cutie-pie policeman."

"I just felt bad for them, Jack. Unless they wanted to travel at least ten miles—and none of them did—they didn't have another restaurant to go to. I mean, lunch at the Joint is their thing. None of them work—at least, not full-time—and seeing one another at Lou's Joint is pretty much the extent of their social calendar." I blew out a breath. "How sad is that? I mean, people like Homer and Dilly are why I want to open my own café—to give the customers, as well as the staff, a better alternative to Lou's Joint."

"And you will."

Princess Eloise sauntered across the back of the sofa. Jackie reached up to stroke her long white fur. The cat gave her a reproachful glare and jumped down onto the floor.

"I don't think she likes me very much," Jackie remarked.

"She doesn't like anyone except Mom. She puts up with me, and to a lesser degree, Rory."

At the mention of his name, Rory popped his head up and wagged his tail. When he saw that no one was eating or offering him a treat, he plopped his head back down onto his paws.

I rested my head against the back of the armchair. "Deputy Hall said that Ivy Donaldson reported Lou Lou was killed with a blunt object."

"That's terrible. And you went in and saw her like that? No wonder you couldn't sleep last night."

"I didn't really see much."

"Thank goodness for that . . . given the circumstances, I mean."

"Pete saw her that way, though. The sheriff asked Ivy Donaldson to take a photo of Lou Lou and show it to Pete so Pete could confirm it was her. It was some sort of technicality, I guess, because we all knew it was Lou Lou."

"How awful."

"I know, right? I wish there'd been some other way. I thought I'd take some food over to Pete's in a little while . . . see if there's anything I can do to help."

"I'll go with you. What're you planning to take?"

"I thought I'd go with a chicken casserole and a pound cake."

"We'd better get started, then, hadn't we?"

* * *

Jackie and I were on our way over to the Holman house when my phone rang. Since I was driving, Jackie fished the phone out of my purse and handed it to me. I answered and was surprised that it was Pete.

"Pete, hi. Jackie and I are on our way to your house with some food. Is there anything you need for us to stop and get you?"

"Uh, no. Thanks, though. I appreciate the offer . . . and the food, of course. But I was calling to ask a favor. Would you care to go over to the funeral home with me to help pick out Momma's casket and make the other arrangements?"

"Yeah . . . sure." Why in the world would Pete ask *me* to help with his mother's funeral arrangements? Surely, there were better choices . . . his girlfriend, for one. Still, the man was grieving. I couldn't refuse. "We can do that. See you in a few." I ended the call and told Jackie what Pete wanted.

She groaned. "Do I have to go?"

"*You* don't. We could make the excuse that someone should stay there at the house in case anyone stops by."

"Are you sure? I hate to leave you stuck like that."

"It's fine. I know how you despise funeral homes."

When we got to the Holmans' small brick home, there were three vehicles besides Pete's truck in the driveway. I parked on the side of the road so I wouldn't block or get blocked in. I carried the casserole, and Jackie carried the cake. The Holmans' neighbor, Shirley Green, saw us coming and opened the door for us.

Ms. Green was a plump rosy-cheeked little woman

whose short gray curls clung to her head like a knit cap. Today she wore a pink floral housedress and a white apron. She lived for occasions like this, where she could insert herself into the situation and mother everyone involved.

"Aren't you girls precious? Come on in, and I'll show you to the kitchen." She lowered her voice. "Poor little old Pete. I don't know what'll become of him now that his momma is gone."

The kitchen reeked of cigarette smoke and a garbage can that needed to be emptied. The round wooden table was full of covered dishes and plates wrapped in aluminum foil that people had brought.

"Has Pete got any other family?" Jackie asked, as she added the cake to the foods on the table.

"Not from around here. And if he has any, they're distant relations at best." Ms. Green clucked her tongue. "Of course, I'll help take care of him as best I can."

I had to bite my tongue to keep from pointing out that the man was forty years old, for pity's sake. Instead, I put the casserole into the refrigerator and saw that it was almost as full as the table. At least Pete wouldn't starve for a good long while.

"Your momma and Bess came by a little while ago, Amy. They brought a lemon pie. It's there in the fridge." She turned to Jackie. "That granny of yours has some wild ideas about her computer stuff. She was telling us about some kinda *boards* she has on her computer?"

Jackie nodded. "She loves pinning things on her social media boards."

Ms. Green continued to look confused. "I don't know anything about computers."

We were saved from commenting further when Pete came into the kitchen.

Jackie gave him a brief hug. "I'm really sorry about your momma."

"Thanks, Amy. As soon as I can get Chris Anne to move her car, we can go."

"Go?" Ms. Green asked. "Go where?"

"To pick out Momma's casket. Amy's gonna help me."

"We can take my car," I offered.

He looked relieved. "I appreciate that. Ms. Green, we shouldn't be too long."

"I'll hold down the fort." She smiled and patted his shoulder.

"And I'll help her," Jackie said.

As Pete and I walked out to my car, I wondered why he hadn't solicited Chris Anne for this job, since she was his girlfriend.

"I'm grateful to you for doing this," he said as I pulled away from the curb. "Momma always appreciated your opinions."

That was hogwash, and we both knew it. But I kept that to myself. No need to speak ill of the dead.

"Chris Anne said she felt like she didn't know Momma well enough to help with the arrangements," he continued. "But I wanted a woman's opinion. I've never been good at picking out things."

Is anyone *good at choosing a casket?* "I understand," I mumbled.

"I guess I could've asked Ms. Green, but Momma always thought she was kind of a busybody."

So Pete's choices had come down to a busybody and an

upstart, as far as his mother was concerned. I suppose upstarts inched out busybodies in Pete's social hierarchy.

"I still want to go after my dream of driving a truck," he continued. "Me and Chris Anne thought maybe we could get married and buy a truck and go into business for ourselves. A lot of couples do that."

"I seem to have heard that somewhere."

"Chris Anne can learn to drive a truck in no time flat and get her commercial driver's license. I already know how to drive a big rig. All I have to do is take the test and get certified."

"That's great," I said. "I hope it works out for you."

"Me too." He paused. "So, naturally, I'll be selling Lou's Joint . . . and . . . uh . . . I was wondering if you're still interested in buying."

Was Pete really this crass? *Hey, Amy, let's go pick out my mother's casket and talk business at the same time.* Or were his supposed shock and grief over his mother's death for the benefit of the police? Or maybe he was simply awkward . . . or, as we used to say, "backward" socially.

"I am, Pete. But we can talk more about that in a few days when everything is settled."

"You mean, like the will? I talked to Billy Hancock, and Momma didn't leave no will."

"Actually, I meant we should give it a few days so you can recover from the blow of losing your mother so suddenly and be absolutely sure about what you want to do."

"Oh, I am sure," Pete said. "But I reckon you've got a point. We ought to get the funeral out of the way and everything before we talk business."

"Right." He'd certainly seemed to have recovered from

his shock and grief much more quickly than I'd expected. Or maybe he was using the business of selling the café and buying a truck as a way to get his mind off his mother's death.

"By the way, Sheriff Billings called, and we're clear to open the Joint back starting tomorrow morning. Would you care to man the grill for the first shift?"

"Of course. In fact, I can work both shifts. No one expects you to come back to work before you're ready, Pete."

"I'll see how I'm feeling tomorrow. Between you and me, I wouldn't step foot in Momma's office again for love or money." He shuddered. "You shouldn't need anything from in there to run the café, though."

"What about money for the cash register?" I asked. "Didn't Lou Lou keep that money in the safe in her office?"

"Yeah. I'll swing by the bank and get you enough to make change."

We arrived at the funeral home, which was a gray stone Colonial home built more than a hundred years ago. As such, it was reputed to be haunted, which is one reason the place freaked out Jackie. Every building a century old (some even less) in Winter Garden was said to be haunted.

When we stepped inside, the thought crossed my mind that maybe Lou Lou's ghost had joined the ranks of the funeral home's restless spirits. I shuddered. *Somebody just walked over my grave.*

U pon returning to Pete's house, Jackie was as glad to see me as I was to see her.

"Get me out of here," she whispered.

"Why don't we go by your place and grab a few things and you can stay over?" I asked on the way to the car. "I'd rather not be by myself tonight."

"Works for me. I'd rather not be alone either with thoughts of Lou Lou's death and the funeral home and Ms. Green's talk about killers so fresh in my mind. I believe that woman quoted statistics on everyone from Jack the Ripper to Ted Bundy."

Jackie lived in an apartment a few miles outside of Winter Garden. She liked to keep things simple—the bare minimum of furniture, no knickknacks, and no pets. Her living room consisted of two mismatched chairs, a coffee table, and a television. In the bedroom, she had a bed and a dresser. The kitchen contained a bistro set, a refrigerator, a coffeemaker, a stove, one frying pan, one saucepan, two sets of dinnerware, and utensils. I figured the only reason Jackie had more than two sets of flatware was because one typically had to buy an eight-, sixteen-, or twenty-four-piece set.

It wasn't just that Jackie preferred to live a simple life. She led a guarded life. Her dad had died in a car accident when Jackie was eight. Then her mother had taken off when Jackie was sixteen years old, leaving Aunt Bess to raise Jackie. Even though her mom, Renee, came around every once in a while, there was no regularity to her visits—one day she was in Winter Garden again, the next day she wasn't. So Jackie was particular about who she chose to trust. Me, Mom, Aunt Bess, Sarah, and Roger were about it.

She went into the bedroom, threw some things into a duffel, and we were off again.

"Was it scary?" she asked as we drove back toward Winter Garden.

"Your apartment? Heck, yeah. Way too uncluttered."

"You know what I meant."

"I'd say the whole funeral home experience was creepy rather than scary."

"I have to wonder why Pete asked you to go help him with the arrangements instead of taking Chris Anne. It might sound callous to say so, but now that Lou Lou is gone, they don't have to be secretive about their relationship anymore, right?"

"I got the impression she didn't want to do it. Pete said I knew his mother better than Chris Anne did and that he needed a woman's opinion," I said. "Plus, he took advantage of the opportunity to ask if I was still interested in buying the café."

"Dang," she said. "Let your mom get cold first, Pete. What'd you say? I mean, is he even sure he *can* sell the Joint this soon?"

"I told him that we should give it a few days . . . get the funeral behind him, let him adjust to the shock of losing his mother and all. He did ask me to man the grill tomorrow morning. That reminds me, did you bring your uniform?"

"No. I'll go get it before work. I figured Lou's Joint would be closed for a few days, didn't you?"

"Frankly, yes. But I'd rather go to the café tomorrow than have it come back to me."

"You've got a point there."

Jackie and I hadn't been at my house long when my mom and Aunt Bess came by. Mom was of average height and thin. She wore her highlighted dark blond hair in a pixie cut that set off her lovely green eyes. Aunt Bess was on the plump side—but I'd never tell her so for a million dollars. I figured she was eighty-two, and she'd earned it. Plus, she looked great. She had a headful of curly white hair, silver-framed oval glasses, and a surprisingly smooth face. She never went out when she wasn't dressed to the nines, including jewelry and makeup.

Jackie and I hugged them both hello.

"Aunt Bess, you're looking as pretty as a pat of butter melting on a short stack," I said.

"Thank you, darlin'. There's no point in people going around like they do. Me and your momma went to the grocery store this morning, and people were walking around in there with their hair uncombed and some of them looked like they were wearing pajamas." She flattened her lips in disapproval. "And, Lord have mercy, what some of them girls were wearing! Or, should I say, *not* wearing. They ought to be ashamed."

"Yes, ma'am, they—"

"Now, I grew up in a time when girls were modest," she continued. "We didn't go around with our hineys and bosoms hanging out of our clothes. The only ones that did that were streetwalkers." She frowned. "And I don't think even *they* did, did they, Jenna?"

"I don't know," Mom said. "I wasn't there."

"No, but your mother was. Didn't she tell you about it?"

"She must not have." Mom was ready for a change in subject. "Tell us about Lou Lou. We didn't find out until just a few minutes ago that you were the one who found her, Amy. Why didn't you call me last night?"

"By the time I got home last night, I was exhausted, and I just wanted to go to bed."

Princess Eloise must've heard Mom's voice, because

she came into the living room and jumped onto Mom's lap, rubbing her head against Mom's chin.

"Hello, sweetums." Mom kissed the top of the cat's head.

"Did you get a picture of Lou's Joint with the crime scene tape up?" Aunt Bess asked.

"No, Aunt Bess, of course not! Why in the world would I do that?"

"I don't know. I just thought if you did, maybe I could start me a Pinterest board on small-town crime."

I exchanged looks of horror with Jackie. Maybe Shirley Green had been right about Aunt Bess's social media addiction getting out of hand. But given what Jackie had said about Ms. Green, the two might have more in common than Ms. Green thought.

"I—I didn't dream you'd want me to take a picture, Aunt Bess."

"Well, you'll know next time," she said.

I prayed there wouldn't be a next time.

"Are you all right?" Mom asked me. "It's bound to be a horrible experience to walk in on . . . on . . . you know, something like that."

"It was. I—"

"Did you see the killer?" Aunt Bess asked. "Do they know who did it? I wouldn't be a bit surprised if it was her boy, Pete. Maybe he finally got tired of taking her guff and just popped her one right in the head."

"Granny!" Jackie cried. "You don't really think Pete would kill his own mom, do you?"

"Why, young 'un, if you're gonna get killed by somebody, nine times out of ten, it's gonna be somebody you love."

She had a point.

"Hey! Why was your yard full of people earlier today?" Aunt Bess barely stopped to take a breath. "Did you have a party and not invite us?"

"Of course not," I said. Aunt Bess was always afraid of being left out of something. I told her and Mom about Homer coming for breakfast and then Dilly showing up wanting lunch.

"You can't let people take advantage of you like that," Mom said.

"That's what I told her," Jackie piped up. "But everything should be back to normal tomorrow. Pete wants us to get back to work."

"Before his mother's even in the ground?" Aunt Bess flattened her palm against her chest. "Lord, have mercy! That makes me want to go back over there and get my lemon pie back. We took that boy a lemon pie this morning, and now I'm wondering if he even deserves it."

"I'll make you another lemon pie," Mom told her.

"Well, I don't want you to go to any trouble on my account, Jenna. If I'd been you, I'd have made two to begin with . . . but that's just me."

Sometimes Mom and Aunt Bess got along great, and sometimes they acted like they couldn't stand each other.

"Amy and I'll be over to cook for you on Sunday, Granny," said Jackie. "And if you want a lemon pie, we'll make you one."

"Well, call me before you go to the store. I might've changed my mind by then."

Mom cut her eyes to Aunt Bess and then back to me. I know she was hoping she'd caught Aunt Bess between breaths. "So what's the sheriff saying about Lou Lou?"

"Not much to me," I said. "He and his deputy questioned me because I was the first on the scene. Neither of them shared any theories with me or anything."

"Do you reckon it was someone just driving by who saw her van there and decided to try to rob the place?" Mom asked. "I mean, Lou Lou usually didn't work late at night, did she?"

"Not often. She generally took the morning shift and left the afternoon shift to Pete. Any work she had to do, she tried to catch up on before she left in the morning."

"Why was she there, then?" Aunt Bess asked.

"I went in yesterday morning and asked to buy the café. She turned me down flat. Later on, Pete called me and asked me to come to a meeting last night. He said he'd talked his momma into selling but wanted to act fast, before she could change her mind. He was having Bobby Hancock come out too."

Aunt Bess squinted. "So Pete Holman was gung ho to sell Lou's Joint?"

"Yes, ma'am. He wants to go into the trucking business."

"Told you," she said, looking at the other three of us in turn. No one asked the question she was waiting for, so she said, "I told you Pete Holman killed that woman."

"Just because he wanted to sell the business?" Mom asked.

"*He* wanted to sell the business. Lou Lou didn't."

"But, Granny, he told Amy he'd gotten her to change her mind," Jackie said.

"He changed her mind by putting a hole in it." She gave a resolute nod of her head. "I reckon he can sell it now, can't he?"

Chapter 5

I was in the kitchen making dinner when Sarah showed up. She'd apparently gone home after work and changed into white shorts and a pink T-shirt. Being fair-skinned, Jackie and I had both always been a teensy bit jealous of Sarah's beautiful caramel-colored skin tone. She looked fantastic in shorts year-round.

"Hey, hey!" she called as she came into the kitchen and gave me a hug.

"You're in time for dinner. Meat loaf sandwiches, kettle-cooked chips, and preacher cookies."

"Sounds great," she said. "And I bet Jackie's in the living room setting up the Scrabble board."

"Yes, she is. Are you up for a game or two?"

"I am," she said. "I'm sorry I didn't call or come by this morning. I didn't know anything about Lou Lou until I got into work and Billy told me about it, and then after that we were swamped. Plus, I heard about your impromptu luncheon. How'd that go?"

"Fine. It wasn't that big a deal. Deputy Hall came by and said I couldn't operate a café without a license. So I told him I was giving a very few people free food and invited him for lunch. But he said he'd already eaten."

She laughed. "You'd better be glad word didn't get out all over town, or else you'd *still* be serving food."

"True. I guess it's a good thing that Pete's opening the café back up tomorrow."

All traces of her laughter dissipated. "Have you seen him today?"

"Yeah. Why?"

"How'd he strike you?" she asked. While I contemplated my answer, she went on. "Did he seem like a guy who'd just lost his mother?"

"Not really," I said.

Jackie came into the kitchen. "Not really what?"

"Pete didn't really seem like a guy who'd just lost his mom today," I said. "But last night, he did. He nearly fainted when the sheriff told him the news."

"Then he recovered quickly," Sarah said. "He was in our office this morning to have Billy get the ball rolling on Lou Lou's estate."

We took our plates and glasses of tea and sat down at the table.

"He seems to be awfully anxious to marry Chris Anne so they can start their own trucking business," I said.

Sarah's eyes widened, and Jackie got strangled on a drink of her tea.

"Are you serious?" Jackie croaked.

"That's what he told me." I spread my hands. "I mean, he could be totally sad about his mom and yet . . . maybe . . . kinda excited about the new opportunities he can pursue now. Right? They say everyone deals with grief differently."

"How was he at the funeral home?" Jackie asked. "I mean, other than asking if you still want to buy the café?"

"Other than that, he was considerate. He wanted to make sure he got the things he thought—and that I thought—Lou Lou would've wanted for the service."

"So we can expect a Hawaiian blue floral-print coffin at the funeral?" Sarah asked.

"No. The Winter Garden Funeral Home would've had to special order that," I said. "We got a tasteful white coffin with a blue satin liner."

Sarah looked down at her plate. "I'm sorry. That was mean of me to say."

"You weren't being mean. You were being honest. How do you think I know for certain that the funeral home would've had to special order the blue floral coffin?"

She grinned at me.

"When will the funeral be?" Jackie asked.

"Day after tomorrow," I said.

Sarah ate a chip. "What did you tell Pete about the Joint?"

"I told him we'd talk about it in a few days. . . . You know, he should get the funeral behind him and make sure selling the café is what he's sure he wants to do." I sipped my tea. "Can Pete legally sell Lou's Joint now?

I'd have imagined there would be some sort of waiting period or something."

Sarah shook her head. "No. Although Lou Lou didn't have a will, Pete is her only heir. He inherits everything, so it's his to sell."

"Do you still want to buy the place?" asked Jackie as she wiped her mouth on her napkin. "I mean, Lou Lou *died* in there. Aren't you going to think about that every time you walk through the door?"

"I don't know," I said. "I guess I'll find out tomorrow."

Jackie left as soon as we'd had some toast and coffee the next morning. She had to go back home and get changed into her uniform before coming back to the café. We were the only two people we knew for certain were going to be working. Hopefully, Pete had called others—particularly Aaron, who bussed tables and washed dishes—but he hadn't mentioned anything about it when he'd lent me a key to the café yesterday.

I saw a police cruiser sitting in the parking lot and my heart began thumping against my rib cage. What were the police doing here? Weren't they done with me? Obviously Ryan had told me I was a person of interest, but I had hoped they would cross me off the list. Why were they here now? What if someone was here to arrest me? What would I do? I knew I was innocent, but I had no way to prove it. What if every cent Nana had left me went for a legal defense instead of for my café?

By the time I'd parked the car and stepped out, tears

had filled my eyes. Deputy Hall got out of the cruiser and came toward me.

He gently took my shoulders. "Hey, hey . . . don't cry. Everything's going to be all right."

"You're not here to arrest me?"

"Of course, not. I'm sorry if you thought that."

"But I *am* a suspect in Lou Lou's murder, aren't I? I found her."

"You are a suspect. But there's no hard evidence indicating you murdered Lou Lou Holman," he said. "Not really. As a matter of fact, off the record, I know you didn't do it."

"Wait. You said *not really*. Do you mean there was evidence found?"

He inclined his head. "Ivy found a necklace beneath Lou Lou's desk."

"What did it look like?"

"A pearl inside a heart. One of the waitresses we spoke with identified it as yours."

"That *is* mine. I lost it more than a month ago." Did he believe that? Or did he think I'd lost it the other night in a struggle with Lou Lou? "My nana gave me that necklace for my birthday one year. I thought I'd lost it for good."

"Well, I'll make sure you get it back . . . you know . . . when all this is over."

Tears filled my eyes again. "The sheriff thinks it's me, doesn't he? But I swear, I didn't hurt Lou Lou."

He spread his arms, and for a second, I thought he was going to hug me. Instead, he simply rested his hands on my forearms. "The sheriff has a lot of people on this case, and we're going to find Lou Lou's killer."

I nodded. "Thank you."

"I hope you'll confide to me any information you remember or come across—like who might've had the motive and the means to harm Ms. Holman," he said. "I also want to warn you. Since you were the first person to arrive at the café after Ms. Holman was murdered, the killer might think you know more than you do." He placed his hands on his hips. "And it's possible you *do* know more than you realize. I want you to take some time to yourself as soon as you can, and write down everything you remember."

"All right. I will."

"And be careful. If you even *think* somebody might be following you or creeping around your house, call the sheriff's department . . . or call me. It'd be better to run the risk of being wrong than to ignore it and be right."

"You're kinda scaring me."

"I don't want you to be scared, only aware."

"I will." I nodded toward the café. "I'd better get to work."

"Me too."

"Thanks for stopping by."

"Please call me if you think of anything I might need to know or if you feel threatened in any way," he said.

"Okay."

I went on into the café and hung my purse on a hook in the kitchen by the back door. Was this door how the killer had entered Lou's Joint that night, or had he—or she—come through the front? Going through the front door seemed awfully brazen to me, especially with the lights in the parking lot. It made more sense that the person would've come through the back. The back of the café led out to just overgrown land. On the other hand, maybe the person had come in the front door, not realizing he'd get angry enough at Lou Lou to kill her.

I shook my head to try to dispel thoughts of that night. I had too much to do to dwell on it right now. Still, it was hard *not* to think about it. Lou Lou had been murdered not twenty feet from where I was standing. Besides, this was a remote area. Sure, it was beautiful, with oaks and maples that had stood for hundreds of years, fields of goldenrod, and cattle grazing in the pasture nearby. But the closest house was half a mile away.

Main Street was three times that distance. And while there were a small grocery store, the newspaper office, a general store, and a hair salon nestled together, none of those businesses were open at six o'clock in the morning.

My mouth suddenly went dry, and I got a drink of water. Jackie had been right. I hadn't realized how I'd be affected by returning to Lou's Joint this morning. I mean, I'd known it wouldn't be business as usual, but I hadn't thought I'd feel so afraid. Of course, Deputy Hall hadn't helped by saying that the killer might come after me. That was something I hadn't even considered.

I downed the rest of the water and made sure the back door was locked. The front door was open, but Jackie should be here any minute.

I had to pull myself together. Pete was counting on me. Lou's Joint patrons were counting on me.

I went out of the kitchen to the counter where the coffeepots were kept. I made two pots of regular coffee and one pot of decaffeinated. I felt better when the scent of brewing coffee filled the air.

I glanced toward the office door and thought about how Lou Lou had looked collapsed across her desk . . . the blood on the desk pad dripping onto the floor.

The front door opened, and I squealed and reeled backward.

"Amy!" Jackie hurried forward. "What is it? Are you okay?"

"You just startled me. That's all." I tried to laugh at myself, but my laugh came out sounding nearly hysterical.

She hugged me. "It's all right. Are you sure you can do this? If not, call Pete and tell him you're leaving. You don't even officially work here anymore, remember?"

"I'd still be working out my notice. Besides, that situation kinda changed night before last. Pete needs all the help he can get right now."

"But that's his problem, not yours."

"Jackie, his mom just died. And I'm the one who found her."

"In this café. Which is the best reason I can think of for you *not* to be here now. Why don't you go on back home? I can take care of things until Pete or somebody else can get here. Pete should have his butt kicked for not shutting down this place for a few days out of respect for his momma in the first place."

"Agreed, but still—"

Brooke, a nurse at Winter Garden Nursing Home, and one of my favorite regulars, came in then. "Am I missing out on a good argument?"

"No," I said. "We aren't arguing."

"Could've fooled me," said Brooke, tilting her head

and pushing her brown corkscrew curls off her right shoulder.

"I'm trying to get her to leave," Jackie told Brooke. "She's as jumpy as a frog dropped on a woodstove."

"Well, I don't doubt it." She turned to me. "I heard about you finding Lou Lou. I'm so sorry. I know that had to have been a shock."

"How do you do it?" I asked. "You go into work every day in a place where people have died."

"That's true, but in my case, they weren't murdered. I think that puts a whole different spin on things."

"Still, it doesn't creep you out to go into a room where some person just died?" Jackie asked. "I'd hate it."

"Well, it's not my favorite part of the job," said Brooke. "But I'm there to help the living. I concentrate on that."

"What about you, Jackie?" I asked. "Is it going to bother you to keep working here?"

"Not as long as I stay out of that office."

"Even if Pete sells, and I completely renovate the office?" Actually, the thought of renovating and using the office gave me pause as well.

"Hey, I heard you were going to open your own café," said Brooke. "I think that would be so cool."

"Thanks, Brooke," I said. "Pete wants me to buy this one, but I have to make sure everyone would be comfortable working here after . . . well, you know." I kept looking at Jackie because I wanted her to answer my question. If she couldn't work here, I wouldn't even consider buying this place anymore. I'd build my own café from scratch.

"I can work here," Jackie said. "We'll wipe away every trace of . . . anything bad that ever happened here, and we'll start all over."

I gave her a hug. "Then we'd better get started. I think we have our first customer of the day."

Jackie grabbed her notepad and pen. "What'll you have, Brooke?"

I went back into the kitchen. I wanted to prepare something different for Lou's Joint patrons today. I looked into the pantry and the refrigerator to see what I could make with the ingredients on hand. I decided to go with a Scottish shortbread.

Jackie brought me Brooke's order and, after making the pancakes, I began mixing up the shortbread. If I could start introducing patrons to new dishes, they'd come to not only accept but expect them . . . and, hopefully, look forward to them.

I thought back to the first time I'd made Scottish shortbread. The dean over the culinary institute was an intimidating man who reminded me of the film actor Robert Preston. Nana had loved older movies, and *The Music Man* had been one of her favorites.

But, anyway, the dean had been observing in our classroom that day. I'd been so nervous that when he'd asked me why the shortbread was baked at 350 degrees for ten minutes and then at 300 degrees for forty minutes, I couldn't sufficiently convey the proper answer—lowering the temperature makes for a flatter, crispier cookie. As I stood there struggling to answer the man, another student in the class stepped up and answered him. He praised her, and she turned to me with a smug smile. I'd decided then and there to stop being intimidated, to never let my fear of failing or looking foolish stand in the way of my stepping up, answering the question, taking a chance.

That's what I was doing with the Down South Café—taking a chance. If I failed, I'd at least know that I'd tried.

Chapter 6

Homer was right on schedule at ten o'clock that morning, and by then, things were almost normal.

"Good morning, Homer. Who's your hero today?"

"Mr. John Lennon."

"Whoa. Are you going to sing 'Imagine' for me?"

"Unfortunately, I have no musical talent. But I do have a cute story to share. When he was in school, the teacher asked him what he wanted to be when he grew up. Mr. Lennon said he wanted to be happy. The teacher said he didn't understand the question. And guess what he said?"

I was familiar with the quote but didn't want to burst Homer's bubble. "What?"

"He said the teacher didn't understand life."

I smiled as I poured Homer a cup of coffee. "I'll have your sausage biscuit right out."

"Take your time."

When I returned with the biscuit, Homer placed a hand on my arm. "Are you nervous being here . . . you know, after what happened?"

"I am, a little." I glanced around to make sure no one was listening to us. "I wish I'd wake up and all of this would just be a bad dream, Homer. I wish I'd never come here that night."

"I know you do." He patted my arm. "John Lennon always said, 'Everything will be okay in the end. If it's not okay, it's not the end.'"

"Thanks. I hope he's right."

I was pressing out hamburger patties when Pete and Chris Anne arrived that afternoon. Chris Anne strode into the kitchen, put her not terribly clean-looking left hand in front of my face, and wagged her fingers.

"Lookie what I got!" she said in a singsong voice. "We're engaged. Pete took me over to the pawnshop and we got the ring last night."

"Congratulations," I said, shooting a look of desperation at Aaron, who had come in not long after Jackie arrived and who could usually interpret my expressions and the telepathy I was trying to convey with them.

"Let me see," Aaron said.

Chris Anne hurried over to show Aaron the ring, thankfully getting her away from the hamburger patties. I mouthed a thank-you to him behind her back.

"Pete says he'll get me an even bigger one once we get our trucking business off the ground."

"Heck, baby, you'll have rings on every finger then,"

Pete said from the doorway. "I appreciate you patting out them hamburgers, Amy. That'll make it easier on me today."

"I'm gonna help waitress," said Chris Anne, tucking a strand of her greasy hair behind her ear. "It'll help me find out what it's gonna be like working side by side with my man every day."

I glanced over her tight black jeans and black T-shirt. "Do you need a uniform?" I didn't think the goth look would go over all that well with our clientele.

"Nope. I'm good. Thanks, though."

"Did everything go all right this morning?" Pete asked.

"Yeah," I said. "I think we were all a little bit nervous at first, but we got through it."

"Good." He looked down the hallway toward the office. "I can't stand the thought of going in there."

"If you need anything, sugar, I'll get it for you." Chris Anne sashayed over to Pete and smiled up at him.

Stan Wheeler came into the café and called out to Pete. Stan rented a mobile home from Lou Lou, and he came into Lou's Joint to eat on occasion. I'd gleaned from overheard conversations between the two that Lou Lou wasn't the best landlord on the planet. But, then, Stan hadn't seemed to be a star renter either. He could be cantankerous, and I preferred to keep my distance from him.

"In the back," Pete answered.

Stan sauntered up and leaned against the other side of the doorjamb. "Need for you to get somebody over to the trailer and fix my leaky roof."

Chris Anne held out her hand. "Lookie what Pete got me."

"Yeah. Nice. About that roof, Pete."

"Stan, my momma just passed day before yesterday. I'm dealing with about everything I can handle."

"Then give me the money to get it fixed, and I'll hire somebody my own self."

I put the lid on the plastic container full of hamburger patties, slipped off my gloves, and put the container in the refrigerator. I was anxious to get out of there.

"How'd we do this morning?" Pete asked me.

"Not good enough to pay for a new roof," I said as I dropped my gloves into the trash.

"What about the safe?" Stan asked. "I know Lou Lou kept money in there."

"She did," said Pete. "But I ain't going in the office after it."

"I'll go," said Chris Anne.

"No, baby, you don't want to be going in there." Pete put his arm around her.

I could tell by the gleam in Chris Anne's eyes that Pete was wrong about that. Was it mere morbid curiosity that had her wanting to look around Lou Lou's office, or was it something more?

"Give me the combination, and I'll go." Stan held out his hand like it was a done deal.

Pete got out his wallet, took out a square of paper, and handed it to Stan. Frankly, I was surprised that he would trust Stan enough to have him go through his mother's safe. Maybe the two of them were closer than I'd thought.

"I never got to use the safe enough to memorize the combination," he said. "Just go ahead and clear it out while you're in there and bring everything out here to me."

"Fine."

"Is there anything else you need from the office?" Chris Anne asked.

"Well, I would like to have the accounts payable, accounts receivable, and payroll ledgers . . . if they're in there," said Pete. "The sheriff said they might have to take some of that kinda stuff for now . . . you know . . . until the person is caught or whatever. But I'm going to need all that stuff to settle the estate."

"I'll help Stan, then. He can't carry all that stuff by himself." She practically ran from the kitchen.

"Get anything else that looks important," Pete called down the hall.

I noticed he'd shut his eyes before turning toward the office.

I walked him into the dining room. "Come on out here and let me get you a cup of coffee. Or would you rather have some water, tea, or lemonade?"

"I don't need anything." He sat down at a table, and I saw that his hands were shaking. The man was an enigma—that was for sure. One minute, he's coming in here bragging with his fiancée that she'll soon have rings on every finger, and the next he's closing his eyes and trembling as he realizes his mother died just a few feet away.

"I can stay and handle the afternoon shift if you need me to," I said. "You don't have to be here today. In fact, I figure most of our patrons probably think we're closed."

"I'll stay," he said. "Thank you, though."

"You're welcome. In addition to patting out some hamburgers, I sliced some tomatoes and onions, shredded some lettuce, and made a chocolate crème pie."

He smiled slightly. "I appreciate that. I know you said you wanted to give me some time to think it over, but I'd like to know if you still want to buy Lou's Joint. If you're not, I'm going to go ahead and put it on the market."

And another emotional shift from Pete. Was he being manipulated by a puppet master who was throwing darts at a list of moods? "I am interested. Have you already scheduled the appraisal?"

"Billy said he'd handle all of that. I need some cash if I'm gonna buy me and Chris Anne that truck."

I nodded. "I wish you all the luck in the world with that."

"I do you too, Amy. I reckon you, me, and Chris Anne are all about to make our dreams come true. I wish Momma hadn't been too stubborn to make hers come true." His eyes filled with tears.

"I'm sure she had everything she wanted," I said. Who was I kidding? I wasn't sure of anything. I had no idea what sort of dreams Lou Lou might have had. Had someone asked me last week, I'd have guessed that maybe belittling her staff was her dream come true. And then I had a stab of guilt for thinking ill of the dead.

Stan and Chris Anne brought out armloads of stuff from Lou Lou's office: a metal bank box, three or four notebooks, a bunch of documents. . . . Chris Anne even had a coffee mug.

"Look," she said. "Still has your momma's lipstick print on the rim."

I managed to suppress a shudder. Jackie didn't.

"Jackie, are you ready to take off?" I asked.

She nodded. "I'll talk to you later."

* * *

I went home, showered, and changed into a navy blue business suit. I didn't have an appointment, but I hoped Billy Hancock would see me anyway. I headed for his office with high hopes.

The office building was small but elegantly decorated. Sarah was sitting at her desk looking beautiful in a pink dress. She loved pink, and the color looked terrific on her.

She smiled up at me. "Hi."

"Hi. Is Billy in?"

"Not back from lunch yet. Want to wait?"

"I do." I sat down on the chair nearest Sarah's desk. "Are you expecting anyone in this afternoon?"

"Not until two, so you have a little while. What do you want to see Billy about?"

"I just need some advice. Before I left Lou's Joint, Pete said he'd talked with Billy about getting the place appraised and that if I didn't want it, he was going to put it on the market."

"He was in here this morning—he and that insufferable Chris Anne. What does he see in her? Not that he's any big catch, but still . . ."

"I think you hit the nail on the head with that 'no big catch' comment. I mean, Pete's nice enough, but he's always struck me as being a sandwich or two short of a picnic. Plus, think about who his bride would have as a mother-in-law."

"That *is* scary," Sarah agreed. "Or was. Maybe Chris Anne is the one who knocked Lou Lou in the head."

We held each other's gazes.

"I was kidding," she said after a moment, "but that's not entirely out of the question."

"She was awfully ghoulish about wanting to go into Lou Lou's office a little while ago."

"Maybe she wanted to make sure she hadn't left any incriminating evidence behind."

I shook my head. "If she did, Ivy Donaldson has already scooped it up."

"Chris Anne might not know that."

It had me thinking. "Hey, can you come over to my house tonight? I'll see if Jackie and Roger can come too."

"Are we having a party?" Sarah asked with a grin.

"No. But what you said about Chris Anne makes sense. I want everybody to toss some theories around, write them down, and see what we can come up with."

"Honey, I'm sure the police are doing all of that."

"I'm sure they are too, but I'm on their list."

"What?"

"I'm a suspect," I said.

"That's total crap!"

"Not if you look at it from their point of view."

"Then let's Nancy Drew the fire out of this thing and get you off the hook."

Before she could say more, we heard Billy's car pull up.

"See you at six?" I asked.

"I'll be there."

"Hello, Amy," Billy said when he came in. "Did you and Sarah have lunch?"

"No, sir. I'm here to see you, if you have a minute."

"I believe I do . . . don't I, Sarah?"

"You're free until two," she told him.

"Good. Come on into my office, then."

I followed Billy into his office. Like the lobby, his office was decorated in forest green and burgundy. He had a high-backed leather desk chair, and there were two small matching chairs in front of the desk. With the exception of an in-box that was full stacked upon an out-box that was empty, the desk was uncluttered. It appeared all of Billy's current case files and other works in progress were on the credenza behind him.

"So how can I help you, Amy?"

"You tell me. I'm afraid I'm a suspect in a homicide, and I want to either buy Lou's Joint or build my own café. But you're probably already aware of all of that."

"I am." He folded his hands. "Whoever found Lou Lou was going to be a suspect in her murder. I don't feel there's anything to worry about unless you're formally accused."

"By 'accused,' do you mean 'arrested'?" My tone was matter-of-fact, but my heart was fluttering up into my throat.

"I do. Is there any reason for you to be arrested, Amy?"

"I didn't kill her, if that's what you mean."

"That's not what I meant. Good to know but not what I'm driving at. Do you have a motive?"

"I resigned from my job at Lou's Joint that morning, and I offered to buy the café. Lou Lou rejected my offer . . . rather soundly, I might add. I was surprised when Pete called to set up our meeting."

"I admit I thought the deed to Lou's Joint would have to be pried out of . . . well, you get my meaning."

"Then you were surprised too," I said.

"Sure, I was. And I let Pete know that I was billing him for the meeting even if his mother backed out."

"He told me this morning that he'd already asked you to get the café appraised."

Billy nodded. "I've called the commercial real estate appraiser, and she's going to get to it as soon as she can."

"Do you think I should buy the existing building or that I should buy a piece of land and build my own café?"

He sat back in his chair and clasped his hands behind his head. "I believe you'd be better off from a financial standpoint to buy Lou's Joint. All the power, water, and sewer lines are already in place. The location is established. And all you'd have to do is renovate." He lowered his arms and rubbed his chin. "Plus, if you don't buy the place, some fast-food franchise might come in and get a foothold while you're still trying to build."

"I hadn't considered that," I said.

"The other thing you have to think about, though, is this: are you going to have the heebie-jeebies working in Lou's Joint?"

"I had my reservations when I went in to work this morning," I began, but he cut in.

"What? Why were you working there? I thought you just said you'd quit."

"I had given my two weeks' notice. But I wouldn't leave Pete in the lurch. He doesn't have anybody else who can cook for him. If I hadn't taken the morning shift, he'd have had to cook all day."

"Or close the place like he had some sense," Billy muttered. "But maybe that's how he's dealing with his grief . . . staying busy."

"Maybe so. Either way, I feel I can't fully commit to buying or building a business until this black cloud I'm under goes away."

"Are you calling your being a murder suspect a black cloud?" Billy waved away that thought with the flick of his wrist. "That's ludicrous. I doubt you'll be arrested."

Doubt? I gulped. "Gee, thanks. I hope and pray you're right. But I'd like to go ahead and give you a retainer so that you can start either planning my defense or working on securing the paperwork I need for the café."

"I do feel the need to tell you that since one of the local churches boycotted Lou's Joint, the place hasn't been in the best financial shape."

"I figured I'd have to do a lot of promotion to let people know the café is something new and different from what they were used to with Lou's Joint. I mean, of course, many of the menu items will remain, but I take pride in my food and I'm looking forward to introducing lots of new dishes too."

"Sounds great. So let's go ahead and incorporate your business," he said. "That way, you'll have something to help distract you from Lou Lou's murder investigation until either the police find out who did it or the case grows cold. We can get the necessary permits and licenses in the business's name, and you can start making a list of your expenses even before you decide whether you'll build or buy. Sound good?"

"I guess so."

"So do you want your business name to be the same as the name of your café?"

"I want to call my café the Down South Café," I said. I'd been thinking on that for quite a while. I wanted people to think of Southern hospitality, a sweet home-town, and a small but bustling café when they thought of my restaurant.

"All righty. Want to call your business Down South Café, Incorporated?"

"Sure. That works."

"Good. I'll get Sarah to start on the paperwork. By this time tomorrow, you'll officially be an entrepreneur."

Chapter 7

I changed into a T-shirt and shorts as soon as I got home. Then I went into the fancy room and cuddled up in the blue chair with my old culinary school textbook. So I was almost an entrepreneur. As I'd mentioned to Billy Hancock, one of the main things I needed to do was establish that Down South Café wasn't simply Lou's Joint under new management . . . even if I wound up building a new restaurant rather than renovating Lou's Joint.

I wanted to continue to serve the foods that the café patrons expected and were accustomed to, but I wanted to give them some more exciting choices as well. My palate had become more sophisticated when I attended culinary school, but I realized that old habits died hard with many Southwest Virginians. Winter Garden residents liked the tried-and-true, and were reluctant to pay for something they might not like. So I'd have to allow

patrons to sample new dishes before I added them to
the menu.

Also, I had to ensure that I could not only acquire all
the ingredients I needed for a recipe, but that their cost
wouldn't make the dish a loss for the café. For example,
I loved cipollini onions, but I couldn't find a grocery
store in our region that stocked them, and ordering them
would be cost-prohibitive.

So as far as breakfast was concerned, I'd serve the
typical fare, offer healthier options, such as turkey bacon
and gluten-free pancakes, and introduce new dishes that
would, hopefully, delight my customers. I made a souf-
fléed cheddar omelet that would nearly melt in your
mouth.

At lunch, I'd also have the menu staples patrons would
expect, but I'd throw in a few surprises there as well. I
felt that most of the patrons would love corn fritters made
with cheddar cheese, but they might be reluctant to try
fried plantain chips. Of course, they could surprise me.
I wanted to give them the opportunity to try a variety of
new foods. I truly felt that offering free samples was the
key to seeing which items would do well on the menu.

I thumbed through the book until I came to the section on food and kitchen safety. That was something I
would certainly need to go over with my staff, especially
those—if any—who came with me from Lou's Joint.
An image of Lou Lou with that ever-present cigarette
dangling from her lip emerged, making me wonder for
the umpteenth time what on earth happened just before
I got to the café that night. And why had Pete been so
willing to let Stan Wheeler pilfer through his mother's
office? I understood why he hadn't wanted to go in there

himself, and I was certainly relieved that he hadn't asked me to go—because I'd have definitely turned him down—but why Stan?

Roger was the first to get to my house. I was surprised. Having his own construction business meant that Roger often worked late hours, especially in the summer. I was also glad he was the first to arrive because I had a lot of questions for him.

He was about five feet nine inches tall and solidly built. He had dark blond hair and brown eyes. I thought he'd been half in love with Jackie since middle school, but he wouldn't ask her out. Maybe one of these days.

I took Roger outside and put him in charge of watching the grill while I set the picnic table.

"I have some questions for you," I said.

"About what, Flowerpot?" The nickname harkened back to our childhood.

"Running your own business. It's difficult, isn't it?"

"Well, yeah. You learn pretty quickly that when you need a helping hand, it's at the end of your arm."

I struck a match to the citronella tiki torch I had standing in the yard. "You mean you don't have anyone you can count on to help you?"

"I have plenty of help . . . a lot of great workers. But at the end of the day, the business is my responsibility. There's nobody but me to worry about overhead and expenses and revenue."

"Is it scary?"

"Heck, yeah, it's scary." He winked and grinned at me. "But ain't anything worth having a little scary?"

I smiled. "You've got a point. Which actually brings me to another question: when are you going to ask Jackie out?"

"Now, don't start *that* again. Jackie's one of my best friends." He took the tongs and turned the steaks. "What if we'd go out and end up not getting along—or even worse, have a bad breakup—and never be able to go back to the way we were before? It would ruin things for our whole group."

"But, Roger, what if you're missing out on the love of your life? And what if Jackie is too?"

"If things are meant to work out between us, they will somehow. Now let's get back to talking about business. Did you ever decide whether you're going to build from the ground up or buy an existing building?"

"Pete's doing his best to get me to buy Lou's Joint, and Billy Hancock says that would be the way to go."

"Billy's right. And I can make that place look like new."

"I know you can." I surveyed the table. All the food was covered and waiting for us to dig in. In addition to the steaks and grilled vegetable kabobs, we were having potato salad, chips and salsa, corn on the cob, key lime pie, and watermelon slices.

"But?" Roger prompted.

"I'm a suspect in Lou Lou's murder. That's one reason I invited all of you over tonight. I have to get this figured out and clear my name."

He shook his head. "Honey, there's no way anyone could think you capable of murdering Lou Lou."

"You're wrong about that. I'm guessing I'm pretty high on the suspect list, since I found her body."

"That's stupid. Why would you kill her and then call

to say you'd found her? If you'd killed her, you'd have done exactly what her murderer did—take off."

"Amen," said Jackie, coming around the side of the house in time to hear what Roger had to say. She gave him a one-armed hug. "Long time, no see. Where've you been?"

"I've been working my butt off," he said.

She took a pointed look at his backside. "Nope, Roger, it's still there." She gave me the "okay" sign but made sure Roger couldn't see.

Sarah was the last to arrive. She'd brought a banana pudding because she said she didn't feel right not bringing anything. We gladly accepted.

"Where's John?" I asked.

John was Sarah's boyfriend. He was in law school at the Appalachian School of Law.

"Had a late class," she said. "Besides, I thought that since we were doing the Nancy Drew and Hardy Boys thing, it should just be us for dinner."

Roger turned the steaks again. "What? Do you think John did it?"

"Did what?" she asked.

"Killed Lou Lou."

She rolled her eyes. "Yes, Roger, I do."

"Good. Get him to confess, and we'll just enjoy our dinner."

"I was being sarcastic," said Sarah.

"I know, but it sounds like a plan. It'll test his legal skills."

"He hasn't graduated yet."

Jackie put an end to Roger's and Sarah's mock argument. "Smarty-pants, you got our steaks ready?"

Roger shook his behind in Jackie's direction. "Don't

rush perfection." Then he called me over to see if the steaks were done.

Once we were seated, I started my spiel. "I went to talk with Billy Hancock today, and he's incorporating my business."

Cheers and congratulations went up from around the table.

"But before I move forward, I need you guys to help me figure out who might've killed Lou Lou. I have to clear myself of any suspicion in her death," I continued. "Who's going to want to eat at the Down South Café if the proprietor is suspected of murdering the previous establishment's owner?"

"Hey, maybe Lou Lou ate some of her own food and died from that," Roger piped up. "I mean, I know they think she was hit on the head, but maybe she hit it on something as she was falling."

"I seriously doubt that," I said.

"No?" he asked. "No chance? I mean, Lou Lou's cooking was pretty nasty."

"That's why the whole town—and all the towns around here—are going to be thrilled with Amy's place," said Jackie. "What did you say you're calling it again?"

"The Down South Café," I said. "But let's be serious about Lou Lou for a minute. Do you guys know of anybody who disliked her enough to murder her?"

"I threw my card on the table when you were at the office today," said Sarah. "My money's on Chris Anne."

"Granny is bound and determined that it was Pete," Jackie said. "And that kinda makes sense too. I mean, Lou Lou was holding him back . . . didn't want him to get married or leave the restaurant business. She wanted to keep him under her thumb."

"What about you, Roger? Any theories other than that she ate her own food and killed herself?" I asked.

He chewed his steak as he mulled over his answer. "Maybe it was a *Murder on the Orient Express*–type deal, and several people took a swing at her. I can imagine some of the waitresses being up for it, and Aaron asked me last week if I was hiring."

I nearly choked on my tea. "What did you tell him?"

"The truth—that I have everybody I need right now but would let him know if anything comes open," said Roger. "Fact is, I could use him while I build or renovate your café."

"You have a point. But I don't want to lose him. He's a great dishwasher and busboy."

Even before I'd approached Lou Lou about buying the Joint, I'd asked Roger to renovate the café for me or to build a new one if she wouldn't sell. The summer months were some of the busiest for him, but Roger had carved out that time for me.

Roger smiled. "Already got him hired, huh?"

"Well, no . . . but . . . I thought at least some of the staff would stay in place," I said.

"I'm only giving you a hard time."

"What do you think drove Aaron over the edge?" Sarah asked. "From what I've heard, Lou Lou was hateful to all of you."

"She was," I said. "I don't know what would've been the last straw for Aaron."

"I do," said Jackie. "Lou Lou accused him of stealing last week."

"When was this?" I asked. "I didn't hear anything about it."

"It was on Monday or Tuesday," she said. "I thought it was typical Lou Lou being Lou Lou, but it really upset Aaron. If he could've afforded to, I believe he'd have quit right there on the spot."

"So put him down on that little list you're making," Roger said.

"Aaron? No," I said. "He's a good kid. He's been helping his parents with their bills since his dad got sick. He wouldn't have killed Lou Lou."

"You said we were here to explore all possibilities. He's a possibility."

"Roger's right," said Sarah. "We need to list everybody with a motive."

"I might as well go ahead and put down half of the population of Winter Garden, then," I said. "How many people rented from Lou Lou?"

"She has the one trailer out on Huff's Pike that she rented to Stan Wheeler," said Roger. "And I believe she has a duplex out on Route Fifty-eight."

"She sold the duplex last year," said Sarah. "I remember drawing up the paperwork for the closing."

"So I guess Stan is her only renter," I said.

"Put him on the list," said Roger. "He's bad news."

"Why? What has he done?"

"According to one of my suppliers, he's a drug dealer. Stan apparently dealt to my friend's sister, and he went looking for Stan. I'd say Stan is lucky my friend didn't find him that night."

"How did I not hear about any of this before now?"

"You were gone, off at school, for quite a while,"

Jackie said. "And then after you came back, you were too busy with work and your nana to get too looped into the gossip."

"So read us that list," said Sarah.

"Me, Chris Anne, Pete, Aaron, and Stan."

Roger leaned across the table toward me. "I think it's that first one."

"*I'm* the first one," I protested.

"I know. Did you kill Lou Lou? I mean, what a shocker it would be if you had. We'd all be like . . ." He clutched at his chest.

"Roger, will you stop?" Jackie slapped his arm. "She's worried enough as it is."

He blew out a breath. "Good gravy! It was a joke! Would one of you *please* bring a boyfriend next time?" he teased. "Or, Amy, invite one of the neighbor men. I don't care if he's a hundred years old. Just get a little more testosterone at the table."

Jackie rolled her eyes. "I am man. See me beat my chest."

"Do not make me club you over the head and drag you back to my cave," he said with a grin.

She leaned back. "Oh, I would *love* to see you try."

"So what do we do now?" Sarah asked. "How do we find out where these people were, if they have alibis for the time of the murder or whatever? My only dealings with criminals are the ones that have already been caught."

"Good point," I said. "What *do* we do now?"

"I'll take Aaron," said Jackie. "I was there when Lou Lou accused him of stealing, and I can ask him in a round-about way what he was doing that night. Plus, he's not afraid to talk to me. You intimidate him, Amy. You're too pretty."

My jaw dropped. "I most certainly am not!"

"You are to him."

Roger tilted his head. "I can see it. If I hadn't known you since you had crooked teeth and skinned knees, I'd think you were pretty too."

I gave him a slow, exaggerated blink. "Thank you so much."

"You're welcome."

By the time everyone left, we still weren't quite sure what to do other than Jackie's plan to talk with Aaron to see what he'd been doing when Lou Lou was murdered. I needed to figure out what to do on my own. Like Roger had said about his business, at the end of the day, this was my own responsibility.

I went and got my phone and Ryan Hall's business card from my purse. As I punched in the number, I knew I was probably making a huge mistake. But I didn't know what else to do.

"Ryan Hall."

"Hi, Deputy Hall. It's Amy Flowers. How are you?"

"I'm fine, Amy. What can I do for you?"

"I've . . . um . . . I've kinda made a suspect list, and I'd like to go over it with you if you have a minute."

"A suspect list?"

I could hear the amusement in his tone, but I didn't let it deter me.

"Yes, a suspect list. Do you have time to talk with me about it, or not?"

"Sure. Let's have it."

I gave him every name on the list, starting with me. "As you know, I don't have an alibi for the time of the murder, other than the fact that I was with my friend Sarah only minutes before I left for Lou's Joint. I haven't had anybody tell me an approximate time of death, but Sarah can verify the time I was with her."

"All right," he said. "Next."

I told him Sarah's theory about Chris Anne, but I didn't tell him it was Sarah's theory. I didn't want him to know I'd been talking about the case with my friends. I didn't think it was breaking any rules to talk with them about Lou Lou's murder, but just in case, I'd rather be safe than sorry.

"Pete also had motive to dispose of his mother," I continued.

"'Dispose of'? Interesting word choice."

"Well, I hate to say Pete had reason to *kill* his mother, but she was terribly hard on him. She wouldn't allow him to have a serious girlfriend, and he desperately wanted her to agree to sell the café so he could pursue other interests."

"She wouldn't 'allow' a forty-year-old man to have a serious girlfriend?" he asked.

"Apparently not. And he's already proposed to Chris Anne and asked me to buy the café so he can put the money toward starting a trucking business." I paused. "You think I'm a fruitcake, don't you?"

"I think you're scared, Amy. And I assure you, we're looking into all the people you've mentioned and then some. We'll find out who's responsible for Lou Lou Holman's death. Just let us do our jobs, all right?"

I didn't say anything. I wanted to trust Deputy Hall. Truly, I did. But this was my life we were talking about. How could I simply take a backseat?

"Please?" he asked. "Trust me."

"I'm trying to."

Chapter 8

Pete called me at just after ten o'clock that night.
"Hey, Amy . . . whatcha doin', gal?" His words
were slightly slurred.

"Pete, are you drunk?" He *had* to be drunk. And he
was drunk-dialing *me*? What on earth for?

"I . . . I might be . . . the slightest bit . . . uh . . .
wasted. Why? Is it . . . is it late?"

"What do you need?" I was not going to deal with
him, not in his condition, and not at this time of night.
I was trying to cut him some slack because of everything
he'd been through, but enough was enough.

"Will you come in . . . in the morning . . . for the grill?"

"You didn't think to call me about this sooner?" I
asked.

"I forgot. Sssorry."

"I'll man the grill tomorrow morning, but I don't
have a key. Would you be able to meet me there and let

me in?" This was ridiculous. I thought—again, and like the rest of the town—that Pete should've had the courtesy to close the café for a few days to mourn. He apparently took his "leave no cent unearned" credo from his mother.

"Use the kitchen door," he said.

"What? Don't you keep it locked?"

"N-no. I mean, yeah. Key's unner the rock by the door."

"Okay. I'll look for it." And then I did something I'm not proud of. I tried to take advantage of his drunken state. "So Pete, do you know of anybody who'd want to hurt your mom?"

"Momma . . . poor Momma." He started blubbering. "Why would *anybody* hurt Momma? She was a saint! A saint, I tell you." He wheezed and coughed before blubbering again. "Except when she was mean. Sometimes she could be a little mean."

"I know, Pete. It's all right."

"It was for my own good. I never learned good judgment. Always hanging around . . . wrong people . . . bad decisions." He sniffled. "She just tried to take care of me. Momma was a saint. Poor, poor Momma!"

"I know," I said again. I didn't know what else to say. I wished I'd never mentioned it, but I thought he might tell me something I didn't know . . . something that he didn't *want* me—or anyone else to know. Now I felt pretty bad. At least he probably wouldn't remember this conversation tomorrow.

"Wh-when you . . . you buy the Joint, Amy . . . will you put a big p-painting of M-Momma on the wall? Y-you know . . . a memorial?"

Uh, no! I most certainly will not!

"Let's talk about it tomorrow, Pete," I said. "You get some rest."

"Nice b-big oil painting. We'll get somebody to do it up real nice. . . ."

"Good night."

"G'night, Amy."

As I got ready for bed, I thought about that key outside the kitchen door. I wondered how many other people knew about that key. It could've certainly allowed the killer to enter and leave the café without being spotted from the road.

The next morning, I found the key just where Pete had said it would be. The rock wasn't even one of those fake rocks used to hide a spare key. It was merely placed under a rock with a flat bottom. The key had apparently been there for a long time, because there was a perfect indentation of it in the earth beneath it. It crossed my mind that I might ought to call Ryan Hall and have him send Ivy Donaldson out to test the key for fingerprints, but I figured that would be useless. The key would have so many fingerprints—even if they were just those of Lou Lou and Pete—that I thought it would be hard to get a distinct print. Add to that the fact that after picking up the key, my own prints were on it. I put the thought aside, unlocked the door, and returned the key to the indentation beneath the rock.

I went into the dining room and retrieved the coffeepots. I thought about going ahead and unlocking the front door, but I decided against it. The café didn't open for another thirty minutes, and I wanted to make sure that no one came in while I was doing the necessary prep work.

As I worked in the kitchen, I thought about uniforms. Should I have uniforms for the staff? Or should I allow the staff to wear their regular clothes covered by a DOWN SOUTH CAFÉ apron? I'd ask Jackie her opinion.

When I did go back through the dining room to unlock the front door, Dilly was standing there waiting for me.

"Good morning, Dilly. I'm sorry you had to wait."

"That's all right. Got any biscuits yet?"

"They're in the oven. Oh, and try this Scottish short-bread I made yesterday morning." I took the cover off the glass cake plate on which I had the cookies.

Dilly took a cookie and then sat at the counter. "I saw Pete Holman and Stan Wheeler going into the pizza parlor last night when I was on my way home from bingo. Why in the world would anybody be having supper that late? It was pert near ten o'clock."

"I don't know," I said. "My stomach would think my throat had been cut if I waited that long to eat my dinner."

"Me too." She shook her head. "And I imagine my raccoon would think I'd left home. He comes to that door every evening as soon as it starts getting dark. You can count on it."

"What happens if you don't have a biscuit for him?" I asked.

"He'll settle for a cookie if he has to. He doesn't like it as well, but he'll take it." She bit into the shortbread. "Oh my goodness! This is good. I bet he'd like this, but he's not getting mine."

I smiled. "Besides two biscuits, then, what would you like for breakfast this morning?"

"Just a scrambled egg, please."

"Hash browns?"

"Oh, yes. That'd be nice."

"Coming right up," I said as I poured Dilly a cup of coffee.

I thought it was interesting that Pete had been out last night with Stan instead of Chris Anne. Maybe the two men were celebrating Pete's engagement. Or maybe Pete had given in and handed over the deed to Stan's mobile home.

While I was preparing Dilly's breakfast, Preacher Robinson came in. He was the pastor of the Winter Garden First Methodist Church. Mom and I had always attended the Winter Garden First Baptist Church, but I was acquainted with Preacher Robinson because the two churches—especially since they were the only two in town—often came together during revivals and community events like buying for needy families during the holidays.

I was surprised to see Preacher Robinson this morning, though. During my time working at Lou's Joint, I'd never seen him in here before. It crossed my mind that he might be preaching Lou Lou's funeral.

"Good morning, Preacher Robinson," I said. "How are you this morning?"

"I'm fair to middling." He nodded to Dilly. "Morning, Missus Boyd."

"Howdy, Preacher."

It struck me that Preacher Robinson probably wasn't

as old as his manner would make him appear to be. He
was a pencil-thin man of average height, with sparse
brown hair and black-rimmed glasses. Even in this heat,
he wore a brown three-piece suit with a tan shirt and a
yellow-and-brown-striped tie.

He was standing awkwardly in the middle of the
dining room, so I invited him to sit anywhere he'd like.

"I'll get you a menu in just a second," I said.

"That won't be necessary. I hadn't planned on staying
to eat. I had some grits before I left the house this morning."

"Okay." I didn't have time to wait for him to tell me
why he was here if it wasn't to eat, so I went ahead and
plated Dilly's food. I brought it out for her and topped
off her coffee.

Preacher Robinson peered down over his glasses at the
meal. "That does look awfully good, though. I suppose it
wouldn't hurt to have some scrambled eggs with a side of
bacon." He grinned and patted his flat stomach. "Just this
once."

"Coming right up," I said. "Coffee?"

"Please."

As I poured the coffee into a white stoneware mug,
I asked, "If you didn't come in for breakfast, Preacher
Robinson, then are you here about Lou Lou's funeral?
Because Pete isn't here."

"Aw, shucks. I mean, I'm not here about the funeral—
there's no way in heck she'd want *me* to preach it if I was
the last pastor on earth anyhow—but I did want to have
a word with Pete."

I glanced at Dilly, wondering if she knew what Lou
Lou had against Preacher Robinson. She was so intent

on eating those hash browns that I doubt she'd even heard what he'd said.

"I can have him give you a call," I said, putting the mug in front of him. The curiosity was killing me. "May I tell him what it's about?"

He sheepishly avoided my eyes and put sugar and creamer into his coffee. As he stirred, he watched the black liquid turn to light brown. "I guess I should've given it a few more days, but our Bible study is coming up, and I'd love to be able to have the meeting here in town for the first time in two years."

"Where have you been meeting?" I asked.

"A diner over in Meadowview." He continued to stir. "Ms. Holman and I had a . . . well, a disagreement, you might say . . . back then, and she threw us out. Wouldn't let us come back either."

What in the world did a preacher and his Bible study group do to offend Lou Lou to the point that she wouldn't accept their business?

He finally looked up at me. "Yes, ma'am, eggs and a side of bacon would really hit the spot."

The conversation was over. I wasn't going to find out what happened from him. I told him I'd get his breakfast out to him right away.

We had a little lull at about a quarter to nine, and I pulled Jackie aside to ask how she felt about uniforms.

"It depends on what they look like. These things Lou Lou made us wear are ugly with a capital *U*." She spread her hands, indicating the pale orange–and-white-checked uniforms. "I'd say she got them on sale somewhere because no one else wanted them. What have you got in mind?"

"I was thinking that the staff could either wear casual clothing covered by DOWN SOUTH CAFÉ aprons, or we could wear matching T-shirts with our logo."

Jackie nodded. "I like that idea. Plus, you could sell the T-shirts and aprons to customers for an additional source of income."

"You really think people would buy them?"

"Sure, they would. Tourists love things like that."

"I guess we could order some extra," I said.

"What about pants?"

"I was thinking jeans."

"Jeans are good," said Jackie.

"By the way, do you know anything about a disagreement between Preacher Robinson and Lou Lou? It would have happened about two years ago." I told Jackie about the pastor coming in this morning wanting to reinstate his Bible study sessions at the café.

Brow furrowed, she stared at the wall just above my head. Suddenly, her eyes widened. "Oh my gosh, I *do* remember that! In fact, it was just after I started working here, and I remember it like it was yesterday! During the Bible study, Preacher Robinson said that in four separate places in the Bible—Genesis, Matthew, Mark, and Ephesians—a man is instructed to leave his father and his mother and cleave unto his wife."

"And Lou Lou thought he was talking about her and Pete?"

Jackie nodded. "Apparently so, because she stormed out of that kitchen and told him that she and Pete were none of his congregation's business and that he needed to do his Bible studying elsewhere."

"Wow. Is it just me, or does it seem kind of extreme that she would make that leap from one passage of the Bible to Pastor Robinson attacking her and her son because Pete still lived at home?"

"Oh, it was extreme, all right. But the thing was, Pete had been dating a woman in the congregation, and I believe her family was putting pressure on her to marry."

"And she was putting pressure on Pete," I guessed.

Jackie chuckled. "Poor woman. I don't know if she encouraged the preacher to have that particular study—and to have it here—or not, but that was the end of her dating Pete too."

"Who was she?" I asked.

"I don't know. She was quite a bit older than us, so neither of us had gone to high school with her. After that, the whole congregation boycotted Lou's Joint, and I think she finally started going to church in Abingdon. Hopefully, she met somebody there."

"Hopefully, someone not quite as henpecked." I shook my head. So maybe that explained why Pete had tried to keep his relationship with Chris Anne from his mom.

"Before I forget," Jackie said, lowering her voice, "I ran into Aaron yesterday evening at the grocery store and *casually* struck up a conversation about Lou Lou's murder. I told him I was at home watching television and had no clue anything had even happened until the next day. He said, 'Same here.'"

"Which, I guess, technically means he has no verifiable alibi."

She turned down the corners of her mouth. "Neither do I. Shouldn't you add me to the list?"

I half smiled. "Nah. If either of us had planned to do someone in, she'd have called on the other to help her."

Jackie laughed. "That's true."

Homer Pickens came into the café and sat on a stool at the counter. I went over to pour him some coffee.

"Good morning, Homer. Who's your hero today?"

"Liam Neeson."

I was eager to hear Homer's reasoning behind his choice. "I like his movies," I said. "If I'm ever kidnapped, I hope he'll come rescue me."

Homer nodded and smiled wistfully. "He's strong. And I love his voice. It can be gentle or menacing." Homer tried to affect Mr. Neeson's voice. He failed miserably. "And don't worry, Amy. If you *are* ever kidnapped, I'll find you. Maybe. I'll at least try."

"Thanks. Sausage biscuit coming right up."

Brooke came rushing into the Joint. "Amy, I need to talk with you for a minute. It's urgent."

I called to Jackie and asked her to make Homer his sausage biscuit, and then I joined Brooke at a table in the far corner.

"What's wrong?"

"Well, I know you were talking about buying this place from Pete Holman, so I thought this news might be of interest to you," she said. "Eddie March, a writer for the *Winter Garden News*, came into the nursing home to see his grandmother this morning. He said that the area immediately surrounding Lou's Joint is about to be designated a historical site because of some Civil War battle that was fought here."

"So what does that mean? Will the government buy Pete out and tear down the café to put up some kind of memorial or something?"

"I don't think so. From the way Eddie talked, it means the café will go up in value. He said that George Lincoln with the Chamber of Commerce had spoken to Lou Lou about buying the Joint, tearing it down, and building a bed-and-breakfast on this site."

"Wow. Thanks for letting me know. When was this?" I asked.

"Only about a week and a half to two weeks ago. It couldn't have been long before you made your offer."

"I wonder if Lou Lou had been considering accepting Mr. Lincoln's offer. She acted to me like she'd never sell her daddy's place, but I have to wonder if she was just holding out for more money."

"Either way, if you want to buy this place, you need to do it," said Brooke. "Mr. Lincoln will be talking with Pete soon if he hasn't done so already."

"Thanks, Brooke."

"You're welcome, Amy. I need to get back."

I passed by Homer and patted his shoulder. "Good?"

"The best. Thank you." He was still trying to talk like Liam Neeson, and it just sounded weird.

I went into the kitchen.

"What's up?" asked Jackie.

I told her about Brooke's news.

"I agree with Brooke." Jackie took off the gloves she'd been wearing while cooking. "If you want to buy this place, you'd better move on it today."

"I will."

"Really?" She smiled. "I'm so excited for you!"

I nodded.

Her smile faded slightly. "Wait. Aren't you excited?"

"Yeah, but I'm scared too. This is a big step."

"One big step for you," she said. "One giant leap for Winter Garden."

I smiled. Although I kept my thoughts to myself, I knew that if Pete could get more money, then he should. He was trying to start a new business too. I'd try to match George Lincoln's offer, but if I couldn't, I'd have to build elsewhere. I wanted to be fair to Pete.

Chapter 9

Pete staggered in at about one thirty that afternoon looking like he'd been bear hunting with a switch. "I'm awfully sorry I didn't get here sooner." He rubbed his forehead. "I wasn't feeling very well this morning."

"You don't look like you're feeling very well now," I said. "Why don't I finish out the day here, and you go on back home?"

"I really would appreciate that. I'll make sure you're paid double time for it."

"Thank you. Also, if you're up to it later, I'd like to discuss buying the café from you."

His eyes sprang from their half-closed state to wide-open. "Are you serious?"

"Yes. If you're sure you want to sell, I'm sure I want to buy."

"Then close up the café an hour early this afternoon

and meet me up at Billy Hancock's office," said Pete. "I'll call him and get him to start drawing up the paperwork."

"Are you certain?" I asked. "You don't have any other offers to consider or anything?"

He frowned. "What do you mean?"

"I heard this morning that George Lincoln wanted to buy the café from your mom. I thought he might've made you an offer too. If he did, I'll try to match it, but—"

"George Lincoln wants to buy the Joint and tear it down. He told Momma that right to her face. He kept coming back and trying to change her mind, but she wouldn't have it, and I won't either. My granddaddy built this restaurant, and I won't have it torn down."

"You do realize that I'm planning on changing the name and the decor, don't you?"

"Sure, I do. But that's all right. I'll still be able to drive by here and see the building and know that it was started by my granddaddy and that there's a Holman legacy right on this very spot."

"All right."

"So I can go ahead and call Billy?" he asked.

"Yep. Just let me know if he can see us today. If he can, I'll close up early."

"Thanks, Amy. I'll call you as soon as I know something." And, with that, he was out the door.

As I stood there watching him back his pickup truck out into the road, Jackie put her hand on my shoulder.

"I heard most of that," she said. "And I'm proud of you. I'm really glad you've finally decided to make your café a reality."

"You don't think I'm hanging my basket higher than I can reach?"

"No way. And if you can't reach it, we'll get you a stepladder."

I hugged her. "I appreciate your confidence in me."

"Look around. See how much happier everybody has been when you've been running things? The waitresses get to keep all their tips. People are laughing and talking while they enjoy their food. Now imagine how much better it will be when we have a pretty new café with cool outfits."

I smiled. "It will be nice, won't it?"

"It'll be the best. You know it will."

That afternoon, I closed Lou's Joint early, and I hurried over to Billy Hancock's office. Like Jackie had been earlier, Sarah was brimming with excitement when she saw me.

"Can you believe it? It's really happening!" she said.

"I know. I'm nervous. I've never done anything like this before. Dang, I've never even bought a new car." I raised a trembling hand to my chest. "This is my first major purchase."

"But it's all right. You have the money to do it with. It's not like you're going into debt forever."

"I know, but what if I fail?" Why was my resolve so quick to run out on me?

"What if you do? You're young enough to start over with something else." She laughed. "Girl, grab that brass ring and hang on tight! You're doing this!"

I knew she was right. But I was just so scared. And Sarah could see that.

"Remember that time when we were about ten years old,

and we went with Roger to his uncle's farm?" she asked. "We all went to the hay barn, and we climbed up to the loft. Roger told us how fun it was to jump off into the hay. Remember?"

"I remember."

"He and I jumped again and again, but you were too afraid to jump. Finally, Roger pushed you. You screamed all the way down, and when you hit the bottom, you laughed. Then you immediately ran back up that ladder so you could jump again. This situation is just like that . . . except safer than jumping into a pile of hay." She smiled. "Making the initial leap is scary, but when you see how great it's going to be, you'll love it."

I laughed. "If I remember correctly, Roger's uncle told our parents and we got grounded for a month for that little stunt."

"Yeah. But it was worth it, wasn't it?"

"It was. Could you call Roger and see if he'd come over and push me into Billy's office?"

"If you need a push this time, I'll do it myself." She jerked her head toward the door. "Now go. They're waiting for you."

O n Friday morning, I woke up with the thought, *I'm a business owner!* The truth was I wasn't *officially* yet—Pete and I still had to meet at Billy Hancock's office again that afternoon to sign the papers—but I was pretty much the proud owner of the soon-to-be Down South Café.

"Thanks, Nana," I said aloud. "If she couldn't hear that, would you tell her for me, God? I'd appreciate it." Like

God didn't have better things to do than to pass along messages to my grandmother.

What a week it had been. On Monday—had it truly been only Monday?—I had resigned from my job waitressing at Lou's Joint and offered to buy the place. Of course, later that same night, I'd found Lou Lou dead. And now I owned the café.

Geez, no wonder the police thought I might've killed Lou Lou. And they probably didn't even know about my actually buying the café yet. In my defense, it was Pete who'd insisted on selling so quickly.

He'd also insisted on manning the grill all day today since I'd handled it yesterday. I'd tried to get him to at least let me take the morning shift, but he wouldn't hear of it. He said that staying busy helped keep his mind off his momma's death. He also told me that after the funeral tomorrow, he wanted to focus on happy memories and moving forward with his life. So this was his last day at Lou's Joint. He said he'd probably feel sentimental, but he was glad the Joint was passing into good hands.

I got out of bed and went to the kitchen. I put food into the pets' bowls and made a to-do list while I ate my cereal. On the list, I put *join the Chamber of Commerce, choose my color scheme, set up a meeting with Roger, publish a website, get business cards made up, get laminated menus printed, prepare a budget.*

I decided to work my way down the list, starting with joining the Chamber of Commerce. I took a shower, French braided my hair, put on a sundress and sandals, and headed downtown.

The Chamber of Commerce was housed in a long,

two-story brick building along with the mayor's office, sheriff's office, and post office. Winter Garden was nothing if not efficient with the limited amount of space it had. The Chamber of Commerce was on the second floor. I took the stairs and met Deputy Hall leaving the post office. It struck me again how handsome he was. If only he didn't think I might be a murderer.

"Morning. Nice dress," he said, then looked a little bashful, like maybe he shouldn't have complimented me.

"Thank you."

"What brings you by?"

"I'm joining the Chamber of Commerce," I said. "Pete practically forced me into making a decision about the café, and I bought it. We sign the papers this afternoon."

"Congratulations." He smiled. "I'll have to stop in sometime."

"Please do." I looked around to make sure no one was paying any attention to us. "Any new leads?"

"I'm afraid not. But we're stringently pursuing the ones we do have. Have you . . . heard anything or come up with any new theories?"

"No, but I'll keep you posted."

"No threats or anything?"

"Not yet."

"That's good." He smiled again. "Although, if you need me, you know how to get in touch."

"Just whistle? Put my lips together and blow?" I laughed. "Sorry. I've seen that movie too many times."

"*To Have and Have Not*. It's one of my favorites too."

"You like old movies?" I asked.

"Yeah . . . I do." His eyes held mine for a long moment. I felt a blush creeping into my cheeks. "See you soon,"

I said as breezily as I possibly could. I felt his eyes still
on me as I walked down the hall to the Chamber of Commerce. I wanted to turn and look back at him, but I didn't
dare.

I pushed open the door and was immediately hit by a
cool waft of air. The entire municipal office building was
air-conditioned, of course, but this office must have
turned its thermostat down to fifty. The slim short-haired
receptionist wore a sweater over her summer dress, and
she still had her shoulders hunched up to her ears like she
was freezing.

"Hi," she said. "How can I help you today?"

"Well, I'm here to join the Chamber, but if you'd like,
I can watch the phones for you for a few minutes if you
want to go outside and warm up."

"Thanks for the offer, but the boss would have my
hide." She handed me a form. "Just fill this out, and we'll
make you official. What kind of business do you have?"

"A café. I'm calling it the Down South Café." I smiled.
"I hope you'll drop in once I get it up and running."

"I sure will." She smiled. "It'll be nice to have a new
café in town. Where are you located?"

"I bought Lou's Joint from Pete Holman. All I have
to do is get it renovated."

A bulky man with a bad comb-over came rushing
out of the office behind the reception area. "Did I hear
you correctly, young lady? Did you say you'd purchased
Lou's Joint?"

"Yes, sir."

"When was this?"

"Yesterday."

He gave his head two fast shakes as if he could

dislodge what he'd just heard. "You moved quickly, didn't you?"

"Actually, it was Pete Holman who wanted to sell the business," I said. "He wants to do something else, and he didn't want to delay."

"Could you come into my office, please?"

He was obviously furious, and I wasn't going anywhere with him. "Given your tone, I'd prefer to talk with you right here." I thought he could fling any accusations at me from behind the receptionist's desk as easily as he could from behind his own.

"I apologize. It appears we got off on the wrong foot. I'm George Lincoln, president of the Winter Garden Chamber of Commerce." He didn't sound all that contrite, and I didn't think his anger could've dissipated that quickly.

"I'm Amy Flowers." I didn't say it was nice to meet him, because it wasn't.

He extended his sweaty hand, and I shook it as briefly as possible.

"Ms. Flowers, I doubt you were aware, but I'd made an offer on Lou's Joint to Ms. Holman some few days ago."

He waited for a response from me, but I didn't know what to say.

"I was planning on speaking with Mr. Holman about the property on Monday, since his mother's funeral is tomorrow," Mr. Lincoln continued. "I felt it would be tacky to discuss business before then."

"As did I, Mr. Lincoln. But as I told you, Mr. Holman approached *me* . . . rather insistently, I might add."

"Very well. Would you consider selling the property and building your café elsewhere?"

"No, sir, I would not. I'm eager to get my business off

the ground and don't want to delay any longer than necessary."

"You might change your mind when you see how much work will go into your venture and how little profit will come out of it." He lifted his chin haughtily.

"If I do, I hope you'll still be willing to buy the café. If not, perhaps someone else will." I gave the receptionist my sweetest smile. "Thanks so much for your kindness. I hope you have a pleasant day. I'll fill out this application and get it back to you as soon as possible." I doubted it would do me any good, though, given the fact that the president of the Chamber of Commerce already had it in for me.

As I left, I decided I wasn't going to let George Lincoln get to me. Sure, the business would be slow starting out and would demand more work than profit, but wasn't that the case for all new entrepreneurial ventures?

Starting down the steps, I noticed Preacher Robinson coming out of the post office. I called to him and waited for him to join me at the stairs.

"Good morning, Amy. How'd you manage to get some time off?"

"Well, Pete wanted to man the grill all day today. It'll be his last time working at Lou's Joint."

He frowned. "Why's that?"

"He wants to go into the trucking business, and he sold the café to me. I'm going to renovate it and call it the Down South Café."

"That sounds charming," he said with a smile.

"And I want you to know that your Bible study group is welcome to meet at the café—once it's reopened—whenever you'd like."

"Well, that's kind of you. I appreciate that."

We began walking slowly down the steps. I wanted to ask about his disagreement with Lou Lou, but I didn't quite know how. I broached the subject tentatively.

"I'm sorry that you had to leave the café," I said. "I can't imagine your parishioners were happy about having to drive that extra twenty minutes or so, especially in winter."

"No. No, they were not."

"I . . . I hope you . . . and they . . . will have a better experience at the Down South Café."

"Yes, well, as a rule, we try not to single anyone out in our sermons or prayers," he said. "But even if we did, I seriously doubt you'd be offended if we called into question the suitability of a grown man not only living with his mother but not being allowed to date." He quickly glanced over his shoulder. "I'm sorry. My wicked tongue got away from me. You know, the Good Book calls the tongue a fire that corrupts the whole body. I'll have to repent of this gossip."

"Oh, now, Preacher Robinson, you didn't say anything that everybody in town didn't already know."

"I imagine not, but as the shepherd of a flock, I'm held to a higher standard, you know." He gently took my arm. "Please don't mention that I spoke out of turn."

"I won't."

"It's a bad habit I'm trying to break."

He looked so concerned that I had to wonder what other gossip had set his corrupt tongue to wagging.

My next stop was the hardware store. I went directly to the paint section and took swatches of yellow and blue. Who knew there were so many variations?

Did I want the interior of Down South Café to be *Sunny Day*, *Hay Bale*, *Daffodil*, *Custard*, *Lemonade*, or *Golden Delight*? And did I want the trim to be *Waterfall*, *Frost*, *Seascape*, or *Riviera*? Hopefully, Roger could help me decide. Yes, he was a construction worker, but I'd have sworn he was also part architect and part interior designer.

I was looking down at the paint swatches and wasn't watching where I was going when I ran headlong into Stan Wheeler. He took me by my upper arms to steady me.

"Hey, there. Somebody's got her head in the clouds."

"I'm so sorry, Stan! I was looking at these paint swatches."

"Oh yeah. Pete mentioned that you were buying the Joint." He snatched the swatches out of my hand. "I like that *Daffodil* and *Waterfall* myself. Of course, I ain't no artist or anything."

"Neither am I . . . but those two do look good together." He seemed in an unusually talkative mood, so I decided to see if I could get some information out of him. "Speaking of buying property, did Pete sell you the mobile home?"

"Uh, we're working on that." He handed back the swatches. "It's gonna take a lot of work to get it fixed back up."

"I heard you talking about the roof at the café the other day," I said.

"Yeah, it needs to be entirely reshingled. Darn thing leaks like a sieve. And not only that, the toilet in the half bath needs to be replaced."

"Owning property can be a money pit, can't it?"

He smiled. "Don't tell me you're having second thoughts already?"

"No. I guess it's too late for that now. At least, while you're renting, the repairs are the Holmans' problem, right?"

"You'd think," he said. "But you probably know how tight Ms. Holman was. She kept promising to send somebody out to patch the roof and to see what was wrong with the toilet, but she never did. I'd been fussing about both for going on three months."

"I do know how she could be," I said. "I'd have hoped she'd have taken better care of her tenants than she did her staff, but apparently she didn't."

"And Pete wouldn't admit it, but she wasn't even that good to him," said Stan. "I'm sorry the woman's dead, but I'm glad Pete has the chance to make a fresh start. I believe he'll do well in the trucking business."

"I hope so. Just don't you two go out partying too much."

He gave a little laugh. "You know about that?"

"Let's just say Pete kinda drunk-dialed me to ask me to work the next morning."

"Oh yeah. Well, Pete just needed to cut loose a little bit . . . let go of some of his grief."

"I understand," I said. "It's good he's got you and Chris Anne to help him through this."

"He's got you people at the Joint too. I mean, I know you wouldn't exactly say you were friends with Lou Lou, but most of you seem to like Pete."

"We do. Pete's a decent guy." I lowered my voice. "You don't know of anyone who might've wanted Lou Lou dead, do you?"

"Only everybody that ever met her. Am I right?" He

laughed again. "You know I'm joshing you. Why would you ask a thing like that?"

"Well, since I found Lou Lou, the police think I look pretty guilty."

"Aw, shucks. That's crazy. Her being hit in the head like that? Killed with one blow? A little thing like you couldn't have done that, and the police know it. I wouldn't worry about that, if I were you. You just concentrate on making the place nice and pretty for your customers."

"Thanks, Stan." I apologized again for nearly mowing him down and said I'd better get on with my rounds.

"That's all right. Just be careful."

The pneumatic doors opened when I approached, and I went from the lovely coolness of the hardware store into the oppressive heat. I was surprised that Stan had been so nice today. Of course, maybe he'd always been in a bad mood when he came into the Joint because of his disagreements with Lou Lou. Or maybe he was high or something today. Roger had said he thought Stan was a drug dealer. But I'd never seen him doing anything that struck me as shady. Was I naïve, or did I just want to think the best of people?

I got into my car and started the engine. Before backing out of the parking lot, I called Roger.

"Hi, Amy," he answered.

"Hi. Could I see you sometime today? I'm meeting with Pete at Billy's office later to sign the paperwork, and then I'll own the café."

"Congratulations, Flowerpot!"

"Thanks!"

"What time do you want to meet?"

"How about this—we'll meet at the café at around five thirty so you can get an idea of what kinds of renovations need to be done. And then I'll buy you dinner somewhere, and we can discuss everything."

"That works. I'll see you at *your* café at half past five."

Chapter 10

&R oger was already at the café when I got there. I
parked my car, got out, and hurried over to him.
He was standing under the front door awning in the
shade. Grinning, I held up the café keys and shook them.

"I wish you'd show just a little enthusiasm about this
place," he said.

I threw my arms around his neck and hugged him.
"Eeeee! The café is officially mine!"

He chuckled. "Congratulations. Now, let's get in there
and see what we can do to make it *look* like it's yours."

"All right."

My hand trembled so badly as I tried to put the key in
the lock that Roger had to unlock the door himself.

"Calm down, Flowerpot." Roger held the door so I
could be the first to step inside.

"We have a lot to do," I said as I looked around.

"I know."

"First things first." I took the paint swatches from my purse.

"Well, that's important, but the *first* thing is to clean out Lou Lou's office. I suggest you get a professional cleaning team to do that. Then once the office has been scrubbed and everything in it removed, we can redo it and you'll never . . ." His voice trailed off.

I smiled slightly. "Oh, I'll still know."

"And you're sure you'll be able to handle that?"

"Maybe you could somehow tear out the office and make it more of a storage room or something." I sighed. "I certainly can't see myself sitting in there working on the books. I'd rather do that from home anyway."

"We'll think of something. Did you talk with Pete about the things in his mother's office?"

"Not really . . . but I will. I know he took some ledgers and things that were in there, money from the safe, some documents. But he might want to keep her desk and the rest of the furniture."

"I have a cleaning team I use out of Bristol. They're really good, and they're reasonably priced. Would you mind if I went ahead and called them in?"

"Not at all. Would you like some coffee or water or something while we talk?" I asked.

"A bottle of water would be great."

I got each of us a bottle of water and sat down at the counter beside Roger. He had taken out a yellow legal pad and was making notes. I looked around the dining room. The walls needed repainting. These ugly chipped tables and chairs would have to go. The counter and stools needed to be replaced. We needed new light fixtures. I wanted a display case for baked goods and specialty items. And, of course, the floor would have to be redone. If I just reopened this place rather than making the café my own, I'd have to call it "Calamity Café."

"Let's see those paint swatches," he said.

I put the swatches on the counter. Roger held different combinations side by side until he finally chose *Lemonade* and *Riviera*. "It's a paler yellow and a bolder blue. What do you think?"

"I defer to your expertise, and I think it'll look great."

"And a soft gray or muted orange for the counters and tables."

I didn't have any swatches for either color. "Which do you think would be best?"

"Personally, I'd go with the gray."

"Gray, it is."

He took out a measuring tape. "I'll need your help with this."

Together we measured the entire café with the exception of Lou Lou's office. Neither of us wanted to go in there until it had been cleaned, and Roger told me he'd be thinking of ways to renovate the café so that it wasn't necessary for anyone to use the office.

"So how do we do this?" I asked. "Do I put you on retainer?"

He smiled. "I'll open an account for you at the home store for all your supplies and everything, and they'll bill you for the materials. I have a contractor discount, so you'll get that too."

"I don't want you to be cheated out of part of your profit," I said.

"I won't be. I never make anyone pay extra for materials. As for the labor, how about I bill you weekly?"

"Sounds good."

"Have you made out a budget yet?" he asked.

"For the renovations? No. I thought you'd help me with that."

"I will. I'm talking about a budget for the café—payroll, supplies, electricity."

"I've got that all worked out."

"Great. I'll get you the renovation budget," said Roger. "I know your nana left you a nice chunk of change, but you won't have it for long unless you take care of it."

"I know, Roger." Once a guy adopts you as his baby sister, you're always his baby sister.

"I know you know, but I figured it would bear repeating. The first thing I'm going to do is change these locks. I took the liberty of stopping by earlier and seeing what kind of locks are used on the front and back doors, and I picked new ones up at the hardware store."

"Wow, thanks." He was a pretty good big brother.

"You don't want Pete or any of his buddies coming back in here when you're not around, now that you own the place," he said. "And I was *real* uncomfortable with that key under the rock at the back door. Who knows how many people knew about that."

"I wonder if that's how the killer got in on Monday night."

"I wouldn't be surprised . . . unless both doors were usually unlocked while Lou Lou was here. Regardless, it's likely that a lot of people know about that key." He shook his head. "That was stupid on the Holmans' part. Why would they put a key right by the door like that?"

"I guess they trusted that the people who knew about the key wouldn't barge in without good reason."

"Well, some folks think hitting a woman over the head and robbing her café would be a sufficient reason."

"Yeah, but Lou Lou and Pete *obviously* trusted the people who knew about the key. I never knew about it until the night Pete drunk-dialed me and asked me to come in to work the next morning."

"I don't know about Lou Lou, but Pete doesn't always exercise the best judgment when it comes to people," Roger said. "Take his girlfriend, for example. She did a stint in jail for drugs."

"Chris Anne did? Are you kidding me?"

He gave an exaggerated blink. "Have you *met* Chris Anne?"

"Well, yeah. . . ." I thought about it for a moment. "I guess you're right. Pete doesn't hang out with the most reputable people."

"Face it. Pete isn't all that reputable either," he said. "You just told me he drunk-dialed you, and I've seen him a few times when I was sure his condition wasn't entirely due to alcohol consumption. And if you're hanging around with drug addicts . . ."

"I know . . . but he never missed work or anything, not that I knew of anyway."

He shrugged. "It just pays to be careful, Flowerpot. You can't be a hundred percent sure of who you're dealing with around here. Don't forget what happened to Lou Lou."

"How could I forget?"

* * *

The next morning, I opened the café early. The night before I'd printed up flyers saying that the café was under new management and would be closed while renovations were under way. I said we would close right after breakfast today so patrons could attend the funeral of Ms. Holman. I had the flyers on the counter, and I taped one to the front door.

Homer came in at his usual time, and I had his sausage biscuit just about ready when he came through the door.

"Am I that predictable?" he asked, as I sat the sausage biscuit in front of him.

"You're that steady." I smiled as I poured his coffee. "So, who's your hero?"

"Yesterday it was Dwight Eisenhower. Today it's Thomas Jefferson."

"You must be feeling presidential."

"Maybe. I've been thinking quite a bit about you and your predicaments."

"Predicaments?"

"Sure. Everybody knows you walked in and found Lou Lou dead, and I can see by this here paper that you've bought the café. Well, good for you. Jefferson once said, 'Do you want to know who you are? Don't ask. Act! Action will delineate and define you.' Do you see where I'm going with that advice?"

"Not exactly."

"You run your business the way it ought to be run and make it a source of pride and happiness to you," he said. "Before long, people will forget about Lou Lou and everything bad that's happened . . . and so will you."

"It going to be pretty hard to forget, Homer. For me and for everybody else too."

He wagged a finger at me. "You can't stop a woman with the right mental attitude from achieving her goal. And you can't help one with the wrong attitude."

"Jefferson?"

"Paraphrased. I know it'll be hard to forget about Lou Lou and what happened here that night, but you have to do your best to put it behind you and move ahead. If you need to, talk with a therapist or something. There's no shame in that."

"I appreciate the advice," I said. "But I think I'll be okay."

"All right. I'm here if you need a friend."

"Thank you, Homer."

I fielded lots of questions throughout the morning about what I was naming the café, whether or not the staff would be kept on, and when the café would reopen. The last one was the only one I couldn't answer for sure. My answer was that I would try to have the café open—all shiny and new—in a month. I knew it was a stretch, but Roger seemed to think we could pull it off if we all worked together.

As soon as the stragglers from the breakfast crowd left, I locked up the café and went home to get ready for Lou Lou's funeral. I took a quick bath and then stood in front of my closet looking for something to wear that would be decent but that I wouldn't burn up in. I wound up choosing a black pencil skirt and a sleeveless black top. I went with black espadrilles because I knew they'd be easier to walk in than heels.

Stepping into the funeral home, I was more nervous than a long-tailed cat in a roomful of rocking chairs. Of course, I'd realized even before Homer mentioned it this morning that everyone knew I was the one who'd found Lou Lou. But there was nothing like somebody saying it out loud to truly drive the point home. Did anyone think I'd actually *killed* her?

Was it my imagination, or did people actually stop talking when they saw me approaching? Were their eyes shooting accusations my way?

I ducked out of the crowded lobby and into the bathroom. I wet a paper towel and cooled the back of my neck with it. I had to get a grip.

I tossed the paper towel into the wastebasket and freshened up my lipstick.

The door burst open and Chris Anne rushed in, threw open a stall, and then threw up her lunch.

"Oh my goodness," I said. "Are you all right? Is there anything I can do?"

Of course, she couldn't speak right then. She was still crouched over the toilet. I felt like an idiot. When she finally emerged from the stall, she was so weak and pale that I rushed to put my arm around her and lead her to a chair that was just inside the door. I got her a damp paper towel and handed it to her.

"Thank you," she whispered. "Do you have a mint or something?"

I did have a peppermint, and Chris Anne took it gratefully.

"Is it your nerves?" I asked.

She shook her head. "It's my baby."

I felt my eyes nearly pop out of my head.

"Don't say anything to anybody, please," she said. "I haven't even told Pete yet. I thought it'd be something good to tell him later today."

"I won't say a word. Congratulations."

"Thank you." She smiled. "I've suspected for a couple of weeks—even took a pregnancy test I got at the dollar store. But I wanted to be sure before saying anything. I knew Pete's momma would hit the ceiling."

"I don't know. She might've been glad."

"Are you serious? Pete was afraid to tell her anything about us. He'd have had to break the news about being in a relationship with me combined with the fact that I'm pregnant. That's why I didn't tell him until it was official. I went to the doctor yesterday."

"Well, I'm happy for you . . . and for Pete."

An odd expression must've crossed my face because Chris Anne said, "Don't worry. I'm not naming my baby 'Lou Lou.' "

I laughed. "Tell Pete that was a one-of-a-kind name for a one-of-a-kind lady. I think he'll understand."

"I sure hope so. Either way . . ."

"Are you feeling better?" I asked. "We should probably go into the chapel."

She nodded. "I think I can do it now. Would you please walk with me? Help hold me up?"

"Of course I will." I was as glad of the support as she was. It was easier for me not having to walk into the chapel alone too.

Either the stares were less accusing than they had been, or I wasn't as paranoid as I had been before. Chris Anne and I walked down the aisle. My plan was to hand her over to Pete and then find my mom, Aunt Bess, and Jackie, and sit with them. But Chris Anne wouldn't let me go. She had an ally, and she was sticking with me for as long as possible.

The funeral service was long and obviously conducted by a preacher who didn't know Lou Lou Holman in the least. I don't know who he was, but he wasn't one of Winter Garden's pastors. I'm not saying it wasn't a nice service—the choir sang, and the preacher extolled Lou Lou's virtues—but it was generic. It was as if the preacher had been given a fill-in-the-blank form prior to preparing for the funeral.

Name of deceased: Lou Lou Holman
Occupation: Business owner
Mother of one

And then he simply recited from the list.

"Lou Lou Holman was a beloved business owner, a pillar of the community, and a respected member of the Winter Garden Chamber of Commerce. She was devoted to her only son . . ."

Naturally, my mind wandered as the man droned on. If Lou Lou was so devoted to Pete, why had he been afraid to tell her what was going on with his life? That he had a girlfriend, that he wanted to get married, that he wanted to buy a truck and go into business for himself? Granted, Lou Lou might not have agreed with all—or any—of Pete's decisions, but they were his choices to make. A forty-year-old man who was still frightened of his mother? What was up with that? Had he been afraid he'd hurt her feelings? Had he been scared she'd write him out of her will? Had he used Lou Lou as an excuse to avoid growing up and having any responsibilities until life—or Chris Anne—had backed him against a wall?

I glanced over at Pete. He was staring at the floor between his shoes. Beside me, Chris Anne fanned herself with a tissue and patted Pete on the back. I merely hoped the service was almost over.

Chapter 11

After the service, I met up with Mom, Aunt Bess, and Jackie in the lobby. I explained that I was going to come and sit with them but that Chris Anne had held on to me for dear life.

"That's all right," said Mom. "We'll see you tomorrow for lunch."

"What're you making?" Aunt Bess asked.

"We haven't decided yet, Granny," said Jackie. "We'll get right on that."

"See that you do."

From the corner of my eye, I saw Sheriff Billings. He was looking straight at me. I nodded in lieu of a better greeting, and he nodded back.

Deputy Hall was behind the sheriff. "Ms. Flowers."

"Deputy."

It felt strange and uncomfortable addressing Ryan that way. Then again, it felt strange and uncomfortable to refer to the deputy as "Ryan," even in my own head. But there was some sort of spark between us. He knew it, and I knew it. And yet, I hadn't been ruled out as a suspect in Lou Lou's murder, so we'd better just dump a bucket of water on that spark and forget about it for the time being.

"Amy?"

Jackie's voice drew me out of my reverie.

"Want to meet at your place and decide what to make for lunch tomorrow?" she asked.

"Sounds good," I said.

"I'll run home and change, and I'll see you in about forty-five minutes."

I nodded, my eyes trailing Deputy Hall as he stepped out into the blinding sunlight.

"He *is* a handsome one," Mom murmured in my ear.

"Who?"

She gave me the "oh, please" look, took Aunt Bess's arm, and left.

By the time Jackie had arrived, I had out the laptop and was looking at Aunt Bess's Pinterest board *Things I'd Love to Eat but Won't Fix*. I looked up at my cousin and shook my head.

"Aunt Bess *does* realize that there are food categories besides desserts, doesn't she?"

"I'm not so sure that she does. Have you made any decisions about what we're going to make?"

"I've narrowed it down. You can make the final choices." I turned the laptop so Jackie could see the screen. "Oven-fried catfish, stuffed shells, or country ham with redeye gravy."

"Let's go with the ham," she said. "I figure the funeral has her in a nostalgic mood thinking of everybody from Winter Garden that she used to know. Maybe the ham and gravy will give her the warm fuzzies."

"All right. We can make biscuits, grits, and maybe a bacon-cheddar quiche to go with it. What do you think?"

"Sounds good. And we can't forget that lemon pie."

"That'll do it." I smiled. "Unless she's changed her mind about the pie."

Jackie took her phone from her purse, called Aunt Bess, and confirmed that she did want a lemon pie.

"Now that we have our menu, should we head to the grocery store?" I asked.

"In a minute. First I want you to tell me what the deal was with Chris Anne. She was practically glued to you at the funeral. It's not like you two are friends or anything."

"We met up in the bathroom. I was having a fit of nerves, and she came in. She wasn't feeling well."

"Why wasn't she feeling well?"

I looked away. Jackie wasn't only my cousin. Being a year older than me, she'd been my best friend all my life. "I promised I wouldn't say anything to anyone."

"You know I won't tell anybody else." She paused. "Wait . . . in the bathroom not feeling well. Oh my gosh! She's pregnant?"

"I didn't say that."

"You didn't have to. Does Pete know?"

"If Chris Anne has any special news to share with Pete, I imagine she'll talk with him about it sometime today. Maybe she hopes to cheer him up . . . if whatever she has to tell him is happy news."

Jackie rolled her eyes. "Okay. Come off it. You didn't

tell me anything, so let's talk straight. Does she think Pete will be happy about her being pregnant?"

"She seemed to think so. And I hope he will be."

"I hope so too. But with all his talk about getting his trucking business started and Chris Anne being his partner . . . he might've preferred to wait a little while before having a family."

"That's true. I hadn't thought of that."

"Well, let's make a list of the ingredients we'll need and get to the store. We don't have time to worry about Pete and Chris Anne right now," she said.

To save us some time on Sunday, I'd gone ahead and made the lemon pie when I'd returned home from the store on Saturday. Now it was in a baker's box in the passenger seat of my car as I drove up to "the big house." The house was close enough that I usually walked when I visited, but I couldn't have carried the pie and the groceries without inevitably dropping something, so today I drove.

Mom heard me coming and opened the door. "Need any help with the groceries?"

"No, but if you'll get this pie, I can bring in all the groceries in one trip."

She took the pie, and I managed to stack the plastic bags onto my arms and muscle them into the kitchen.

I heard Aunt Bess hurrying into the kitchen like a little girl on Christmas morning. "What're we having?"

"Ham and redeye gravy, a bacon-and-cheddar quiche, biscuits, grits, and—by special request—a lemon pie."

She licked her lips. "Um-mmmm!"

"Where's Jackie?" Mom asked.

"I haven't talked with her this morning, but she should be here soon. I'll get started on the biscuits."

As I mixed up the ingredients for the biscuits, Mom and Aunt Bess sat down at the kitchen table to drink coffee and watch me work. I'd come by my culinary skills from Nana. Mom didn't like to cook. She did it when she had to, but she certainly didn't enjoy it. Same with Aunt Bess.

"That was a nice service yesterday," Aunt Bess said.

"I thought it was kinda sad." I mixed the dough with my hands. "The preacher didn't even know Lou Lou."

"Course he didn't! How else were they gonna get him to say nice things about her?"

"Aunt Bess!" Mom scolded.

"Now, Jenna, the truth'll stand when the world's on fire."

I hid my smile as I turned my dough out onto the floured board. "Were all of Lou Lou's people ornery, Aunt Bess?"

"Her daddy wasn't too awful bad. And he was nice-looking too. It was a shame Lou Lou and Pete turned out so homely."

"So Lou Holman was a nice man?" I prompted.

"I don't know that I'd call him nice, but he wasn't as bad as his daddy and his uncle," she said. "One time when I was young, I heard that Lou's daddy, Bo, and his uncle Grady had gone over to North Carolina and robbed a bank. That was along about the time that Lou was building the Joint."

I froze, doughy hands in the air. "Did you just say that Lou Lou's granddaddy robbed a bank?"

"That's what I heard. It was over in Boone or somewhere. But it might've just been a tale, honey. They weren't ever arrested, and I never heard tell of anybody finding the money they were supposed to have stolen. Maybe somebody just made it all up."

I washed the dough off my hands and got the rolling pin. "Why would somebody make up a story like that?"

"Aw, you know how things get started. They didn't have television or Internet. Plus, Grady and Bo—Lou's daddy—were as crooked as a dog's hind leg and twice as dirty. It wasn't hard to imagine them going across the border, robbing a bank, and hightailing it back home."

"Didn't the North Carolina police investigate the matter?" Mom asked.

"Of course, they did—at least, that's what I heard—but since they couldn't find the money and the men had worn masks while robbing the bank, the police couldn't prove the Holmans did any wrong."

Jackie was breathless when she rushed into the kitchen. "Sorry I'm late. I overslept."

"You've done missed out on a wild tale," I said.

"And I ain't repeating it." Aunt Bess gave a resolute nod.

Jackie merely rolled her eyes. "Granny tells lots of wild tales. What do you need me to do?"

"You can start frying the ham while I finish getting the biscuits ready to go into the oven."

"I grew up hearing wild tales," said Aunt Bess. "I'm just passing on the oral history of my people."

Mom laughed. "Whether they're true or not isn't the point."

Aunt Bess huffed. "Do you always believe what those people on television tell you? Or are they just telling you what they're paid to say?"

"Well, I think that depends," said Mom. "If they're telling me to buy XYZ shampoo because it's the best thing on the market, I'm going to be suspicious. But if they're telling me someone's hair fell out after using XYZ shampoo, then I'm going to think twice before I use the stuff."

"Either way, you're being swayed by the television. I was swayed by my parents, my grandparents, my aunts, and my uncles."

Jackie and I shared a glance. Aunt Bess had a point. But I knew that those old tales handed down from generation to generation could also become like that old game of telephone, where one person whispers something into someone's ear who then whispers it to someone else and by the time the story gets back to the originator, there's seldom much resemblance to that initial report.

By the time we were finishing lunch, all thoughts of wild tales had been replaced by the yumminess of lemon pie.

"Your meringue is always so good, Amy," said Mom.

"Yeah. Around here, nobody makes good meringue." Aunt Bess cut her eyes toward Mom. "What's your secret?"

"Well, for a cream pie like this, I make a Swiss meringue rather than a common meringue," I said.

"That's it, Jenna," said Aunt Bess. "Amy's meringue is uncommon. She does it like they do in Switzerland." Aunt Bess then nodded at me as if she, the Swiss, and I had it all figured out.

Later that afternoon, I was in the fancy room reading a small-business magazine when Roger dropped in. I took him to the kitchen. The fancy room wasn't Roger's style, and I figured he'd want a glass of tea or a cup of coffee while we talked.

I was right. He wanted a cup of coffee and the last of the preacher cookies.

"I've got an idea." He brought out his yellow legal pad. "What would you think of this? We do away with the office completely. In its place, we build a screened-in porch with picnic tables. Patrons could enjoy the space most of three seasons out of the year." As he talked, he was drawing the café and how it would look with the screened-in side porch.

"I think that's a terrific idea! I love it."

"Really?"

"Really." I smiled. "You're a genius."

"Oh, I *know* that. I just thought this way, you wouldn't have to go into Lou Lou's office again. We can completely demolish it and turn it into something new. And the something new adds value and an additional aesthetic to the café."

"Brilliant. Thank you."

"That's what you're paying me the big bucks for." He popped the last bite of a preacher cookie into his mouth.

"Have you . . . have you looked at the office?"

He nodded, swallowed, and wiped his mouth on his napkin. "The cleaning crew spent hours in there yesterday. I went by before heading over here to make sure we won't have any trouble tearing out the office."

"Wh-what does it look like?"

"You'd never know what happened in there. The place is spotless." He took a sip of his coffee. "Here's the thing, though. You have to decide what you're going to do with all the stuff still in that office. Do you want any of the furniture?"

"No. I don't want anything from that office. I don't need any reminders."

"That's what I figured. But we need to do something with it. Does Pete want it?"

"I don't know," I said. "I'll call him and ask him."

"He really needs to sort through the documents to see if there's anything important there. But, if he doesn't, we can simply take them to the recycling center. I can call and see if Goodwill or the Salvation Army would take the furniture if Pete doesn't want it. Find out today, and let me know in the morning."

"All right, I will. What time should we be there tomorrow?"

"Daylight," said Roger. "If you want to reopen the café in a month, we're going to have to put in a lot of hours."

"Fine by me. I'll bring sausage biscuits for everybody."

"They'd appreciate that." He finished off his coffee, stood, and patted my shoulder. "The Down South Café is going to be beautiful, Flowerpot."

"Thanks."

I put off calling Pete for as long as I could. He'd only buried his mother yesterday, and now here I was calling to ask if he'd like to go through the things in her office. I knew he'd said earlier that he'd gotten what he'd needed from Lou Lou's office; but I thought that maybe after the finality of her death had set in, he'd reconsider.

I finally dialed the Holman home at around nine

o'clock that night. The phone rang three times, and I was getting ready to hang up when Pete answered.

"Hello." His voice sounded flat and empty.

"Pete, hi. It's Amy. How are you?"

"I'm getting by. How are you?"

"I'm all right. I'm sorry to disturb you, but I need to ask you something. As you know, I'm renovating the café. The builders are going to take out your momma's office."

"Well, that's fine, Amy. Do whatever you want to do. It's yours now."

"Um . . . thanks . . . but I thought you might want to go through the contents of the office," I said. "You know . . . the furniture, the filing cabinet, the knickknacks . . . just to see if there's anything there you might want to save."

"I don't care about any of that. Just throw it all out."

"No, wait!"

Is that Chris Anne's voice?

It was. She'd grabbed the phone away from Pete.

"He doesn't know what he's saying, Amy. Save all Lou Lou's stuff for us somewhere on the property. We'll be there first thing in the morning to go through it all."

"Chris Anne, I don't want to," I heard Pete tell her.

"You might not right now, but if you let them throw away that stuff without even seeing what it was, you'll regret it."

I was inclined to agree with Chris Anne, but I kept my opinion to myself.

"If it's so important to you, *you* go!" he shouted.

"Fine! I will!"

She directed her next comment to me rather than Pete. "See you tomorrow, then. Thanks for holding that stuff for us."

"No problem," I said.

After I ended the call, I wondered about the couple. Had Chris Anne told Pete about the pregnancy? Had Jackie been right that Pete would be upset by the news? After all, his dream did involve him and Chris Anne hitting the open road in a tractor-trailer. That would be hard to do with Chris Anne pregnant, and it would be practically impossible once she'd had the baby.

Maybe she hadn't told him about the pregnancy yet and he was merely morose about his mother's death. I could understand his not wanting to go through her things, but I thought he should. They could bring him some comfort. I'd been consoled when I'd looked through some of the things Nana had left behind. They'd reminded me of her sense of humor, how much she'd loved us, how thoughtful she'd been. Those things had been in Nana's home, but if she'd had an office, I'd have wanted to see those things too. I'd have wanted to look at everything she'd left behind.

Of course, this was Lou Lou Holman we were talking about now. As far as I'd ever seen, she'd had no sense of humor and she'd certainly not been thoughtful. But, hopefully, she had been considerate toward her son, and he'd find something from her office that would make him smile.

Chapter 12

Since I had to be at the Down South Café so early—that sounded so cool in my head that I had to say it out loud just to bask in the words—I got up an hour before daylight so I could make the sausage biscuits I'd promised Roger. Of course, I'd chosen sausage biscuits because I thought it was likely that Homer would be coming by. And Dilly might also stop by so she could have her biscuit and take one to the raccoon.

I arrived at the café with a plastic container filled with sausage biscuits—I'd say I had about thirty-five. Roger and his crew were already there. He'd kept a key when he'd changed the locks so he could work whenever he wanted.

I put the biscuits on the counter and told the workers to help themselves while I made coffee. In addition to Roger's workers, Jackie, Aaron, and a couple of the other café staff came to help us. I was paying the café staff to help. The ones who didn't come in either wanted time off or they intended to find jobs elsewhere. Either way was fine with me. I didn't want to have to replace any members of the existing staff, but I had a month to do so if need be.

After we'd had breakfast, I put the leftovers in the refrigerator.

"What do you want us to do?" I asked Roger.

"You guys need to move these tables and chairs out into the parking lot and stack them up. Since you're getting new ones, we'll have these hauled off."

"All right. If anyone comes by and wants a set, they can have them."

He nodded. "Okay. We're going to get started tearing down the office as soon as we move everything out of it. Did you talk with Pete?"

"I did. He told me to get rid of everything, but Chris Anne said they'd come by this morning and look through it first. I thought we could move it all outside and see whether or not they show up today." I put my hands on my hips. "After we get everything hauled out, then what?"

He pointed to a stack of paint cans, brushes, rollers, pans, and masking tape in the corner. "Get to taping off the dining room."

"Got it, chief."

Aaron and Jackie were already carrying chairs outside, so I began helping Roger bring everything out of the office. I still had the heebie-jeebies about returning to that room, but I was curious about what Lou Lou had been working on the night she was killed.

Either Roger or the cleaning crew had put everything into banker's boxes with openings on the sides so they could be carried easily. I was lugging a box outside when I noticed a sheet of notebook paper sticking out. It caught my attention because it had STAN WHEELER written on it. I set the box down and removed the sheet of paper. Beside Stan's name, Lou Lou had drawn a fish.

I dug a little deeper into the box and found a list of suppliers. I thought that would come in handy, although I was still going to research suppliers of my own. When possible, I wanted to buy from the local farmers. I also found an old ledger with accounts payable and accounts receivable. I knew Pete had the newest ones—which was good, since he'd be dealing with those on behalf of Lou Lou's estate—but I thought I might want to look through it later just to see what Lou Lou's bookkeeping had been like.

The café staff had just finished moving all the tables, chairs, and other fixtures outside and stacking them when Pete and Chris Anne arrived. Fortunately, Roger's crew and I had moved everything from the office out here too.

I went out to greet Pete and Chris Anne. "Hi. I'm glad you decided to come by."

"She twisted my arm," Pete said.

"I figured as much."

Chris Anne simply smiled and then got started going through Lou Lou's filing cabinet. I didn't really think that was her place, but then it wasn't *my* place to say so. I told them to let me know if they needed anything.

I went back inside, cringing at the sound of a sledge-hammer pounding away at the office walls.

"So Aaron and I are going to start taping around the windows and doors," said Jackie.

"Okay. I'll help you."

Before I could begin helping Jackie and Aaron, Homer came in.

"Good morning, Homer," I said. "You're early today. Who's your hero?"

"Henry Ford. He once said that coming together is the beginning, keeping together is progress, and working together is success. I'm here to help."

"Oh, Homer, you don't have to do that. I do have a sausage biscuit for you, though."

"It isn't time for my biscuit yet, but I'd like to help you with your café. What can I do?"

"Will you give me a hand in taping around the trim?"

"I sure will." He beamed. "Like Mr. Ford always said, 'Nothing is particularly hard if you divide it into small jobs.'"

"He was a smart man."

"One of the smartest."

Homer and I had barely taped off one wall when Stan Wheeler poked his head into the café.

"Hey, Amy, can I see you for a second?" he asked.

"Sure." I wiped my hands on my shorts and stepped out into the parking lot. "What can I do for you?"

"Are you selling these tables and chairs?"

"Nope, but you can have a set if you'd like."

"I'll be glad to pay for them."

"Not for sale," I said. "But please take a set."

"I appreciate that."

"We're taking a set of them too, if that's all right," Chris Anne said. She was still busily loading things into the back of Pete's pickup truck while he sat on a chair, looking miserable.

"That's fine." I went over to Pete. "May I get you anything? Coffee? Water?"

He shook his head. "Naw, I'm fine."

I knew he wasn't, but I also knew there was nothing I could do to help. "Let me know if you change your mind."

I went back inside to help Homer with the trim. I was relieved a few minutes later when I heard Pete's truck drive off . . . although I half expected to learn that Chris Anne had left in it, leaving poor Pete behind to wait for her to return for another load. I glanced out the window, and it appeared that she, Pete, and Stan were all gone.

Listening to Roger—or one of his crew members—pounding on that wall made me wish I'd thought to bring a radio or MP3 player this morning to give us something more pleasant to hear while we worked. But the slamming sledgehammer would still be audible above the music. I reminded myself of how great the screened-in porch would look when the work was finished.

"Amy! I need you in here!" Roger called.

I told Homer I'd be right back and hurried into the hallway. My steps faltered as I approached the open door to the office. "Wh-what do you need?"

He was holding a green metal lockbox. "This was in the wall."

"What is it?"

"I don't know. Let's go find out." He jerked his head toward the opening in the wall, and I followed him out to the backyard. He called out to his crew to keep busy and that he'd be right back.

Roger used a screwdriver and a hammer to break the lock. He glanced at me before opening the box.

My jaw dropped when I saw the contents of the box. "Is that *real*?"

The box contained stacks of hundred-dollar bills.

"Appears to be."

"Oh my gosh! What're we gonna do?"

"You're going to calm down," he said.

"Right. Right." I calmed down for nearly two seconds. "What're we gonna *do*?"

"Look, the money was hidden in the wall for a reason. I'd say there's something not right about it, wouldn't you?"

I bobbed my head. "Oh my *gosh*! The bank robbery! This is the money from the bank robbery!"

"What bank robbery? And keep your voice down."

"Aunt Bess told us Sunday that Lou's dad and uncle robbed a bank in North Carolina, but it was never proven and the money was never found." I shook both arms at the box. *"That's the money!"*

"We don't know that," he said.

"What're we gonna do?"

"Will you please stop asking me that? You sound like Prissy from *Gone with the Wind*."

"I'm sorry, but I don't know what to do." Tears welled in my eyes.

"Call that deputy you know."

"I don't *know* him, know him. I just *kinda* know him . . . because I'm a murder suspect." The tears spilled onto my cheeks.

Roger sighed and pulled me into a one-armed hug. "Stop crying. If most people found a box containing stacks of money in their wall, they'd be thrilled."

"I'm not most people. Most people didn't walk into an office to find their boss dead. Most people's necklaces aren't found beneath the dead woman's desk. Most people's great-aunts didn't tell them about a bank robbery that happened years ago when this café was being built." I just wanted to start my business. I didn't need any more drama. It was bad enough the building was part of a murder investigation. Was I now going to be slowed down for weeks while the police dug into a cold case—another investigation that involved *me*? It was too much.

"Calm down and call the deputy. You obviously had nothing to do with a bank robbery that occurred before you were even born."

"But what if the money *isn't* from the bank robbery? What if it's from something else?"

"Fine. I'll call the deputy," he said.

"No! I'll call him. I don't want him to think I'm trying to hide something."

Roger stared at me blankly. "I've slung a sledgehammer all morning, and now *you're* giving me a headache."

"Sorry. I'll make the call."

He handed me the box. "Keep this with you. Or, at least, put it in the kitchen. And don't mention it to anyone else until after the deputy tells you what to do with it."

"All right."

We went back around to the side of the building and stepped through the wall. I took the box into the kitchen, where Jackie was warming up Homer's sausage biscuit.

"What's that?" she asked.

"Just something Roger found."

She left with the plate, and I called Deputy Hall.

"Ryan Hall."

"Hi. This is Amy Flowers."

"Good morning, Ms. Flowers. What can I help you with?"

"Um . . . Could you come to the café? Alone, maybe? I mean, we—the workers . . . you know, the construction crew—they found something in the wall when they tore it out . . . and I don't know. . . . Could you come over?"

He chuckled. "What'd you find? A body?"

"No! I mean, not yet. There *is* one wall still standing. You don't think there's a body in there, do you?"

"It was a joke, Amy. I'm on my way."

"Th-thank you." With shaking hands, I ended the call.

I'd placed the box on the counter in front of me, and now I decided to look in it again. Maybe the money was fake. Maybe we'd been so surprised to find it that we had taken it at face value, when a closer examination would prove that we were all up in the air over nothing. Okay, so Roger wasn't up in the air, but I was in orbit.

I opened the box and peered inside. That money certainly looked legitimate. I mean, Ben Franklin's head wasn't enormous the way it was on newer bills, but it was Franklin. It wasn't some superhero or cartoon character. I wondered how much was there, but I didn't dare touch it. I quickly closed the box.

"Are you okay?" Jackie asked, returning Homer's plate. "You look pale."

"Yeah, fine. Hard work, I guess. Taking its toll on me."

She frowned. "You don't seem all right. You're talking like you've been sucking helium."

"Nope. No helium for me. I'm going to have some water. You want some water?"

"I'm good. I'm going to get back to taping. You should rest for a few minutes."

"Okay. Thanks."

She gave me another odd look before going back into the dining room. I needed to get back to work too. But I was going to have that water first. And try to get my trembling hands under control so my tape wouldn't be as crooked as a rainbow.

Luckily, Deputy Hall arrived before I'd even finished my water. I heard his car pull up, and I hurried to the doorway between the kitchen and the dining area and motioned him back. I didn't look directly at Jackie, but I could see from the corner of my eye that she was giving me the "I knew it!" look.

"Thank goodness you're here," I told Deputy Hall as I took his arm and pulled him the rest of the way into the kitchen.

He put his hands on my shoulders and examined my face. "Are you all right?"

"I'm better now."

He smiled.

"Here." I hurried over to the counter, got the box, and shoved it toward him.

"What is this?"

"Money."

He lifted the lid. "Wow." He put the box on the counter and slipped on some latex gloves. "Let's see how much is here." He took the stacks out of the box and began thumbing through one of them. "There appear to be fifty bills in a stack, so each of these stacks contains five thousand dollars."

I gasped. "And how many stacks are there?"

"There are four stacks here. That's twenty thousand dollars."

"Why would somebody have twenty thousand dollars stashed in a wall?"

"I don't know," said Deputy Hall. "But I'll take this with me and let you know what I can turn up."

"Thank you."

I watched him put the money back into the box.

"I want you to know I had nothing to do with any of this," I said.

He grinned at me. "I know."

"I wasn't even the one who found it in the wall. That was Roger."

"I believe you."

"You might want to check into a bank robbery that happened about the time those bills were minted." I told him Aunt Bess's story about the rumored North Carolina bank robbery.

"Thanks. I'll take all of this under advisement and be in touch when I know something. In the meantime, don't say a word about this to anyone. And caution your friend who found the box to keep it under wraps too. We don't want people to know we have this much money in the evidence locker at the jail."

"Right. Roger won't say anything. And, of course, I won't either. Neither of us will say anything about finding money stashed in the wall of Lou Lou's—*dead* Lou Lou's—office. I mean, first I stumble onto Lou Lou lying dead across her desk and now we find money hidden in the wall? What next?"

"There's really no need to be upset about this." He placed his hand gently on my arm.

"I—I know. It's just . . ." I took two deep breaths. "I've been through so much over the past week."

"Maybe whatever happens next will be something great," he said.

"I hope it will be." I gave him a bag to put the box in so no one would notice it when he left.

"So do I. I'll call you as soon as I know something."

Deputy Hall had barely backed out of the parking lot before Jackie hurried back into the kitchen.

"What's going on?"

"Nothing," I said.

She put her hands on her hips.

"Roger found something in the wall. We aren't supposed to talk about it. In fact, I need to go tell Roger not to say anything about it."

"What was it?" she asked.

"What did I just tell you?"

She pressed her lips together. "Fine. I won't say anything."

"I know. And I'll tell you all about it as soon as I can." I went out the kitchen door to find Roger.

Chapter 13

We stopped working at lunchtime and had ham sandwiches, and then we all—including Homer—resumed work on the café until five o'clock that afternoon. After that, I invited everybody to the pizza parlor for dinner. There were a couple of Roger's workers who had families to get home to or had already made other plans, but everyone else went to the pizza parlor.

It was a ragtag crew that ambled into Winter Garden Pizza, and we took the entire back corner of booths and tables. A waitress came over and took our drink orders, and I went ahead and ordered one of nearly every pizza on the menu.

As soon as the waitress left, I looked at Roger, who was seated to my left. "What's the plan for tomorrow?"

"You and I need to go to the restaurant furniture

wholesaler and pick out your tables, chairs, countertops, and stools . . . plus any other fixtures you might want."

"Okay. What about everyone else?"

"My workers know what they need to be doing," he said. "Do yours?"

Jackie was sitting directly across from me.

"Jackie, do you know what needs to be done in the dining room tomorrow?" I asked her.

"Sure do. Why? You bailing on us already?"

"I have to go with Roger to pick out furniture."

"We need flooring too," Roger said. "I'm thinking laminate wood flooring for the dining room and treated hardwood for the screened-in porch."

"And a sign," Jackie said. "See about getting your sign done."

"You want us to do all of that tomorrow?" I asked.

"You're the one who wants to be open in a month," Roger reminded me. "You need to get things ordered so they'll be finished and installed by then."

"All right. Do you have a list of what needs to be ordered?"

He tapped his temple. "It's all up here."

"Heaven help us," Jackie said. "You'd better make him write it down, Amy."

Roger blew her a kiss, and she countered with an unladylike gesture. Then they both laughed. Was I the only one who could see how crazy they were about each other? What a good couple they'd make?

The waitress brought our drinks then, and the group split into conversations about sports, television shows, and a new shopping center that was being built nearby.

We were all tired and weary of work. None of us really wanted to think about the café any more until tomorrow.

As soon as I got home from the pizza parlor, I took a long, relaxing shower. When I got out of the tub, I wrapped myself in a knee-length plush pink robe and went into the living room to curl up on the couch. I was reaching for the remote when my doorbell rang.

Rory went ballistic, barking and jumping near the door. Princess Eloise ran down the hall to parts unknown.

I wasn't expecting anyone. Remembering Deputy Hall's warning about the killer still being on the loose, I looked out the window and saw a red convertible in my driveway. Surely, Lou Lou's killer wouldn't drive a red convertible. Okay, so that was illogical. But, in my defense, I was tired and not thinking very clearly. I did, however, leave the chain on the door until I opened it and saw Deputy Hall standing there in faded jeans and a white T-shirt.

"Did I catch you at a bad time?" he asked.

"No. Please come in." I closed the door enough to undo the chain and then opened it to let Deputy Hall inside. "Have a seat, and I'll slip on some clothes and be right back."

I hurried to the bedroom and threw on some shorts and a sweatshirt. When I returned to the living room, he was sitting on the sofa with Princess Eloise perched on his lap and Rory lying by his feet. Rory I understood—he loved everybody—but Princess Eloise threw me for a loop.

"How'd you manage that?" I asked.

"Manage what?"

"To win the affection of Princess Eloise. She's not crazy about most people."

He shrugged. "Just lucky, I guess."

"May I get you something to drink? Are you hungry?"

"I'd love some water, please."

"Anything else?" I called over my shoulder as I went to the kitchen for two bottles of water.

"No, thanks."

I returned, handed him his water, and sat on the chair across from him. "What brings you by, Deputy Hall?"

"The money box. And please call me Ryan."

"Ryan," I repeated.

"As you can see, I'm here unofficially—plain clothes, my personal vehicle—and I'm not here to discuss the ongoing investigation of Lou Lou Holman's murder."

"All right." I drew the word out, indicating he should go ahead and make his point. Not that I minded sitting here looking at Mr. Handsome out of uniform, but I'd had an early morning today and there was another one ahead of me tomorrow.

"I just wanted to tell you that I was intrigued by that box you found and the story you told me. Since it was a slow day at work, I did some digging."

I leaned forward, elbows on my knees.

"There was a robbery in Surry County, North Carolina, in the spring of 1936."

"Do you think the robbery was committed by Lou Holman's dad and uncle like Aunt Bess said?" I asked.

"No one was ever convicted of the crime. I looked through some newspaper archives. You may be aware that the *Winter Garden News* was pretty gossipy in the 1930s."

"Was?" I barked out a laugh. "It hasn't evolved much, then."

Ryan laughed too. "This is what I was able to piece together. Lou's dad's name was Bo, and Bo's brother was Grady. The bank was about to foreclose on Grady's farm."

I took a sip of my water. "The Surry County bank?"

"No, the local bank here in Winter Garden—or, rather, the bank that was in business at the time—is the one that was about to foreclose. But the men knew they'd likely be recognized if they robbed their own bank, even if they wore masks, so they went across the border."

"How did the newspaper say this stuff if the Holman brothers were never even arrested for the crime?"

"The newspaper was privately owned, and they put the information in their *gossip* column," Ryan said. "They basically said, 'this is all conjecture,' but I think they had the story right."

"So Bo and Grady robbed the bank in Surry County. How much did they get away with?"

"Twenty thousand dollars."

I frowned. "The exact amount in the lockbox? They didn't spend any of it. Were they lying low or what?"

"The gossip columnist said that Grady Holman had a change of heart. He felt like he'd besmirched the whole family's honor, and in fact, told a friend what had happened."

"Which is how the gossip columnist got his or her information. But wait. According to Aunt Bess, both Holman brothers were pretty mean. Why would Grady have a sudden change of heart?"

"Grady told this friend that he didn't want his brother to go to jail for Grady's mistakes and that he was going to turn himself in and give back the money," said Ryan. "He hoped the authorities would go easy on him. The friend didn't see Grady anymore after that."

"Why? Was Grady murdered? Did he run off somewhere?" I couldn't figure out why Grady's disappearance was a big deal.

Ryan inclined his head. "I'll get to that. As you already determined, Lou was building his café at the time and provided his dad with the perfect hiding place for the stolen money."

"How did Lou have the funds to build a café when his uncle's farm was being foreclosed on?" I asked. "That seems wrong somehow."

"It might seem unfair, but I have to think that Lou had also worked hard, saved his money for a down payment, and taken out a building loan. He had the right to pursue his dream as much as Grady had to pursue his, didn't he?"

"Of course. I'm sorry. I wasn't thinking."

"You're family-minded." He smiled and took a drink from his water bottle. "Had you been in Lou's position, you'd have used your money to try to help bail out your uncle."

"Yeah, but that doesn't mean Lou should have. Who knows? Maybe Grady had squandered all his money somehow, and Lou knew he would do the same with any more he received. So what happened to Grady?"

"The gossip columnist said Grady 'wasn't seen around these parts again.' He didn't know whether Grady had simply run off, committed suicide, or—and I quote—'*met a darker fate.*' The columnist supposed that Bo and Grady might've argued—they were both known to drink a lot—and the argument might've escalated into a physical altercation."

"So I'm assuming that Grady never showed back up in Winter Garden," I said. "Aunt Bess didn't mention that. But, then, she's been known to leave bits out of her stories so she can come back with a jaw-dropper later on. I'll have to see what else she knows."

"I could find no record of Grady Holman after 1936."

"Okay, so let's say that Grady was dead. Why didn't Bo spend the money? Guilt?"

"Maybe. He could've also been waiting for news of the North Carolina robbery to die down. People would've likely forgotten it in a year or two, and he could've started to spend it a little at a time," Ryan said. "But Bo was killed when the tractor he was driving overturned on him in 1937."

"Wow. A lot of people around here would consider that money cursed, then."

"Maybe it is."

"You don't think it played into Lou Lou's murder?" I asked.

"I can't see a connection right now, but then, it *was* in the wall of the office where she was killed."

The thought gave me chills. "Do you think she knew about the money?"

"I don't know. I don't even know for sure that Lou knew. His dad might've put the money in the wall without Lou's knowledge."

"So what happens to the money now?"

"I turned it over to Sheriff Billings. We have no hard

evidence that this money even came from a robbery. That's conjecture. But since we're not sure what to do with the money, right now the box is sitting in an evidence locker."

"Thanks for sharing that story with me," I said.

"You're welcome. I thought you should know."

"My cousin Jackie is dying of curiosity about what was going on this morning. Do you mind if I tell her? And Roger—he found the box. I promise not to tell anyone else."

"You can tell Jackie and Roger, but I would appreciate it if you didn't spread the word that there's twenty thousand dollars sitting in evidence in our jail." He chuckled. "Sure as the world, some knucklehead would try to break in and steal it."

"Isn't that the truth?" I laughed.

"And I wouldn't put it past someone to try to break into the café to see if there was more money hidden there somewhere."

"The less said, the better."

"Right." He took Princess Eloise off his lap and stood. "I'd better be going."

"Thanks again for stopping by." I stood and walked him to the door. "And thank you for trusting me enough to talk with me about this stuff."

"I've already told you, I don't believe you murdered Lou Lou Holman." He lowered his eyes. "I'm anxious to get this case solved so . . ."

"So what?"

He brought his eyes back to mine. "So we can all move on."

He walked down the porch steps to the driveway. I

closed the door. I didn't want him to think I was weird for standing there watching him. Princess Eloise brushed against my ankle, gave me a haughty look, and left the room.

Roger and I had a good hour's drive the next morning to get to the restaurant furniture wholesaler. Along the way, I told him about Ryan's visit and the tale the gossip columnist had woven about the bank robbery.

"Ah, so the deputy finds an excuse to let you see his ripped muscles in a T-shirt and to show off his flashy car."

"That's not the subject we're addressing. We're talking about the money you found in the wall yesterday."

He laughed. "All right. All right. Ignore what's right in front of you in favor of a mystery that's what—eighty years old?"

"*I* ignore what's in front of *me*?"

"Yes, you do," he said.

"Well, Mr. Pot-Calling-the-Kettle-Black, I need a favor. Jackie was dying to know what was going on yesterday, and I didn't tell her because Ryan asked me not to."

Roger affected a falsetto voice. "Dreamy Ryan asked me to keep mum about the box in the wall." He then mimicked buttoning his lip.

I lightly slapped his arm. "Take Jackie to dinner tonight and tell her about the box. Just make sure that neither of you tells anyone else. The last thing I need is someone breaking into the café and tearing all the walls out to see if there's more money inside them."

"All right. Why do I have to take her to dinner, though? Can't I just pull her aside?"

"Roger, take Jackie to dinner already. How long are you two going to deny your feelings for each other?"

"We don't have those kinds of feelings for each other. We've been friends forever."

"So have we," I said. "But you and I don't look at each other the way you and Jackie do."

"Do you want me to?" He glanced away from the road to look cross-eyed at me.

"I'm serious."

"I am too. I don't want to ruin a perfectly good friend-ship."

"Then take Jackie to dinner as a friend."

"You're a pain in the butt, you know."

"I do know. And if you don't want me to sound like a broken record for the rest of the way to the wholesaler's shop and back, you'll agree to take Jackie to dinner this evening."

He sighed. "I'll see if she has plans. Satisfied?"

"Yes." I looked out the window at the wildflowers grow-ing in the median. "How long do you think it'll take for our tables and chairs to be delivered?"

"Two months."

I jerked my head at him. "What?"

"Kidding. I owed you one."

Chapter 14

Roger and I got to the café around lunchtime. We brought burgers and potato chips for the entire crew.

I sat at the counter beside Homer to eat. "Did Jackie take care of your sausage biscuit this morning?"

"Yes, she did. Thank you for asking. And, in case you're wondering—Napoleon Hill is my hero for the day."

"How about that? I'm reading one of his books right now."

"Which one?"

"The Law of Success."

"That's a good one," he said. "I have *Think and Grow Rich*, if you'd like to borrow it after you finish the one you're reading."

"Thank you. I appreciate that. And I also appreciate all your hard work here." I'd had to insist on paying him to the point of refusing to allow him to help if he didn't accept a paycheck.

"Aw . . . it's like Mr. Hill once said: 'If you cannot do great things, do small things in a great way.' By doing small things, I'm helping y'all do something great."

"You sure are, Homer. And, trust me—where these renovations are concerned, there are no small things."

Jackie came up and sat on the other side of me. "Roger just cornered me and asked me to go to dinner tonight."

"Did you say yes?"

"Yeah, but that's weird, don't you think?"

"No, I don't." I debated on whether or not to tell her I'd had to talk him into it, but I decided not to go there. He'd asked and she'd accepted. That was all that mattered.

"Did you guys find everything you were looking for at the wholesalers?"

"Yup. We ordered bamboo flooring. It's tongue-and-groove hardwood but is the most durable and scratch-resistant. Also, Roger was thrilled that it's environmentally conscious. I mean, I am too, but I'd have thought all wood was . . . well . . . green, you know?"

"I'd have thought so too." She looked down at the scuffed brown linoleum. "It'll sure beat this all to pieces."

"Won't it, though? It'll be here tomorrow."

"Then we need to finish painting today," Jackie said. "I'm so excited!"

She gave me a quick hug. "Me too. Hey, what about the uniforms? What did you come up with there?"

"I thought I'd order blue T-shirts with DOWN SOUTH CAFÉ written on them in yellow. We'll also have yellow aprons. Other than that, you can wear jeans or a skirt—whatever suits you."

"Jeans suit me. Don't forget to order extra T-shirts for the tourists."

"I'll do it," I said. "Even if the tourists don't buy them, we'll have them on hand when we need them."

"The tourists will buy the shirts. Trust me. We'll be famous."

"I'll buy one," Homer piped up.

"No way. You'll get yours for free. You're part of the staff now."

He puffed out his chest. "I'm proud to help."

"Lunch break is up, people!" Roger called from the other side of the room. "This café won't renovate itself!"

I was tidying up the kitchen area after everyone else had left that evening. The chime Roger had installed over the door alerted me to someone coming in the front. I wiped my hands on a dish towel and went to see who was there.

Stan Wheeler was standing in the middle of the dining room, gazing around and nodding. "This place is looking good."

"Thank you."

"Thank *you*. The table and chairs in my trailer were getting pretty ratty, so I was tickled to get one of those sets you were giving away."

"I'm glad it worked for you."

He nodded toward the window nearest where the screened-in porch would be. "I see that you've torn out the office."

"Yeah. We're going to make it additional dining space."

"Huh. Did Pete get everything he wanted or needed out of there?" He held up his hands. "I mean, I know you'd give him anything he'd want, but he acted the other night like he didn't want any of the stuff his momma had here."

"I know. I hope he and Chris Anne got what they wanted yesterday. A couple of Roger's guys hauled the rest of it off this morning."

"I imagine Chris Anne took everything she could carry," he said. "When I was here yesterday, it looked like she was packing that truck full."

"She was. Pete mainly just stood around looking sad. I think it bothered him to be here." I shrugged. "I guess Chris Anne was trying to look out for him."

Stan scoffed. "Make no mistake. If Chris Anne was looking out for anybody, it was for herself. I warned Pete when he started up with her that she was trouble."

"What makes you say so?"

"She served jail time for drug possession, for one thing. She's younger than Pete, but she's a lot harder than he is. He's been pretty much sheltered. And, you know, I served a nickel for drugs myself, but I'm clean now."

"You don't think Chris Anne is?"

"No, I don't. It'd take a miracle for that girl to get sober."

I thought about the miracle she had growing inside her and hoped it would be enough to convince her to change her ways, if she hadn't done so prior to finding out that she was going to be a mother.

I also wondered again if she'd told Pete about her pregnancy. Could that be why he seemed so distraught yesterday? Had he realized his mother wouldn't get to see her grandchild or be around to see the child grow up? Or was he upset that Chris Anne's pregnancy interfered with his plans for the two of them to go on the road?

"I won't keep you any longer," said Stan. "You care if I walk around there and take a look at what the workers are doing with the office?"

"I don't mind. Just be careful. There might be nails lying around or something."

"I'll watch my step."

I locked the front door before going back to the kitchen. Even though Stan had been acting much nicer of late, and he'd just told me he wasn't doing drugs anymore, I didn't really trust him. And I didn't want to be caught off guard again.

A fter leaving the café, I went to Pete's house. He'd called earlier asking me to stop by, but he didn't say why.

I realized what a mess I was as I was knocking on the door. I hadn't brushed my hair—which now had paint in it—since this morning. My clothes were dusty and paint-flecked. I imagined I looked like a ragamuffin standing on the Holmans' doorstep.

Chris Anne came to the door. "Hey, Amy. How're you?"

"I'm fine. Is Pete here?"

"Not right now, but he'll be back in a minute. He went up to the pizza place to get us some dinner. We're tired of casseroles." Her eyes widened as if it had just dawned on her that I might've brought over one of those casseroles—which, of course, Jackie and I had. "I mean, we're keeping them in the freezer, and we'll certainly eat them. . . . We just wanted a change, is all."

"I understand. It's like a day or two after Thanksgiving when you don't want to even think about turkey again for a month."

"Exactly like that! Come on in. We'll talk while we wait for Pete."

I stepped into the living room. Even more than with the café, Lou Lou's influence was everywhere. A print of a Hawaiian landscape hung over the couch, and an Elvis clock sat atop the television. Chris Anne sat on the couch, and I sat on the chair across from her.

"Have you told Pete about the baby?"

"I have."

Was there a delicate way to ask her if she was sober? "Are you taking good care of yourself . . . and the baby?"

"I am." She grinned. "The doctor put me on them prenatal vitamins. They're big as half outdoors, and they taste nasty, but I'm taking them."

"That's good. I guess Pete's over the moon."

She studied her fingernails. "He wasn't as happy as I'd hoped he would be, but he'll come around."

"I'm sorry. It was probably bittersweet news for him, since he realizes his mother won't be around to see the baby."

Chris Anne looked surprised. "I hadn't thought of that. I figured he was just mad because it's going to be hard for me to drive a truck with a belly out to here." She held her hand out in front of her to show me how big she thought her stomach would get.

I laughed. "And I don't think tractor-trailers are particularly built for car seats either, are they?"

"No, I don't believe they are. I told Pete to get Stan

to go in with him. They've become like best friends or something here lately."

"Well, there you go. That sounds like the perfect solution."

She put her index finger to her lips. "Pete just pulled up. I don't want him to know what we've been talking about."

"Sure."

Pete came in carrying a pizza box. "Chris Anne, get this thing. It's hot."

Chris Anne hopped up off the couch and got the box. "I'll put it in the kitchen. Amy's here."

"Yeah, I saw her car. Hey, Amy." He took Chris Anne's vacated seat. "You doing all right?"

"I'm fine. How are you doing?"

"I'm okay. Getting there, anyway. It ain't easy."

"No, it's not. My nana dying was the hardest thing I've ever had to deal with. I can only imagine how hard this is for you."

He bobbed his head. "You want some pizza? We've got plenty."

"No. I need to leave here in a second. I only stopped by because I got your message."

"Oh yeah. I found another set of keys to the Joint. I'll get 'em for you." He went into the kitchen and got the keys.

"Thanks, Pete." I didn't tell him that Roger had already changed the locks. "You guys have a good evening."

"We will. Thanks for coming by."

The first thing I did when I got home was feed Rory and Princess Eloise. As soon as I'd done that, I took a shower. It felt good to wash away the grime and fatigue of the day, but it also felt wonderful to have made so much progress on the café in such a short amount of time.

When I got out of the shower, I made myself a peanut butter sandwich. Luckily, Rory had gone out into the backyard after he'd eaten, so he didn't realize I had more food at his disposal.

While eating, I looked through my cookbooks to find something interesting I could make and take the crew for breakfast tomorrow morning. I decided on baked cinnamon-sugar doughnuts.

I preheated the oven, got out my doughnut pan, and sprayed the pan with nonstick spray. As I mixed up the batter for the doughnuts, I thought about Pete. He'd been so delighted with Chris Anne only a few days ago that he'd gotten engaged to her the day after his mother's murder. Now he seemed sullen and resentful toward her. What had happened between them since then? Was it her pregnancy? Or was there more to it?

I put the batter into a pastry bag and piped six doughnuts, filling the pan. I put that pan in the oven and melted a small bowl of butter in the microwave. I got another bowl and stirred together the cinnamon and sugar.

I planned on making two dozen doughnuts for the crew. I decided to make an additional half dozen and take them to Mom and Aunt Bess. I wanted to tell them about the money we found in the wall and its probable connection to the bank robbery Aunt Bess told us about on Sunday. I knew I was supposed to be keeping it a secret. But Ryan had said I could tell Roger and Jackie. Letting just two more people know—especially a pair as trustworthy as Aunt Bess and Mom—wouldn't make a difference.

* * *

Aunt Bess was delighted with her box of doughnuts. "And it's not even Sunday!" she exclaimed. "Get us some plates, Jenna. And some milk too. I like milk with my doughnuts." She bit into one of the doughnuts. "Mmmm. Merciful goodness! These are still warm."

"I'm glad you like them."

Mom brought plates and glasses of milk for everybody. "We *could* go into the kitchen and eat, and I wouldn't have to vacuum crumbs up when we're done."

"Where'd be the fun in that?" Aunt Bess asked. "Besides, I can tell by the look on her face that Amy has some juicy gossip to fill us in on. I want to be on this comfy sofa when she does."

Mom arched a brow at me. "Do you have juicy gossip?"

"As a matter of fact, I do. Would you like for me to start with what Roger found hidden in the office wall of the Joint? Or would you like me to tell you about Pete and Chris Anne?"

"Tell us what was in the wall," Aunt Bess said, licking the sugar and cinnamon off her fingertips. "Was it Grady Holman's body? Did you get us some napkins, Jenna?"

She *had* known about Grady's disappearance and had left that out of her story.

Mom sighed. "Be right back. Don't start without me."

When Mom returned with napkins, I extracted promises from her and Aunt Bess not to say a word about what I was telling them to anyone. After they'd both sworn solemn oaths, I told them about the money in the lockbox hidden in the wall. I went on to tell them the story Ryan had told to me from the gossip columnist's point of view.

Aunt Bess looked up at the ceiling. "You know, for a fact, nobody saw Grady Holman around here right after the news about that bank robbery got stirred up. I didn't really know the Holmans and didn't give it much thought, but folks said they wouldn't be a bit surprised to find out that Bo killed Grady so he could keep all that money. So it very well could've been Grady you found holed up in the wall."

"I guess anything's possible, but it wasn't Grady," I said. "And Ryan said that Bo died in a tractor accident the next year."

Aunt Bess nodded. "I remember that well. The thing overturned and the back tires ran over his chest. Crushed him all to pieces."

"Why do you think Lou didn't spend the money?" I asked. "Why would he leave it hidden for all this time?"

"My guess is he didn't know about it," Mom said. "If I was going to hide ill-gotten gains in your café, I certainly wouldn't tell you about it."

"Gee, thanks."

"Where would you get these ill-gotten gains?" Aunt Bess asked. "Have you been up to something?"

"Of course not. But if I *had*, I wouldn't want to drag my daughter into it. Even if I had nowhere else to stash the money except her café, I wouldn't tell her. Then she'd have deniability if I was caught and the money was found."

"So you think it's been there all this time because Lou—and then Lou Lou and Pete—knew nothing about it," I said.

"I know Lou Lou Holman didn't know anything about money being hidden in that office, or else she'd have clawed through that wall years ago," said Aunt Bess. "She sure wouldn't have left it alone. You know as well as I do that she was so tight her toes curled every time she blinked."

"That's true," I said. "But being as tight as she was, maybe she was keeping it there in case of an emergency."

"What news were you going to tell us about Pete and Chris Anne?" Mom asked.

"Chris Anne is pregnant."

Aunt Bess shook her head. "Saints preserve us. Those two need a baby like an alcoholic needs to tend bar. It's all they can do to take care of themselves."

"A lot of people never quite grow up until they have to," said Mom. "I actually thought I had until I had a child and realized how immature I was."

"Ain't that the truth? But you turned out just fine," said Aunt Bess. "And Amy did too."

Chapter 15

I got to the café the next morning even before Roger and his crew arrived. I preheated the oven to two hundred degrees so I could warm the doughnuts before everyone else got there.

I heard a truck pull into the parking lot and went out front, expecting to see Roger. To my surprise, it was Pete.

"Pete, is everything all right?" I asked when he stepped down out of the truck. "What on earth are you doing here at six o'clock?"

"Everything's fine. I was up anyway and got to wondering how the renovations are coming along."

"Come on inside and see for yourself."

He looked around the dining room. "I like these colors. They really brighten up the place."

"Thank you."

"Momma talked a lot about fixing up the Joint, but she never did," Pete said. "She just never had the time."

I nodded. "Time certainly can slip away from you in a hurry."

"Ain't that the truth? Seems like only yesterday, I was a little ol' thing running around here with dirty hands and skinned knees. Momma was waitressing, and Grandpa was at the grill." He grinned. "You don't know how good you've got it when you're a kid, you know? It's only looking back that you realize how nice it was."

I smiled. "I guess so."

His grin faded as he shook his head. "I can't quite come to grips with Momma being gone. She was always here. I know she could have an ornery turn to her sometimes, but she was always trying to do right by me."

"I know she was." I didn't really know whether she always tried to do right by Pete or not, but I felt that it was proper to say she did.

"I'm glad Chris Anne saved a bunch of the stuff from the office."

"I thought you would be," I said. "It helps you grieve when you have something to hold on to. It's not that you need something to remind you of her, but it's nice to have something of hers to sort of ground you to the past. I have one of my Nana's rings. I wear it sometimes when I want to feel especially close to her."

"Last night, Chris Anne got out Momma's photo albums. She wanted to see what I looked like as a baby and then as a boy." He blew out a breath. "I finally had to leave the room—brought up too many memories."

"It'll get easier. Congratulations on the baby."

"Thanks." He ran a hand through his thinning hair. "I wish me and Chris Anne could've done things differently, planned things out a little better, but I guess this is how it's supposed to be. I mean, I'd have liked to have waited . . . just had it be me and her before having kids. But it is what it is."

"Chris Anne said you're thinking of asking Stan to be your business partner. I hope that works out for you."

"So do I. Maybe it's better not to be in business with my fiancée anyway, right?"

"Maybe." I told him that Aunt Bess had told me the legend of the Holman brothers who'd robbed a bank in North Carolina.

Pete did a snort-laugh combo. "Lordy mercy, I heard that story so many times growing up. At nearly every family reunion and every holiday, Grandpa would gather around anybody who'd listen and give them an earful." He gazed at the back wall as if seeing it all play out on a movie screen. "After he'd tell the bank-robbing story, he'd tell us that Uncle Grady disappeared after that and that maybe he took the money with him. Then he'd lean in like he was telling us a secret and say that maybe Uncle Grady had left that money hidden around here some-where. Then all us kids would go on a treasure hunt."

"Did you ever find anything?"

"Poison ivy a time or two. Like as not, every cent of that money—if there ever was any—went for liquor or was gambled away two weeks after they got it."

I bobbed my head in a way that couldn't actually be called a nod. I didn't want to be mistaken for being in agreement with Pete when I knew full well that the money was in evidence at the Winter Garden Police Department.

"So what kind of tall tales did your grandpa tell you?" Pete asked.

"He mostly told us about working in the coal mines. And, with every story he told, I became more convinced that I never wanted to work in a dark, scary mine."

"I heard that."

Roger and his crew pulled into the parking lot.

"There's the boss," I told Pete. "Time to get to work."

"Thanks again for letting me look at the place. It's nice. Momma would be proud."

I knew that was a lie he could've kept from telling, but it was nice of him to say so all the same. "Thanks, Pete. Stop by anytime."

I brought out the warm doughnuts and hot coffee, and they were enjoyed by all. Homer still liked his ten-o'clock sausage biscuit, but he wouldn't turn down a warm doughnut at six thirty.

Homer's, Jackie's, and my job today was to tear out the old floor. We had heavy gloves and chisels.

"Who's your hero, Homer?" I asked.

"James Arthur Baldwin. Have you heard of him?"

"He wrote essays, right?"

"Novels too. And poems . . . plays."

"Sounds like an accomplished guy," said Jackie.

"Indeed he was."

"Pete stopped by today," I said. "He told me he was glad Chris Anne didn't let him throw out all of Lou Lou's things from the office."

"Yeah, I guess he was when he had time to stop and consider it," she said.

"Any word yet on who killed Ms. Holman?" Homer asked.

"Not yet." I pushed my chisel under a particularly well-glued stretch of linoleum. "I wish they'd find whoever did it, though. I'd love to know what the crime scene technician found."

"Let's think about who Lou Lou's enemies were," Jackie said.

"Mr. Baldwin said that people who treat others as less than human must not be surprised when the bread they've cast upon the waters comes floating back to them poisoned," said Homer.

"That guy had a good point." Jackie stopped in mid-scrape. "Lou Lou alienated almost everyone who'd ever met her."

"Even Pete said this morning that his mother could be ornery sometimes," I said. "But he said he knew she always had his best interests at heart."

"I'm not sure I believe that," said Jackie. "Do you?"

"I don't know. Maybe she *thought* she was doing the right thing for him, but she was actually smothering him." I frowned. "Is that the right word?"

"I believe the word you're looking for is 'overbearing,'" said Jackie. "But 'smothering' fits too. All the psychology and parenting articles warn that being too controlling really screws up your kids."

I dropped my chisel. "You've been reading parenting articles?"

She put the chisel back into my hand. "No. I mean, I thumbed through some when I was still in school and babysitting to pick up some extra money. And I did take a psychology course at the community college when I was taking secretarial classes."

I remembered that now. Jackie had dropped out of

college after one of her mother's visits to Winter Garden. It was the first time Renee had been back since she'd left Jackie with Aunt Bess, and Jackie had been devastated when her mom had left again.

"It shouldn't take a trained therapist to see that Pete's relationship with his mother was messed up," said Homer. "The man's forty and seemed to be afraid to tell his mother he had a serious girlfriend."

"No words of wisdom from Mr. Baldwin?" I asked.

"Only this—and I'm paraphrasing, of course. People pay for what they do and for what they've allowed themselves to become, and they pay for it by the lives they lead."

"Oh man, you're right. I never stopped to consider it, but Lou Lou must've been miserable," I said. "Maybe that's why she treated us all so badly."

Jackie stabbed her chisel into the linoleum with a vengeance. "I refuse to make excuses for that woman. She was wicked. I only went to the funeral because I felt sorry for Pete. After all, wasn't it ultimately her choice to be miserable?"

"Jackie, that's an awful thing to say!"

"I understand exactly what you mean, Jackie," said Homer. "Despite Ms. Holman's hardships, it was she who chose to wallow in self-loathing or self-pity or whatever other destructive emotions she was filled with rather than rising above them and making a better life for herself and her child."

Jackie smiled. "Homer, you are one deep dude."

"Thank you. I have my mom to thank for that . . . and my heroes." He smiled and went back to tearing up the floor.

"You grew up around here, right, Homer?" I asked.

"Nearby."

"Did you ever hear any stories about the Holmans? Aunt Bess told me that it was rumored that Lou Lou's grandfather and uncle robbed a bank in North Carolina once. Have you heard that story before?"

He shook his head. "Nope. Must've been before my time. The only stories I ever heard about the Holmans was that Lou—the original owner of this café—was a very hard man. He was said to have been rough on his wife and daughter. I always heard that he doted on his grandson, though. It seemed he'd wanted a boy when Lou Lou was born."

"So Lou Lou has no siblings," Jackie said.

"No." He looked at his watch. "It's ten o'clock."

I gratefully put down my chisel. "Let me get that sausage biscuit for you."

It did strike me odd, though, that Aunt Bess had believed Lou Holman to be such a peach of a guy when Homer had heard the exact opposite.

I didn't get a minute alone with Jackie until she and I were in the kitchen making sandwiches for everyone's lunch.

Speaking in hushed tones, I asked, "So?"

"So what?" She opened a loaf of bread and made a row of slices across the countertop.

I rolled my eyes. "How was your date with Roger?"

Jackie lowered her voice too. "I don't know that I'd classify it as a *date*. I mean, it was dinner with Roger. We've had dinner lots of times."

"Not by yourselves. Come on. His telling you about . . .

the thing we found . . . was just an excuse for the two of you to go out."

She tried to hide her smile. "Okay, okay. It was . . . nice."

"Nice?"

"It was *Roger*." She huffed. "We've known each other practically all our lives."

"But not like *this*. Not as dates. You've known each other as friends."

"I'd like to think we're still friends." She put mayo on half the slices she'd laid out and mustard on the other half.

"Jackie!" I wailed.

"Shhh!" She smiled. "It *was* nice. Maybe a little better than nice."

I squealed. "I knew it! You guys have liked each other for so long."

"Keep your cool. He might've had a lousy time."

"I'll do some recon later," I said.

Her eyes widened. "Don't you dare."

"Why not?"

"Because he'll know we've been talking about him . . . about our date," she said.

"As you pointed out, he's known us most of our lives. He already knows we've been talking about him and your date. He also knows I'm going to ask *him* about your date and that I'm then going to report back to you."

"Fair enough. But you know Roger well enough to know that he'll say it's none of your business."

I raised an index finger. "Unless he wants me to tell you something in particular."

She shook her head and took some turkey out of the refrigerator. "Do you think everybody's good with turkey?"

"I don't know. We'll make several turkey-and-cheese sandwiches and some peanut butter–and-jelly sandwiches too. That should cover everyone."

"So . . . what do you think he'll say?"

I made my own row of bread slices and got out the peanut butter. "Only one way to find out." My best guess was that Roger was dying to know what Jackie was saying about last night and that he'd seek *me* out after lunch. "Did you kiss good night?"

"None of your business."

"I'll take that as a yes." I spread peanut butter on the slice of bread nearest me.

"Fine. He kissed me once . . . when he dropped me off at home."

"And?" I looked up in time to see Jackie blush and drop her head.

"Tell me about your date with the deputy."

"What date?" I asked.

"The one where he came to your house to tell you all the important stuff about the thing that happened forever ago that couldn't wait until the next day."

"It was interesting . . . and it *was* important." I tried to concentrate hard on spreading my peanut butter to perfection. "I think it was great of Ryan to come to my house during his off-duty time to fill me in on what may be a . . . another . . . clue . . . or something in Lou Lou's case."

"Ah. Does *Ryan* think the box in the wall is a clue?"

"It certainly *could* be." I moved on to the next slice without looking up from my work.

"Sure. Because anything that happened—what—seventy-five . . . eighty . . . years ago would naturally have some bearing on a murder that took place just over a week

ago." She snorted. "That kind, thoughtful deputy . . . rushing over on his own time to make sure you were safe from
the centenarian bandit killer!"

"Will you just hush and make your turkey sandwiches? We have hungry people to feed."

Chapter 16

After lunch, I went to take a look at the side porch to see how much progress had been made. I truly wasn't going to talk with Roger about his date. I knew he was busy and that I'd have plenty of time to speak with him after work.

"Amy . . . good . . . glad you're here," said Roger as I stepped around the side of the café. He pointed. "We need to turn that window into a door. The original door that opened into the office will be fine for staff taking dishes out or bringing them back inside, but you don't want your patrons having to use the same door."

"You're right. I hadn't considered that, but no, we don't want customers coming through the back, where we're working."

"I want to get that door cut out today. The flooring should be here later this afternoon, but we can't start putting it down until the door is finished."

"What about the painting we've already done?"

"It won't be a problem," said Roger. "If we mar any-thing, we'll touch it back up. But the molding around the door should hide where the window has been enlarged."

"Okay. So what do you need me to do?"

"Get out of here."

"Excuse me?"

He grinned. "You and the café staff should take the rest of the day off. I talked with Aaron about it over lunch, since he's been really interested in construction, and he'd like to stay."

I huffed. "Roger! I knew Aaron was interested in con-struction, but he's the best busboy and dishwasher we have!"

"He's really getting the hang of construction, and he's enjoying it. Would you prefer he stay a busboy forever?"

"No." I felt a stab of guilt for my poutiness. "Of course, I want Aaron to do whatever will make him happy. I'll talk with him."

"He's a good kid and a fast learner. I think he could do well in construction."

"I know, but I thought you didn't have an opening."

"I didn't, but I believe one of my guys will be leaving in late summer or early fall. That gives me time to get Aaron well trained."

"Then I guess I'm looking for a new busboy."

"I'm pretty sure you are, but talk with him first and make sure that's what he wants."

"I will." I turned to go back around the building to the café and saw Stan Wheeler pulling into the parking lot. "Wonder what he wants."

Roger stepped up next to me. "I don't know. Wait and we'll see."

Stan got out of his car and walked toward Roger and me. "Hey, folks, how're y'all doing?"

"Good, thanks," I said. "How are you, Stan?"

"To be honest, I'm as broke as a convict. I was wondering if Roger here could use an extra man."

"I don't know," Roger said. "Do you have any construction experience?"

"I do."

"Were you only wanting to work today? Or do you want to make it a regular thing?" asked Roger.

"Well, I'm mainly interested in helping with the café," Stan said. "Maybe we could see how it goes."

"All right. I could use some extra help for the next day or two." Roger nodded toward a tall, heavyset man holding a clipboard. "Go talk with Johnny and see where he'd like you to work today."

After Stan headed in Johnny's direction, Roger muttered to me under his breath, "Wish me luck."

"Good luck." Given Roger's warning about Stan, I had to wonder why he'd agree to take him on, even if it was only for a day or two. Could it be a case of keeping your friends close and your enemies closer? I left to find Aaron.

Aaron was in the café tearing up a section of flooring with Homer.

"I have good news," I said. "Roger wants us to clear out of here to let his guys turn a window into a door. So we can relax for the rest of the afternoon."

A little cheer went up.

"But," I continued, "I'm going to pay y'all for a full day. You guys have been working so hard, and I truly appreciate you."

"We're almost finished with what we're doing," Homer said. "Do you think Roger would mind if we clear this section here before we go?"

"Probably not. Aaron, could I talk with you for a second?"

"Yes, ma'am."

He was only a couple of years younger than me, but sometimes Aaron made me feel like I was ancient.

We walked over to the counter, and I handed him a bottle of water. He thanked me but looked at me expectantly rather than opening the bottle.

"Roger said he'd told you about converting the window to a door and that you'd like to stay and work with his crew this afternoon."

He nodded. "Yeah. That might be handy to know sometime . . . like if I buy a house and want to do my own renovations or something."

"True. Roger says you're a fast learner, and he's impressed with the work you've been doing."

He opened the bottle then and took a drink. "Thanks."

"What I'm asking is if you'd prefer to go to work with Roger."

His eyes widened. "You mean it? You wouldn't be mad?"

"Of course not. I'd miss you. You're our best busboy, but you need to follow your heart and do what you enjoy."

"Are you sure?"

"Positive," I said with a smile. "I would like to ask you something while I'm thinking of it, though. Were you working that Monday afternoon? You know, *the* Monday?"

"Yes, ma'am."

"Did anyone come in acting angry toward Lou Lou or anything?"

"No. Pete almost always worked the afternoon shift, and Monday was no exception. If anybody would've been mad, they'd have been mad at Pete . . . right?"

"Good point. Did anyone come in acting like they had a beef with Pete?"

"Nah, Pete didn't make people mad. He just went along with whatever they said. It was his momma who ticked everybody off."

"That's true." I patted his shoulder. "Thanks again for all your hard work."

"The only person who came in who was disagreeable at all was that Mr. Lincoln from the Chamber of Commerce. He wanted to buy the Joint, but Pete told him his momma had already given him her answer." He looked toward the door. "Is it all right if I go ahead and tell Roger I'd like to work with him?"

"Sure." I had a couple of errands to run. I supposed I needed to add a stop at the *Winter Garden News* to the list.

The first errand on my agenda was to go to the print shop and order business cards and menus. Now that we had the colors for the café, I could take the swatches to the printer to get an exact match . . . or, at least, fairly close.

I thought this would be a simple, quick trip. I was

wrong. Once I'd explained to the printer what I wanted, she got out books to show me examples of business cards and menus. I looked through pages and pages of samples until I found the styles that I felt best exemplified Down South Café.

My choices made, I was ready to leave. And then the printer asked about letterhead and checks and envelopes— with windows for paychecks and without windows for correspondence. I told her I'd think about those and talk with her again when I returned to pick up the business cards and menus.

I had to take care of my budget. I knew it would be easy to spend a small fortune on things that would be nice to have but that I didn't necessarily need. A paycheck written on a plain check and put into a regular envelope would spend just as well as one written on a fancy check and put into a window envelope with a preprinted return address.

I still had checks and envelopes on my mind when I left the print shop and nearly collided with Chris Anne.

"Oh, goodness! I'm sorry, Chris Anne. I wasn't pay-ing attention to where I was going."

"It's probably my fault. I'm so mad I could spit."

"What's wrong?"

"I went in there to the bank to get a loan. I want to build onto the house, get me some maternity clothes, buy a few things for the baby . . . stuff like that."

I was thinking, *Didn't Pete just come into an inheri-tance? And money from selling the café? Wouldn't that money buy you clothes and things you two need for the baby?* I didn't say anything, though. It wasn't any of my business.

Chris Anne anchored one bony fist to her hip. "Do you know they had the nerve to tell me that I couldn't use our house as collateral on a loan?"

"Your house?" I asked. "I thought you lived in an apartment building in Abingdon."

"I'm talking about my house with Pete. *Our* house."

"You and Pete bought a new house?"

She rolled her eyes. "Pete's house is now *our* house." She held up her left hand and waggled her fingers. "We're engaged?"

"True, but that doesn't make it your house too until Pete either adds you to the deed or the two of you get married."

She let out a growl of frustration. "Now you sound just like those bank people! They said I have no right to use Pete's home as collateral, and they wouldn't even tell me how much he has in his bank account."

"Huh." That's the only sound I could manage that wouldn't let her know that I was absolutely astounded by her incomprehension.

"I told them Pete was fine with it and told them to call him. They said he'd have to come to the bank in person." She huffed. "I told them he couldn't come today because he was out looking at trucks and getting ready to start his business. Don't they *know* they're dealing with a businessman now that could have a big impact on their bank?"

"I guess not." I wondered if Pete really *was* fine with Chris Anne trying to get a loan against his house. Did he even know?

"Oh well. I'll see you later, Amy."

"See you."

As I walked on up the street toward the *Winter Garden News* office, I marveled at Chris Anne's actions. Had she honestly thought that since she was Pete's fiancée, the bank employees would give her information on Pete's financial accounts? *And* a loan secured by his house?

And what about Pete and Stan? Both Pete and Chris Anne had indicated that Pete was considering asking Stan to go into the trucking business with Pete. Yet Stan had stopped by the café looking for work. If Stan was as broke as he said he was, how was he supposed to become a partner in a business? He couldn't afford to help pay for a truck. Maybe Pete intended to hire Stan as an employee rather than take him on as a partner. Or, it could be that they both thought they'd make so much money once the business got rolling that the truck would practically pay for itself.

I walked into the office of the *Winter Garden News* and was happy to see that it hadn't changed since the last time I'd visited, about nine years ago. I'd gone to have a classified ad put in proclaiming Mom's age on her birthday: *Lordy, lordy, Jenna's forty!* Mom had not been amused.

Anyway, the walls were still the same flat beige. The globe still stood in the corner, surrounded by floor-to-ceiling bookshelves to the left and right. And the scarred wooden desk stood in front of the office's only window—a picture window that looked out onto the street.

Ms. Peggy, who'd run the *Winter Garden News* for as long as anyone could remember, sat in her huge leather office chair with the wood scroll arms and the nail-head accents.

"Hello, dear," said Ms. Peggy in her reedy voice. "What can I do for you today?"

"I'd like to put in a classified ad to hire a busboy for the Down South Café."

I'd also put an ad on Craigslist. But even though not everyone in Winter Garden was computer savvy, everyone read the *News*. Hopefully, I could get my ad to run for a couple of weeks and have a few applicants by the time I needed to staff the café. Most of the high schoolers on summer break already had jobs, and there weren't many others beating a path to Winter Garden for its employment opportunities.

"All right." Ms. Peggy pushed away from the desk, got up, and handed me a pad of paper and a pen. "Twenty-five words or less, twenty dollars per week. Anything over twenty-five words will be an additional forty cents a word."

"Thank you." As I sat and tried to concentrate on what I wanted to say, I thought about how long Ms. Peggy had been here in Winter Garden. I got up and went to stand by the desk so she could hear me. "Ms. Peggy, have you lived here all your life?"

"Yep."

"My aunt Bess was telling me about a bank robbery that Lou Holman's dad, Bo, and his brother Grady were supposed to have committed back in the thirties."

"Over in North Carolina. I remember. What about it?"

"Do you believe the Holman brothers did it?"

"Course I do. Didn't she?" Ms. Peggy asked.

"I think she thought they were guilty."

"I'd bet you five dollars to ten they did it. Though why they didn't use that money to get Grady out of hock is beyond me."

"Aunt Bess said that Grady disappeared right after the robbery."

"Disappeared, my eye," she said. "Lou killed him."

"Lou?"

"Yeah, Lou. He was furious that Grady had dragged his daddy into something that could cause him to have to rot in prison for the rest of his life, and he killed Grady."

"Are you sure?" I asked.

"I wouldn't swear to it on a stack of Bibles or anything, but I'm fairly certain. And so was my father. He's the one who told me." She leaned back in her chair. "Lou Holman was a mean man. Why'd you think Lou Lou grew up with such a wicked look and a mouth that didn't spout nothing but vitriol?"

"Well, I figured it had something to do with her upbringing."

"Then you figured right. That little ol' girl never could do anything good enough to suit her daddy. And still, she worshipped the ground he walked on. It was a crying shame."

"I'm sorry," I said.

"Yeah, well, honey, what's done is done. Can't fix it now." She nodded toward the paper, which I hadn't even begun writing on. "You got that ad ready?"

After I got back home, I went into the fancy room, lay down on the sofa, and called Ryan.

"Hi," I said when he'd answered. "I was wondering if you've had any new leads on the Lou Lou Holman case."

"I haven't, but we're fully investigating the leads we

have. Is there anything new that has come to light on your end?"

"Not about this case, but maybe about one that happened around the time the lockbox was hidden in the office wall." I told Ryan about my visit with Ms. Peggy and what she'd told me about Lou Holman killing Grady.

"That's certainly possible. Of course, she has no proof, and it wouldn't matter if she did, since Lou Holman has been dead for more than sixty years."

"I know," I said. "I just wondered if Lou *had* known about the money hidden in the wall of his office. If so, isn't it possible that he told someone about the money? Or that he maybe left a note?"

"What're you getting at?"

"Let's say Lou did leave a note in case something happened to him. He'd want his family to have the money, right?"

"Maybe."

I huffed.

"Okay, probably," Ryan conceded.

"So the note gets lost for all this time, and then someone finds it and wants Lou Lou to cough up the money," I said.

"Doesn't it stand to reason that if her father had left a note, Lou Lou would be the most likely person to have found it?"

"Yeah, but what if she wasn't? What if someone else found the note and wanted that money? That could be the motive behind Lou Lou's death. Isn't that possible?"

"It is possible."

"So if Lou Lou didn't find it . . ." I gulped. And then

I swallowed again because my throat had become thick and dry. "Pete?"

"I'll look into it," Ryan said.

"Do you really think Pete could've had something to do with his mother's death?" I asked.

"He has always been a suspect. We typically look the hardest at the person with the most to gain from the victim's death. In this case, it was the victim's son."

"Wow."

"You had to have known we were looking at Pete."

"I did, but in my mind, the possibility was too unlikely to honestly consider. Now I'm not so sure."

"Why don't we discuss happy things? How are the renovations going?"

I began telling Ryan about what we'd got done so far. But in my mind, I was still ruminating over the idea that Pete could've killed his own mother.

Chapter 17

I decided it might be good for me to get out of Winter Garden for a little while. I could do some shopping, pick up some dinner . . . If it wasn't too late when I started back home, I could see if Mom and Aunt Bess wanted me to pick up something for them too.

Tucking a couple of foldable totes into my purse, I got into the Bug and backed out of the driveway. It was sunny, and since I had my hair in a ponytail, I put down my windows. The breeze not only felt good, it smelled like freshly mown grass. I turned on the radio and was delighted to hear Don Henley singing to me about the boys of summer.

On the way out of town, I drove by the mobile home Stan rented from Lou Lou . . . or Pete, I guessed, now. The roof had been patched in places using mismatched shingles. Hadn't Stan asked Pete for money to completely replace the roof? Maybe whoever he'd hired hadn't got around to doing it yet, and Stan had just put the other shingles over the holes until the new roof was put on. It looked pretty bad. I hoped the roofer would get around to Stan's home soon.

I spent the rest of the afternoon looking at clothes, shoes, makeup, purses, linens, baking pans, and picnic tables with umbrellas—I made a mental note to ask Roger about what type of tables we planned to get for the patio. Fortunately for my wallet, I bought nothing.

Before heading back to Winter Garden, I called the big house. Aunt Bess answered.

"Hi, Aunt Bess. It's Amy. I was wondering if you and Mom would like me to swing by a drive-through and get us some burgers and fries for dinner."

"You're going to *buy* us some cheeseburgers and French fries when you could make better-tasting ones right here yourself?"

"Yes, I am. I'm not cooking this evening. So when I get my food, do you want me to pick y'all up something too?"

"Well, yeah. I'd appreciate that, and I imagine your mother and Jackie would too."

"I didn't realize Jackie was there," I said. "I'll get dinner for everybody and be there in about twenty minutes."

Mom had set the table by the time I got there with our bags of burgers and fries.

"The drinks are still in the car," I said, putting the bags on the dining room table.

"I'll grab them," said Jackie.

Aunt Bess instructed Mom to "light up the candles, since we're eating all fancy."

Whether it was out of spite or not, Mom lit the white taper candles. When Jackie returned with the drink tray, she passed out the drinks. We put our burgers and fries on the good china plates and used the linen napkins rather than the paper ones that came with the food.

Mom gave me a little smirk behind Aunt Bess's back, making me think that the fancy table *had* been an act of spite since Aunt Bess had disparaged my bringing us fast food for dinner. Mom was probably of the same mind as I was—it sure beat having to cook this evening.

"What have you done today?" Mom asked me.

I told her about tearing up linoleum all morning and then shopping this afternoon. "I didn't buy anything, but I feel that it did me good to have a change of scenery for a while."

"I bet it did," Jackie said. "I've been taking 'before' pictures of the café as well as photos of the progress we're making. I'm looking forward to seeing the café once all the work is done."

"How long do you think it'll take?" Mom asked.

"Roger told me it would take a month at the outset, but it seems to be going quicker than I thought it would. How about you, Jackie?"

"Yeah, I think that with us working too, Roger has had help he wasn't originally counting on."

Aunt Bess scoffed. "So you and Amy are doing the work of a whole crew of men?"

"No, Granny. But Amy is paying any of the café staff who wanted to help with the renovations to work."

"Yeah. Homer's even working for us," I said. "The only bad thing is that we've now lost Aaron as our busboy."

"What?" Jackie asked.

"He's found that he really enjoys construction work. He's going to work with Roger."

"That's good for Aaron and Roger, but what're *we* gonna do?" Jackie popped a fry into her mouth.

"I put an ad in the *Winter Garden News* before I came home after lunch. I put it on Craigslist too. Come to think of it, I'm not sure how many of our waitresses will be back either. There are only two who agreed to help renovate."

Jackie waved her hand dismissively. "We'll be fine."

Aunt Bess finished off her cheeseburger. "That was awfully tasty. We ought to do this more often."

W hen I went home, I got out my laptop. Ever since Roger had found the lockbox with the money hidden in the wall, I'd been curious about the bank robbery and the Holman brothers. So I did an Internet search for *Bo Holman, Winter Garden, Virginia*. As expected, there were genealogy sites with references to Bo's death, his marriage to Lou's mother, things like that. I hadn't expected the fount of information Ryan had been able to uncover, but I'd hoped for a little more than this.

Not getting my hopes up, I opened a new tab and typed *Grady Holman, Winter Garden, Virginia* into the search engine. Nothing. I went back to the results page for *Bo Holman* and found that he had a brother named *Grady Walter Holman*.

Thinking maybe Grady had started going by his middle name in an effort to remain hidden, I did a

search for *Walter Holman*. The first thing that popped
up was an obituary from 1984.

> Walter Holman, 88, originally of Winter Garden, Virginia,
> died today at his home near Boone, North Carolina.
> Mr. Holman was preceded in death by his beloved wife,
> Millicent, and is survived by his daughters, Anna and
> Sadie; son, Philip; and numerous grandchildren. A
> beloved member of the community, Mr. Holman . . .

I merely scanned the rest of the listing. Could this
really have been Lou Lou's great-uncle Grady? Had he
just walked away from Winter Garden and made a new
life for himself?

I did a search for *Philip Holman*. As the only boy, I
figured he'd be the easiest to find, because it was less
likely he might have changed his last name. There was
a phone number for a Philip Holman living in Knoxville,
Tennessee.

I grabbed my phone and punched in Mr. Holman's
number. As soon as this man answered, I could tell he
was too young to be Grady's son. Still, I soldiered on.

"Hello, Mr. Holman. My name is Amy Flowers, and
I live in Winter Garden, Virginia. I'm calling to ask if
your father was Grady or Walter Holman, who was also
originally from this area."

"No. My dad was from here in Tennessee."

I thanked him for his time and called two other rela-
tively local Philip Holmans. Both times, I struck out.

I put Anna Holman's name into the search engine. I
found an Anna Holman Carter who lived in Boone and
was sixty-nine years old.

Fingers crossed, I punched in Anna Carter's phone number. When she answered, I introduced myself and asked if her father was Grady or Walter Holman, originally of Winter Garden, Virginia.

"Yes, he was. He hated the name 'Grady' and went by 'Walter.' Why? What's this about?"

"Well, I've got a crazy story to tell you."

Ms. Carter laughed. "Daddy was full of crazy stories. Let's hear yours."

I told Ms. Carter about my buying the café from Lou Lou Holman, leaving out the part where I'd found the woman murdered in her office. "When we renovated the café, we found a lockbox hidden in the wall. Inside we found a little money." I didn't want to tell this woman we'd found twenty thousand dollars in the box. After all, Ryan had asked for my discretion.

"Oh, heavens!"

"We turned the lockbox over to the police because we didn't know what else to do with it. My aunt remembered hearing rumors of Bo and Grady Holman robbing a bank in North Carolina. It was never proven, of course," I added quickly, "and no money was ever recovered, but no one here in Winter Garden could seem to figure out what had happened to Grady. Frankly, I think many people were afraid that either his brother or his nephew had done him in."

Ms. Carter chuckled. "Our family heard all about that bank robbery growing up. You see, the bank there in Winter Garden was about to foreclose on Daddy's farm. His brother Bo offered to take him to a bank here in North Carolina to see if they'd give Daddy a loan.

Daddy didn't realize Bo intended to rob the bank until Bo handed him a ski mask and a pistol."

"Poor Grady . . . or *Walter*!"

"Well, I don't know if it was 'poor Walter' or not. He went along with the plan. Course, if you'd ever met Daddy, you'd have seen he was one of the most easygoing men in the world."

Given Aunt Bess's description of Grady, he must've really changed his ways after moving to North Carolina.

"He'd have gone along with Bo just because Bo was his older brother and wanted him to do it," Ms. Carter continued. "I mean, what kind of man allows his brother to rob a bank by himself?"

She laughed, and I did too.

"After they'd got back to Winter Garden, though, Daddy's conscience started to eat at him, and he wanted to give back the money. Bo told him no, they'd go to jail. To hear Daddy tell it, Daddy wanted to put the money in a sack and leave it by the bank's front door."

"Somebody else would've surely come along and got it if they'd done that," I said.

"That's exactly what Bo told him. Bo said he'd hide the money and that when things died down, they'd figure out how to get the money back to the bank. But Daddy figured Bo was lying, and he just left. He knew the bank would foreclose on the farm, and he didn't care. He just wanted to start over somewhere new."

"Well, I'm so glad nothing bad happened to him."

"Me too, or else I wouldn't be here." She chuckled again. "We didn't hear that story until all of us young 'uns were grown and had children of our own. My sister, Sadie, was incensed that Daddy had taken part in a bank robbery, but my brother, Phil, and I thought it was kinda neat. We never would've dreamed Daddy had an adventurous streak."

"Did Sadie eventually forgive him?"

"Not until he was on his deathbed," she said, an edge to her voice. "By the way, what ever happened to Bo?"

"He died in a tractor accident the year after he and his brother robbed the bank."

"Huh. And Lou. Did you ever meet him?"

"No. I did know his daughter, though."

"What was she like?" Ms. Carter asked.

I paused, trying to think of a nice way to describe Lou Lou.

Ms. Carter giggled. "That bad, huh?"

"A little bit. She was . . . a rough person to have to work for."

"Which is why you bought the café?"

"That, and I wanted to either buy Lou Lou's café or build my own," I said. "Buying an existing café was easier in the long run."

"I imagine it was."

"I appreciate your talking with me. I was just so curious about what happened to Grady. The rumors were that he'd died. And when I did the search and found his obituary, I wondered if Walter was *the* Grady Holman."

"Well, he sure was. Do you have any photos of the Winter Garden Holmans?" she asked. "And I'd love to meet some of my relatives if they're amenable to it."

"I'm sure I can round up some pictures from the newspaper office."

"Thank you. I'd enjoy looking at them."

"Tell you what," I said. "I'll see what I can dig up, and I'll talk with Pete Holman—he'd be your great-nephew—and give him your number. And maybe once the café is renovated, I can come over and have coffee with you sometime. I'd like to look at your photos too."

"I'm going to be in Mountain City late tomorrow afternoon. I know you're in the middle of a big project, but you've got my curiosity up. Is there any way you could meet me for coffee there somewhere? Mountain City is about halfway for both of us, isn't it?"

She was right about my stirring her curiosity. Surely, Roger could spare me—and Jackie—for a couple of hours. I told Ms. Carter yes, I'd love to meet.

As soon as I was finished talking with Anna Carter, I called Jackie.

"What's up?"

"I'm calling to see if you're up for a road trip tomorrow afternoon," I said.

"Where are we going?"

"Mountain City."

"What's in Mountain City?"

"Grady Holman's daughter."

She was so quiet that for a second I thought we'd been disconnected. "Grady Holman's daughter?"

"Yes."

"Why would we want to go to Mountain City to see Grady Holman's daughter?"

"Why wouldn't we?" I explained about my search for Grady and then filled her in on my chat with his daughter Anna Holman Carter. "Who knows? Maybe whatever happened to Grady—or Walter, as he called himself after leaving Winter Garden—has some bearing on what

happened to Lou Lou. What if getting to the bottom of
the old mystery could help us solve the new one? So what
do you say? Will you go with me?"

"I guess. I don't know what good you think it'll do,
though. An eighty-year-old crime has nothing to do with
Lou Lou's death. Have you talked with your hunky deputy
about this?"

"No, I haven't mentioned it to him yet. I want to see
if anything comes of it first. I figure it can't do any harm
to talk with this woman."

She blew out a breath. "Okay. I'll go."

Chapter 18

George Lincoln came by the café on his way to work the next morning. I was making coffee and didn't realize he was there until the café became dark, and I looked around to see where the sun had gone. It was being blocked by Mr. Lincoln standing in the doorway.

"May I help you with something this morning?" I asked.

"I was on my way to work and merely stopped by to see how the renovations are coming." His upper lip curled as he looked around at the café. "You do realize this paint will have to go, don't you?"

"Excuse me?"

He spread his hands as if he were dropping a basketball. "This color scheme doesn't fit in with the historical society's guidelines. I'm afraid you've wasted your time and money on your yellow and blue paint. If you'll come by the Chamber of Commerce, I'll get you a list of acceptable colors."

"But my entire color scheme has already been established! Everything we've ordered complements these colors!" It would cost so much time and money to completely repaint the café. Who did George Lincoln think he was coming in here telling me what colors were suitable for the historical society?

I heard Roger's voice from behind George Lincoln. "Coming through with some flooring!"

Mr. Lincoln moved aside and allowed Roger to pass. I noticed a red SUV parked outside and realized it must be Mr. Lincoln's vehicle.

Roger set the box he carried onto the floor. "Did I hear you say something about Amy's color scheme not working?"

"Indeed you did. It won't do at all."

"Everyone is entitled to his opinion," Roger said. "I think it'll do nicely."

"Not according to the historical society guidelines." Mr. Lincoln raised his chin.

"And when was this café declared a historical site?" Roger asked.

"Well, it hasn't been yet. But only because the meeting isn't being held until next month. It's only a matter of time." Mr. Lincoln looked from Roger to me. "You could've saved yourself a great deal of trouble had you checked with me prior to choosing your colors. In fact, you could've saved yourself even more trouble had you sold this place to me as I asked you to."

"I'm not selling the café, Mr. Lincoln," I said.

"Suit yourself." He looked around the café again.

"Although if you change your mind, I might still consider taking the place off your hands." He nodded to both Roger and me, and then he left.

I waited until he'd started the engine on his car before asking Roger if what Mr. Lincoln had said about the color scheme was true.

"I doubt it. But you might want to call Sarah and find out what Billy thinks about it."

"I will. Thanks." I put my hand on Roger's arm because he was about to go back and get another box of flooring. "Wait. While it's just the two of us, I wanted to talk with you for a second."

He squinted at me.

"It's nothing bad, I promise," I said.

"I know what it is, and I don't want to discuss it with you."

I changed tactics. "Fine, then. I *won't* tell you that Jackie and I are going to Mountain City after work today to meet with Grady Holman's daughter."

"What?"

I nodded. "Yeah. I found the woman yesterday when I was poking around on the Internet trying to find out what happened to Grady. Turns out, he died in 1984, but he left behind three children. One of them is Anna Holman Carter, and Jackie and I are meeting her for coffee."

"Why?"

"Ms. Carter wants to look at photos of the Holmans she's never seen. I'm going to the newspaper office at lunch to see what I can find."

"Are you sure about this?" he asked. "What do you hope to gain from meeting this woman?"

"I'm hoping she can give me a little more insight into the

Holmans, the bank robbery, and the money we found." I huffed. "You sound like Jackie. And speaking of Jackie, how did your date go?"

"I *knew* that's what you wanted to talk with me about."

"Of course it is." I grinned. "So?"

"So you were kidding about meeting this woman?"

"No," I said. "We're meeting her."

"Do you want me to come with you?"

"No . . . unless you'd like to go."

"I'd *like* to work over this evening and get this as much of this floor done as possible," he said. "But you know absolutely nothing about this woman."

"I know that she's, like, seventy years old. I think the meeting will be fine."

"And the date was nice, but don't you *dare* repeat that, Flowerpot," he said over his shoulder as he strode outside to get another box.

Smiling, I went to the kitchen to check on the biscuits. They weren't quite done, and it was too early to call Sarah. I fried some sausage.

As I was assembling the sausage biscuits, everyone else started coming in to work. Jackie wandered into the kitchen to see how I was doing.

"Need any help?" she asked.

"Nope, I've about got it."

"Were you and Roger here alone this morning?"

"We usually are. I told him that you and I are going to meet Grady Holman's daughter. Like you, he didn't think that was such a swell idea. But I'm dropping by the newspaper office at lunchtime to see what old photos I can dig up to take to Ms. Carter."

"That's nice. What else did you guys talk about?"

"George Lincoln's assertion that my color scheme will violate some sort of historical society code. Which reminds me, I need to call Sarah." I handed her the tray of biscuits. "Would you mind taking these out to the workers?"

Jackie took the tray outside, and I called Sarah.

"Good morning. Hancock Law Offices. How may I help you?"

"Hi, Sarah." I told her about George Lincoln's visit to the café earlier this morning.

"I think that man is just trying another tactic to get you to sell him the café. Billy is walking in the door now. Let me put you on hold while I get his take on this situation."

I listened to some instrumental pop music while waiting for Sarah to talk the matter over with Billy.

"Hey," Sarah said when she came back on the line. "Billy says Lincoln is blowing smoke. The café hasn't been deemed a historic site, and you can do anything you want with it. Even if the *land* is deemed a historic site, that has nothing to do with the café. You aren't in a historic *district*. So you're good. If Lincoln keeps hounding you, we'll file a harassment suit."

"Works for me. You know, I'm beginning to think George Lincoln might be as big a bully as Lou Lou was. It makes me wonder what else he might've done to get his hands on the café." I blew out a breath. "Thanks for your help, Sarah."

"Anytime. How are the renovations coming, besides the inappropriate color scheme, I mean?"

"Things are going great. I can hardly wait for you to see the place."

"I'll come by soon," she said. "Got another call. See ya!"

I left the kitchen and joined everyone else in the dining room. They were either sitting on the floor or standing as they ate their biscuits and drank their coffee. I grabbed a cup of coffee and wandered over to Homer.

"I'm having my biscuit early today," he said.

"Good for you. Change can be a positive thing. Who's your hero today?"

"The great jazz saxophonist John Coltrane. He died young at only forty, you know. But he teaches us that men are here to grow into the best good that they can be," he said. "That's what I'm trying to do."

"I think you're doing a wonderful job, Homer."

Roger gathered us around in a circle and gave us our assignments. The café crew was going to be helping him and one other man put down flooring here in the dining room.

"Johnny and I will help with the harder areas—corners and edges. The rest of it should be simple and straightforward. We'll go over it with you a couple of times before we actually get started. Don't hesitate to let us know if you have questions. Better to ask than for us to have to tear something out and redo it."

The construction crew would be working on the patio.

I stood, dusted off my shorts, and slipped on my heavy canvas gloves.

Knowing I wouldn't have time to make lunch for the workers, given my planned trip to the newspaper office, I called the pizza parlor and had them deliver pizza and breadsticks for lunch. It was a good thing I did. We weren't even halfway finished with the floor by then. The work was harder than it had looked.

I grabbed a breadstick and a bottle of water before heading out to search through the *Winter Garden News* archives.

Ms. Peggy looked up from her perusal of a crossword puzzle when I walked through the door. "Back to run another ad?"

"No, actually I'm here to see if the newspaper would have any old photographs of the Holmans."

She frowned. "Why in the world would you want those? Honey, let the past be. That café is your place now."

I smiled. "I know. But Grady Holman's daughter wants to see some of her Winter Garden relatives."

"Grady Holman's daughter!" Ms. Peggy brought her palm up to rest just below her throat. "I didn't know Grady had any children!"

"He had three—two daughters and a son . . . after he moved to North Carolina."

"Land's sakes! Grady didn't die way back in the thirties, then?"

"He didn't die until 1984."

"Well, I'll be," she mused. "I always thought Bo killed Grady. I'd have gone to my grave thinking it if you hadn't just told me different."

I quickly explained about doing an online search and finding Grady's obituary as Walter Holman and then locating Anna Carter from that.

Ms. Peggy took a business card out of her desk drawer. "Ask Ms. Carter to call me. I want to do a story on Grady and let people know what became of him."

"I'll tell her." I took the card and slipped it into my purse. "About those photos?"

"Your best bet would be to do a search for the grand opening of Lou's Joint. Also look for Lou Lou's engagement and marriage announcement."

"Lou Lou was married?" I asked.

"Well, sure she was. You know good and well that Pete's her son."

"I know. But since everybody in the family is named *Holman*, I assumed that Lou Lou had . . . you know . . . given birth out of wedlock."

"Nope. She was married to Sherman Harding," she said. "They didn't stay married long, though. And when they got divorced, Lou Lou took back her maiden name and gave the baby her name too, since she was no longer a Harding when Pete was born."

I went into the archive room and sat down at the computer. Ms. Peggy was right. There were photographs from the grand opening and ribbon-cutting ceremony of Lou's Joint. Lou Lou had looked a lot like her father. There was an older man standing next to Lou. The caption indicated it was Bo Holman, Lou's father. He had bushy white hair and the appearance of a mountain man, but he didn't strike me as a bank robber. I supposed looks could be deceiving.

Bo's obituary was in the *Winter Garden News*, of course, but there wasn't a photograph to accompany it.

The Holman–Harding engagement was announced. I pulled up that article and saw a photo of a younger, thinner, smiling—that was the strangest part, since the woman seldom smiled—Lou Lou and a man who didn't look half bad. In fact, there was something about him

that seemed familiar. The pair actually made a handsome couple.

I looked at the wedding announcement. Lou Lou,
again smiling, was in a tea-length white gown with a hat
and gloves. Sherman Harding stood beside her in a black
suit. They were looking at each other rather than at the
photographer. I wondered what could've possibly gone
so wrong between them that Lou Lou would even strip
their son of Sherman's last name. And Pete had obviously
not grown up with Sherman Harding being a part of his
life . . . at least, as far as I knew.

I retrieved the photos I'd printed and went back out
to the front office.

"Ms. Peggy, what happened between Lou Lou and
Sherman Harding? They seemed so happy in their
engagement and wedding photos."

She smiled. "Everybody looks happy in their engagement and wedding photos, don't you reckon?"

"Yeah, I guess they do."

"It's too bad they can't stay that way. With Lou Lou
and Sherman, rumor had it that he never stopped loving
his first girlfriend, Becky. Sherman had taken up with
Lou Lou while he and Becky were broken up. Becky
even left here for a while and went to stay with some
relatives up north somewhere."

"And let me guess," I said. "Becky came back, and
she and Sherman rekindled those old feelings?"

"She came back with a son. He was born just a few
months before Pete was."

"Dang. Sherman must've been a fast worker."

"I reckon Becky's parents thought people would think
the boy was adopted or something if she went away for

a few months, but everybody knew. Everybody always knows," she said. "But, anyhow, that was the end of his romance with Lou Lou. When he saw his first love with his firstborn child, he left Lou Lou for Becky." She nodded toward the papers in my hand. "Did you get everything you need?"

"Yes." I paid her for the copies. "Thanks for everything."

"Don't forget to ask Grady's daughter—Ms. Carter, did you say?—to call me. I'd bet she has an interesting story to tell."

Chapter 19

When I got back to the café, I went around the side of the building to look at the patio. The builders had made a lot of progress today. They'd put up support beams and should be able to construct the roof next.

"Looking nice, don't you think?" Stan said, coming to stand next to me.

"It sure is." I studied his profile. There was something so familiar about him . . . something I couldn't quite figure out. "Y'all are doing a fantastic job. Thank you."

"I just do what I'm told. I'm tickled Roger saw fit to give me this job, even if it *is* only for a few days. I'd like to earn enough money to go home for Independence Day."

"So you haven't always lived here in Winter Garden, Stan?"

There were very few people who lived here who weren't born here. Some were born here and stayed, some left and later returned, but there weren't many transplants. Mainly because it was such small town. Folks had either never heard of Winter Garden, or they wanted to live closer to the shopping malls and restaurants.

"No, ma'am. I'm originally from Pulaski."

"And your parents are still there?" I asked.

"My mom's passed on, but my dad is. I can't imagine him ever leaving . . . though if I do ever make enough money, I'd like to have him come here and live with me."

"That'd be nice. I think he'd like it here."

He smiled. "Me too."

I went back into the café and got to work on the floor.

After we'd finished up for the day, Jackie and I went into the kitchen to pack ourselves some dinner to take with us. I was making ham sandwiches, and she was putting chips into plastic baggies.

Roger walked into the kitchen. "Getting ready for the road trip, I see."

"Yep," Jackie said.

He ran his hand lightly down her arm. "Be careful. I think it's weird that this woman wants to meet with strangers to compare notes about her family."

"*She* probably thinks it's weird that I called her out of the blue about her dead father," I said.

"You've got a point there," Roger said. "You're both weirdos."

"And what am I?" asked Jackie.

"I guess you're the person going with her to make sure she doesn't get killed."

"As long as I'm not a weirdo."

"I didn't say that," he corrected.

I put our sandwiches into baggies and then put the sandwiches, chips, and packages of apple slices into an insulated tote.

"Did you find lots of interesting photos to share with Anna Carter?" Jackie asked.

"Yeah. You'll find them interesting too."

She and Roger exchanged glances.

"One of you let me know when you get back," Roger said.

"I will." Jackie smiled.

Once we were in the car, I said, "I take it you and Roger had a talk."

"We did. And we're on the same page with wanting to take things slowly but to see if there's more between us than friendship. We're going out again on Saturday night."

"Oh, good. Glad you're taking it *slowly.*"

"What did you mean about my finding the photos interesting?" She got our sandwiches out of the tote. She took mine from the baggie and handed it to me.

I accepted the sandwich. "After we eat, you can look through them, and you'll know exactly what I mean. They're on the backseat."

"I can wait." She dropped her sandwich back into the tote, undid her seat belt, and reached into the backseat for the manila envelope. She refastened the seat belt and slid the photos from the envelope.

I ate while Jackie flipped through the photographs.

"Oh my gosh!"

"I think you just found the most interesting one," I said.

"Can you believe Lou Lou was ever this thin?"

"I can't believe she ever looked that happy. I imagine she was devastated when Sherman left. You see how happy she looks in those photos."

"Yeah, but come on, Amy. Who looks sad in engagement and wedding photos?"

"That's what Ms. Peggy said."

"And she said Lou Lou's husband left her—while she was pregnant—for another woman?" Jackie asked.

"Apparently. And the other woman also had a child by him."

"Did this Harding guy know Lou Lou was pregnant when he abandoned her?"

"I don't know. Maybe he didn't realize it."

"I'd hope not. I'd hate to think the man would abandon his child as well as his wife, but this could explain why Lou Lou never wanted to cut those apron strings."

"Yeah. It looks as if Pete really was all she had."

Lou Lou had been a miserable person. And she'd held to her son so tightly that, in ways, she'd lost him too. He hadn't even been able to share some of the most important parts of his life with her. I felt that she'd have been happy—or, at least, I wanted to hope she would have been—to have known her grandchild. Maybe she'd have adored the baby and given Pete her blessing to start his trucking career.

The coffee shop was in the middle of a strip of store buildings. There was an antiques store on one side and an art gallery on the other. The Hill o' Beans was a tan building with kelly green trim. Inside, floral curtains were pulled back to let the waning sunshine in, and there were sofas and armchairs in addition to bistro tables and chairs.

A waitress spotted Jackie and me standing just inside the front door, looking clueless. Smiling brightly, she hurried over.

"Hi, there! Is either one of you Amy Flowers?" she asked.

"I am," I said.

"Ms. Carter is waiting for you right over here." She led us to a table where Anna Carter sat nursing a cup of coffee.

Ms. Carter stood when Jackie and I reached the table. "Hello. Thank you so much for coming."

I introduced her to Jackie, and we all sat down around the table. Jackie and I ordered coffee from the waitress, and she scampered off to get it.

"I'm looking forward to seeing what some of Daddy's relatives looked like," said Ms. Carter. "Did you have a chance to talk with my great-nephew yet? Pete, did you say his name was?"

"I haven't had a chance to speak with Pete yet, but I will." I took Ms. Peggy's business card from my purse and slid it across the table. "When I went to the newspaper office to get the photos, Ms. Peggy was interested in doing a story on your dad. She thought people—especially the older folks—would enjoy knowing how he spent his life after leaving Winter Garden."

"Okay. I'll consider giving her a call." She took a photo album from a tote she had sitting on the floor beside her chair. She opened it. "This is Daddy."

The sepia photograph had been taken when Grady

Holman was in his early twenties. His hair was dark, and
he was smiling impishly at the photographer. He had on
overalls and what appeared to be a white shirt. I glanced
up at Ms. Carter, but I didn't see much of a resemblance.
I passed the photo album on down closer to Jackie.

"He was a cutie pie, wasn't he?" she said to Ms. Carter.

"He certainly was." She sat a little taller in her seat.

I opened the manila envelope and took out the photo
taken at the grand opening of Lou's Joint. "I can see the
resemblance between your dad and Bo." Grady hadn't
been as tall or as broad as Bo, nor did he have a beard,
but their faces looked similar.

"And Lou took after them too," said Ms. Carter, her
lips slowly curving into a smile. "Daddy was the better-
looking of the two brothers, though, don't you think?"

Jackie and I agreed that he was.

Ms. Carter flipped through the photos. "And this was
Lou's daughter? Poor thing . . . to be named Lou Lou."

"I always heard Lou wanted a son," said Jackie.

"Apparently, he wanted two of them." Ms. Carter
chuckled.

Jackie and I thumbed through the photo album.

"You must take after your mom's side of the family,"
I said, noting that the diminutive Ms. Carter looked
nothing like the Holmans I knew.

"I do. My brother is tall and muscular." She grinned.
"Mother always said thank goodness we girls took after
her people."

"Did your dad ever talk about his family back in
Winter Garden?" Jackie asked.

"He spoke of Bo pretty often. I believe he missed his
brother." She ran a fingertip over the photocopy of Bo's

obituary. "I wonder if he knew Bo had died, or if he just thought his brother had forgotten about him."

"If Grady was in touch with anybody back home, then he knew what happened," I said. "You mentioned over the phone that Grady had told you about the bank robbery."

"He had." She shook her head. "I always figured it was one of his tall tales. I mean, some of the stories he told about growing up in that little town in Virginia with Bo . . . they couldn't possibly have been true." She looked again at the photo of Bo and Lou at the café's ribbon-cutting ceremony. "I thought there was maybe a grain of truth to them but that Daddy had exaggerated."

"So you didn't believe that he and Bo had robbed a bank?" Jackie asked.

"I thought maybe they'd tried . . . or even that they had made a teller slip them a few dollars. But Daddy told me his conscience bothered him too bad to keep it, and he gave the money back."

"I don't imagine Bo was very happy about that," I said.

"No, he wasn't. That drove the wedge between them that made Daddy leave Winter Garden and head for North Carolina to look for work," said Ms. Carter.

When Jackie and I were in the car on our way back home, I mentioned that Ms. Carter had changed her story about the bank robbery.

"Over the phone last night, she told me that Bo had driven Grady over to the bank in North Carolina and that Grady hadn't known they were going to rob the bank until Bo handed him a ski mask and a pistol."

"And then Grady just went along with it?"

"According to Ms. Carter, he did. She spoke as if Grady would've done anything his big brother wanted him to do."

"But she also told us that Grady had given the money back," Jackie said. "If that's the truth, where did the money in the lockbox come from?"

"I mentioned the lockbox to her over the phone too. I said there was money inside, but I didn't tell her how much. Now I wish I hadn't said anything about it."

"Amy! She might come looking for that money!"

"You saw her. Do you really believe she'd burst through the doors of the café, guns blazing, to demand her daddy's stolen money? Besides, I told her the money was in police custody."

"I don't think she'd do it herself, but her children might be like Bo, Grady, and Lou. Or, worse yet, Lou Lou!" Jackie said. "If they think there's anything to be gained here, they might come after you."

"I rather doubt it. I imagine the woman simply wanted to paint her father in the best possible light. Or what if Grady told his daughter the truth, and he really *did* return the money to the bank?" I asked. "Do you think the twenty thousand dollars was Bo's part of the money? Or do you think the money found in the lockbox had nothing to do with the bank after all? Maybe the money belonged to Lou."

"That's possible." She frowned. "Now I'm wondering what other skeletons linger in Lou Holman's closet."

"We know Sherman Harding was one. Wonder whatever became of him."

"I don't know, but I'm guessing you'll be burning up that laptop of yours tonight to try to find out."

"You've got that right," I said.

* * *

Jackie had been right. I wanted to find out more about this man who'd been married to Lou Lou Holman and had then thrown her over for another woman. So I got out my laptop as soon as I got home to see what I could learn.

I had no luck finding Sherman Harding until I downloaded a free trial for a genealogy site and searched for him there. That's where I found Sherman Harding, who had been married to Rebecca Minton Harding. And they had one son—Stanley Wheeler Harding.

Wait . . . what?!

I sat staring at my laptop as my cursor kept blinking on the name "Stanley Wheeler Harding." Stanley Harding. Stan Harding. Stan *Wheeler* Harding.

Oh my goodness. Was that true? It had to be. It's why Stan's profile had looked so familiar after I'd seen the photo of Sherman Harding. Stan Wheeler was Sherman Harding's son. He was Pete's half brother.

Had Lou Lou known? I thought back to the paper I'd seen in the box from her office. Was that why she'd written Stan's name and drawn the fish beside it? Did she think Stan was fishing for something? Or did she think there was something fishy about Stan?

At least, I now knew why, after seeing the photograph of Sherman Harding, something about Stan struck me as being familiar. And if I saw a resemblance, even though I couldn't quite recall why, surely Lou Lou—having been married to Sherman—could see his likeness in his son. Funny, though, Pete looked nothing like Sherman. He took after the Holman side of the family.

I thought about my conversation with Anna Carter and promising I'd talk with Pete to see if he'd be willing to talk with her. There might be another family member he'd be even more interested in speaking with.

So what was Stan doing in Winter Garden? Why was he here as Stan Wheeler rather than Stan Harding? And how long had he been here? It had obviously been long enough to establish a seedy reputation. Maybe I should talk with Ryan about this. He'd told me to let me know of any leads I came across. This could be considered a lead. I'd give him a call tomorrow.

Something very, very strange was going on with Stan Wheeler.

Chapter 20

The shrill noise woke me, but it was Rory's barking along with it that fully brought me from sleep to wakefulness. I rose up onto my elbow, gently pushed Rory's face out of mine, and answered the phone.

"Hello?"

"Morning, Flowerpot! Rise and shine!"

It was Roger. I looked at the clock. It was six a.m. "I refuse to rise or shine this early. What's wrong?" I had a sudden fear that the café was on fire.

"Nothing really. I just wondered if you'd give your staff the day off. It's pouring rain, and my guys can't work on the patio today, so I thought we'd work inside."

"And you don't want us in your way," I said.

"Precisely. You catch on quickly for a foggy-brained sleepyhead."

"What would you like me to bring for breakfast?"

"Nothing, thanks. I'll stop and get a box of doughnuts. We wouldn't turn down lunch, though."

"You got it. Are sandwiches all right?"

"That'll be great," said Roger. "Thanks."

"Thank you. Not having to come in so early will be
wonderful."

"Rub it in, why don't you?"

I laughed. "Do I need to tell Jackie, or does she know
already?"

"I told her when we spoke last night that if it rained
like the forecast was calling for, I was going to ask you to
give the café staff the day off. You might want to remind
her, though."

"I will. See you at lunchtime."

I hung up the phone. Rory had already snuggled back
up against me. He was so warm and cozy. And I could
hear the rain pounding against the roof. I dropped my
head back onto my pillow. My alarm was set for six thirty.
I'd snooze until then.

It was seven o'clock before I finally dragged my butt
out of bed and called the café workers. Like me, they
were thrilled not to have to work on such a rainy day.
Jackie offered to come by and help with lunch, but I
assured her that I had it under control. I'd planned to make
sandwiches, potato wedges, and cookies. Easy to make,
and easy to transport.

While I was at it, I thought I'd make a small tray of
sandwiches to take to Pete and Chris Anne. I wanted to
talk with Pete about his father and find out what he knew
about Stan.

When I spoke with Homer, I promised to add a sausage biscuit to the lunch and have it for him at the café. He understood that he didn't have to work today, but he said he would drop by anyway to see if Roger needed his help. Homer was such a good guy.

I washed the potatoes, dried them, and cut them into wedges. I preheated the oven while gathering my spices. I put salt, pepper, and garlic powder into a large plastic baggie. I then added the potato wedges. I gave the mixture a good shake, added olive oil, and shook them again.

While the potatoes were baking, I made turkey, ham, tuna, and pimiento cheese sandwiches. I cut them into fourths, so they'd stand up nicely on the trays and the workers could see what kinds of sandwiches there were to choose from. When I took the potatoes from the oven, I sprinkled them with Parmesan cheese. I put the potato wedges in a pan lined with parchment paper to transport them to the café.

Fortunately, I had some frozen biscuits in my freezer, so it was no problem to add Homer's sausage biscuit to the food I was delivering. I also had frozen cookie dough, so while the oven was hot, I was able to make three dozen chocolate chip cookies.

I dropped off the food at the café. Homer was there, helping Roger's crew with something in the kitchen. I gave him his sausage biscuit, and he thanked me.

"Who's your hero today?"

"Jacques Cousteau, Mademoiselle."

I smiled. *"Fantastique!"*

I found Roger, told him I was delivering a sandwich tray to Pete and Chris Anne, and said I'd be back to help afterward.

"You don't have to do that. We've got everything under control. Enjoy today."

"But Homer is here. I can't *not* be here when Homer is here working. This is my café. I should be here."

"And, like Homer, you'll be underfoot and kinda in the way," Roger whispered. "And we'll have to give you something to do so you don't realize that you're underfoot and in the way."

"Fine, but I'll still come back by here after I go to Pete's house to make sure you don't need my help with anything."

"All right. Take your time," he said.

"Gee, you know how to make a girl feel appreciated."

"You want to feel appreciated? Be here when we dive into those boxes of food."

I laughed. "See you later."

I flipped the hood up on my jacket as I sprinted back out to the car. The rain was still coming down hard. I slid behind the wheel, put on my headlights, and drove to Pete's house.

I pulled into the driveway and was glad to see only Pete's brown pickup truck there. It might be easier to talk with him without Chris Anne around. I went to the door and rang the bell.

Pete answered the door and invited me inside.

"Where's Chris Anne?" I asked, carrying the sandwiches through to the kitchen. "I brought you two some lunch."

"That's thoughtful of you, and I'll try to save her some, but she's out garage-saling. I told her I doubted there'd be many people having sales today since it's raining so hard, but she hopes to find some bargains for the baby."

"Maybe she'll have good luck," I said. "I've heard you can find some great baby items at garage and thrift sales."

"That's what she's counting on."

"So, Pete, what are you hoping for? A boy or a girl?"

He shrugged his bony shoulders. "I don't reckon it matters. We're just praying the baby'll be healthy."

"How about your trucking business? Any luck finding a tractor and trailer yet?"

"I believe I've found the semi I want. Right now I'm dickering with the salesman to get him to come down a little on the price."

"Well, I'm glad you can haggle. I sure don't like to."

He chuckled. "Live with Momma for forty years. I don't know how *not* to haggle!"

I laughed but saw the opening I'd been waiting for. "What about your dad, Pete? Is he still in your life?"

His smile completely disappeared, and his lips curled in revulsion. "My daddy was never part of my life. He took off on Momma when she was pregnant."

"I'm so sorry to hear that."

"Yeah, well, that's just one of them things." He jerked his head toward the tray I'd sat on the table. "I appreciate the lunch. I'll save it until Chris Anne gets home. Does it need to go in the fridge?"

"It does," I said. "Just one other thing, Pete. I know you're considering Stan Wheeler for your partner. How well do you know him?"

"Pretty good, I guess. We've been friends since he moved here"—he squinted up at the ceiling—"a little over a year ago now."

"I don't know that I'd trust him enough to go into business with him," I said. "You've got this fresh new start. I don't want anything to jeopardize that for you."

He laughed. "Listen at you sounding like a baby

sister! I kinda like it. I always wanted a brother or a sister."

If he only knew. I wanted to tell him about Stan, but I was afraid to. For one thing, I wasn't sure what game Stan had been playing, coming here to Winter Garden under an assumed name . . . or, at least, not his full name. And for another, Pete had been through so much with his mother's death already. I didn't want to be the one to add to his stress.

"I'd better be getting back to the café. If y'all need anything, let me know."

"Thank you, Amy. We appreciate the kindness."

I got back into the car, shivering slightly from the onslaught of the cold rain, and backed out of Pete's driveway.

I couldn't imagine Pete would entertain friendly thoughts toward Stan Wheeler if he knew Stan was his half brother. He certainly had no warm, fuzzy feelings toward his father. Did he even know his father's name? I wondered what story Pete had been told . . . and who might know.

I went back to the café. The workers were taking their lunch break. Homer was sitting at the counter, sort of off to himself. I sat down beside him.

"Homer, may I ask you something?"

"You can ask me anything. I might not know the answer, but maybe I'll be able to help you find it."

I told him about my visit to Pete and my mentioning his father. "It's apparent that Pete can't stand his dad. I didn't know the Holmans personally until I came to work here last year. When Nana was living—before she got sick, I mean, and while I was growing up here in Winter

Garden—we didn't eat out much. Nana was an absolutely wonderful cook." I realized I was getting off track. "Anyway, I'd never heard anything about Pete's father or Lou Lou's situation. It had never really crossed my mind until now."

"Word around town at the time of Mr. Harding's departure was that he'd either been in an auto accident and had been placed in a rehab facility close to where his parents lived or that he'd returned to his first love," said Homer. "But, of course, Lou Lou went back to using her maiden name and gave the name to her child as well. That made us all believe that he'd just thrown Lou Lou over, and we correctly assumed that the Holman family didn't want mention made of Mr. Harding anymore."

"Pete told me his father ran out on his mother when she was pregnant. Why didn't anyone tell him the story about the auto accident?"

"Listen, *chérie*, Lou Holman was as hard as nails, and he laid down the law where his family was concerned. I have no doubt that he got rid of Sherman Harding—paid him to stay away or threatened him or something—and then told Lou Lou what she was to tell her son."

I glanced around to make sure Stan Wheeler wasn't within earshot, and lowered my voice. "Did you know that Stan is Pete's half brother?"

"I did not. I'm guessing no one else here does either. These people aren't Lou Lou's contemporaries; they're Pete's. Pete's father left Winter Garden before he was born. None of these younger people remember him."

"No, of course, they wouldn't." I told Homer about my findings the night before. "But Lou Lou *had* to have guessed who Stan Wheeler was . . . or, at least suspected.

He looks a lot like his father, judging from the photograph that was in the newspaper."

"I imagine she would have."

"Then why didn't she turn Stan away?" I asked. "Ask him to leave Winter Garden?"

"Perhaps Stan held the truth over her . . . threatened to tell Pete what he knew if she didn't do as he asked. Or maybe Lou Lou never recovered from her lost love, and she wanted news of Sherman. She might've even entertained thoughts of the two of them reuniting." He spread his hands. "The only person who could tell us her reasons has been silenced . . . that is, unless Stan knows."

"Yeah." I wondered if Sherman Harding might be able to give me some insight into Lou Lou's behavior. "I have to run. I'll check with Roger before I go to see if he needs anything."

"*À bientôt!*"

The French thing was odd. It was okay for a day, but I think it would wear thin after a while. Luckily, Homer would have a new hero tomorrow.

At home, I discussed the feasibility of calling Sherman Harding with Rory. I tried to include Princess Eloise in the discussion; but she merely gave me a disdainful look, turned her back, and glared out the window at the rain. I didn't know whether to interpret her silence as disapproval or not, so I continued to hash out my reasoning with Rory.

"What harm could it do?" I asked the furry little terrier. "I could tell Mr. Harding that I was going through some archives for a relative of Grady Holman—which

was true—and that I came across a wedding announcement for Lou Lou Holman and Sherman Harding. Then
I could ask if *he* is that Sherman Harding and then tell
him I thought he might be interested to know that Ms.
Holman passed away. And maybe he'll open up and give
me a clue as to what his son is doing here in Winter
Garden. What do you think?"

Rory barked.

"Okay." I got the phone. "Let's do this."

He wagged his tail and looked up at me expectantly.

"Let's see how this goes, and then I'll get you a treat.
I might need one myself."

I used the phone to look up listings for Sherman
Harding in Pulaski, Virginia. There was only one number. I called it.

After what seemed like forty rings but was probably
more like five, a gruff, wheezy male voice answered. "Hello."

"Hi. Is this Sherman Harding?"

"Yes. Who's this?"

"My name is Amy Flowers. I live in Winter Garden."

My announcement was met with silence, so I plunged on.

"I was going through some of the *Winter Garden News*
archives for a relative of Grady Holman, and I came
across a wedding announcement for Sherman Harding
and Lou Lou Holman," I said. "Were you ever married
to Lou Lou Holman?"

"For a very short while. Why do you ask?"

"Well, I thought you might want be interested to know
that she passed away about a week ago."

"Sorry to hear that."

He didn't seem surprised. He didn't sound particularly sorry either.

"Also, there's a man named Stan here in town, and I wondered if you were any relation."

"Yes, but I don't see how my relatives are any of your business," said Mr. Harding. "Anything else you need to know?"

"Well, actually, I wondered if Ms. Holman had been in touch with you before she died."

"Nope. Hadn't talked with any of the Holmans in years."

"Were you aware that Ms. Holman had a son named Pete?" I asked.

"Yep. Seems like that was her business."

"You're not Pete's father?"

"Didn't say that," he said. "I want to know how you figure any of this is *your* business, miss?"

"It isn't—"

"Right," Mr. Harding interrupted. "So stay out of it."

"But wait! Please!" I listened to make sure he hadn't ended the call.

"What?"

"Ms. Holman was murdered. I found her, and I'm trying to find out if anyone had a motive to kill her."

"And what? You think I did it?" He began to laugh, but it turned into a coughing fit.

"No, sir," I said once he'd recovered. "I don't suspect you at all. It's just that you have a history with the Holmans, so I thought you might be able to provide me with some insights."

"That girl should've never allowed her daddy to keep her under his thumb the way she did. But she made her choice. That's why I'm here and she and her boy are not. I imagine Lou Holman made a lot of enemies in his day, and given Lou Lou's penchant for being the spitting image of him, she probably did too. I'd appreciate it if you don't call here again."

"All right. Thank you for your time."

He wheezed. "I'm sorry for your troubles, miss. But I can't help you."

"I know. Again, I appreciate your talking with me."

"You're welcome."

After talking with Sherman Harding, I felt deflated. I went into the kitchen and got Rory a treat, and I got myself a cookie. Then I went back to the living room and flopped onto the sofa.

I felt that what Mr. Harding *hadn't* said was as important as what he had said. He'd given me the impression that had Mr. Holman allowed it, he'd have stayed married to Lou Lou. But he'd been shut out—and possibly paid off—by Lou Holman. And Lou Lou had apparently let it happen.

So why had Lou Lou rented a home to Stan when he'd arrived in Winter Garden? Had she made the connection between Stan and her former husband? Or had she known that Stan was Sherman's son and had she rented the mobile home to him so she could find out why he'd come to town? Did Stan know about his father's brief marriage to Lou Lou and the fact that Pete was his half brother?

And had someone killed to make sure one or all of these secrets stayed buried?

Chapter 21

I called Ryan to get his thoughts on the situation. When I explained that I'd both met with Grady Holman's daughter and talked with Sherman Harding, he told me he was in the area and would stop by my house.

I put some chocolate chip cookies on a plate and made a fresh pitcher of iced tea. I also brushed my hair and freshened my makeup. I realized it was a police investigation and not a date, but that didn't mean I had to look my worst.

When Ryan arrived, we decided to speak on the front porch. I put the cookies, pitcher of tea, and plastic tumblers on a tray and placed it on the table between the two white rocking chairs.

"Thank you," he said with a grin. "Southern hospitality at its finest."

"I try. I hope that's what people will say about the

Down South Café once it's up and running. Well, that and that the food is delicious."

"If these cookies are any indication, your food is outstanding."

I smiled. "Thank you."

"So, you've been investigating, huh?"

"In a way . . . I guess I have."

"You do know that's the sheriff's department's job and that it's also our job to protect the citizens of Winter Garden—including you—right?"

I nodded.

"And unless I've missed some background on you somewhere, you aren't trained to investigate crimes."

"No, sir."

"All right," he said. "Tell me what you've got."

I told him about calling Grady Holman's daughter and later meeting her for coffee. "She told two different stories about the bank robbery, but in both versions, she said Grady gave the money back."

"It could be nothing," Ryan said. "Maybe Grady really did give the money back and the money found when the office wall was torn down belonged to either Bo or Lou. We're trying to track the money and see where it came from. But it's taking some time since it's so old and the original bank that was robbed back in the thirties is no longer there."

"When I was searching for photographs of the Holmans for Grady's daughter, I ran across Lou Lou's engagement and wedding announcements. That's when I realized she'd been married to Stan Wheeler's father." I took a drink of my tea. "I didn't know at first that he was Stan's father, but now I do, and I can't help but think that somehow Lou Lou's secrets about her past played some part in her murder."

"We need to figure out where Lou Lou stood with regard to Sherman and Stan. Did she want to reconnect with her ex-husband?" He bit into a cookie while he studied the situation. "Who would Lou Lou have confided in? Who were those closest to her?"

"In the year that I worked with her, I don't know of anyone who struck me as being Lou Lou's friend. She had employees, suppliers, customers, and Pete. That was about the extent of her social circle."

"I'll see what Ivy confiscated from Lou Lou's office. Maybe there's a date book or something that might provide some answers for us."

I gazed at his profile. "Could I maybe help?"

"If there is a date book or planner among the items Ivy took from Lou Lou's office, it would be potential evidence, Amy. You aren't supposed to be around while I'm examining evidence."

"Please, Ryan. This is my life on the line here. I want to help."

He glanced over at me.

"Please."

His expression softened. "Of course, if you were to be at the library in half an hour and I happened to be there looking at the documents, I couldn't very well ask you to leave." He held up a hand. "I'm not going to let you look at anything, but you might be able to give me some insight into the names I'm not familiar with."

I smiled. "I'll see you then."

* * *

The Winter Garden Library was housed in a small brick building with floor-to-ceiling windows trimmed in white. The door was also white and heavy, and there were window panels on each side.

I walked inside, my sandaled feet clicking on the tile foyer until I reached the gray industrial carpet covering the floor inside the main part of the library. The building smelled fresh and clean. It had been remodeled since I'd been here as a little girl. Back then, the entire floor was tile and the library had smelled of leather book spines and old musty pages. I was sure there must still be some ancient leather-bound books around here somewhere, but most of the books sitting on the carts to be reshelved were brand-new, current bestsellers.

I looked around the room. Ryan hadn't said where he'd be. I supposed I could ask for him at the circulation desk, but he might not appreciate that. He might prefer I pretend our meeting was accidental. Either way, the clerk sitting behind the long wooden desk was chatting on the phone and didn't appear to be inclined to do anything else.

I spotted Ryan at a rectangular wooden table at the back of the room. He sat on the chair facing the door, and there was an empty chair in front of him.

"Is this seat taken?" I asked, pulling out the chair.

"Why, no. What brings you here, Ms. Flowers?"

"I thought I might take a look at some of the cookbooks of old to see if there's anything I might want to revive for the Down South Café."

"Then please grab a book and join me."

"Oh . . . yeah." I stood and took a book off the nearest shelf. It was a psychology textbook that had nothing to do with cooking. Still, it was a book. "Have you found anything?"

"There doesn't seem to be anything out of the ordinary in these ledgers."

"Wait. I thought Pete got the ledgers from the safe."

"The ledgers from the safe were probably old ones. These are current."

I tried not to look, but I couldn't help but see that the dates on the page Ryan was looking at were from two months ago. "Did Lou Lou have a date book?"

"She kept a calendar," he said. "It looks like she was seeing someone named Sissy every Wednesday. Do you know anyone named Sissy who might've visited Lou Lou at the café?"

I shook my head slowly. *Sissy . . . Sissy . . . Why did that name ring a bell?* "Sissy's Scissors!"

"Excuse me?"

I lowered my voice. "Sorry. Lou Lou left every Wednesday to have her hair done. She must've gone to Sissy's Scissors in Meadowview. Nana used to go there."

"Lots of women gossip with their hairstylists . . . or so I've heard. I'll see if anyone has talked with this woman yet, and if not, I'll get right on that. Thanks for your help."

I wasn't content to let the matter lie. I went out to my car, called Sissy, and learned that she had had a cancellation and would be able to see me in the next thirty minutes if I could get there by then. I said I'd be right over.

*   *   *

Apparently, Sissy had just finished giving an elderly woman a perm when I walked into her salon. The smell nearly brought tears to my eyes.

"Hi, hon!" Sissy, a woman with the top half of her hair platinum and the bottom half jet-black, called to me. "I'll be finished up here in a minute!" She was teasing the white tightly curled hair of the woman in the chair in front of her to the point where the hair was probably thinking it had had enough of this nonsense. She was about go from teasing it to making it downright mad.

I sat on a nearby black vinyl and stainless steel chair to watch Sissy—a wisp of a woman dressed in black capris, a black T-shirt, and silver ballet flats—poof up the rest of her client's hair. When she was finished, she instructed, "Close your eyes, sweetie!" before blasting the hair with so much hairspray that I could've sworn a mushroom cloud lingered over the poor lady's head.

"All done!" Sissy announced brightly. "You're beautiful!"

"Thank you." The woman reached into a large brown purse that she held on her lap and took out a wallet.

"No, sweetie, your daughter has done paid for you this week. Remember?"

"Oh. Well, here's a little something extra." She handed Sissy a dollar.

"You're so sweet. Thank you." She shoved the dollar into her pants pocket before helping the woman to the door and holding it open for her. "See you next time." When the woman left, Sissy turned to me. "What're we doing for you today, hon?"

"I thought I'd like an updo . . . something kind of intricate." I wanted to make sure I had adequate time to talk with Sissy.

She smiled. "Got a big date, huh? Good for you! Come on over and have a seat."

I sat down on the chair vacated by Ms. Perm, and Sissy draped me with a black cape. She took a book and showed me the hairstyle she had in mind. It appeared that it would certainly take a while, so I went with it.

"I don't think you've ever been here before," she said. "I never forget a face. Unless, of course, you were here when Tina or one of the other girls was working."

"No . . . this is my first time."

"How'd you hear about us?"

"Well, I worked for Lou Lou Holman," I said. "I know she came by here every week."

"Oh yeah . . . God rest her poor soul. What's gonna happen to the Joint now that Lou Lou's gone?"

"I bought it. Pete wants to go into the trucking business, so he sold Lou's Joint to me. I'm in the process of doing a little remodeling, and I hope to reopen as the Down South Café in a few weeks."

"Kudos to you, darling! It does my heart good to know somebody is going to run the place. The good Lord knows Winter Garden needs something better than that pizza place to keep us going . . . am I right? I mean, I like pizza all right, but theirs isn't the best in the world, and besides that, we need some variety. Am I right?"

"You're absolutely right," I said, wanting to steer the conversation back to my reason for being here. "Poor Lou Lou. I never knew her to miss a hair appointment."

"Yep. She had a standing Wednesday appointment.

Had it for as long as I've been in business, as a matter of fact." She took a small comb from a container of disinfecting solution, shook it out, and then began using it to separate my hair into sections. She took clips and secured the sections of my hair out of the way of the one she planned on working with first. "Gosh, I guess it's been twenty years since I started doing her hair."

"Wow. So you've known Lou Lou a long time."

"I reckon I have."

"I'm beginning to feel like I didn't know her at all," I said. "I mean, I'd been working for her for a year, but I didn't know anything about her marriage until just the other day."

"Oh yeah, that was a sore spot for her." Sissy began curling tiny sections of my hair and pinning them on top of my head.

"About that. I made the mistake of asking Pete about his father. You know, I wondered if maybe they were close. Pete took his mother's death so hard and everything."

"Hon, I know your heart was in the right place, but Pete knows absolutely nothing about his daddy. He thinks his daddy was some kind of jerk who just ran off and left his mother while she was pregnant," Sissy said. "Lou Lou said she told him his daddy's name was Joe Smith or something because she never wanted Pete to try to find the man."

"I can understand Lou Lou's pain, but didn't she think Pete deserved to know the truth about his father?"

"Well, you see, Lou Lou thought for years that Sherman had left her because he was in love with that other girl," said Sissy. "But he wasn't."

I winced as a bobby pin poked a little too enthusiastically into my scalp. "Then why did he marry the other girl?"

"I guess he figured he might as well. And he got to raise one of his children that way. Anyhow, Lou Lou's momma finally told her on her deathbed that her daddy was the reason Sherman left."

"Lou paid him off," I mused.

"I believe it started out that way, but Sherman wouldn't leave for money. Mrs. Holman told Lou Lou that Lou and Sherman had fought and that her daddy had stabbed Sherman. Sherman nearly died." Sissy nodded at my shocked expression in the mirror. "Lou and one of his friends took Sherman to the emergency room and dumped him out of the car. Then they took off. But they made it clear to Sherman that if he stayed in Winter Garden, they'd kill him. They told him to leave and never come back."

"And Lou was never arrested for the assault?"

Sissy shook her head. "Sherman just got out of town before Lou made good on his promise. Lou Lou said she wondered if Sherman had thought she'd reach out to him, but she didn't. She believed the tale her daddy had told her. And then she'd gone for so many years hating him for breaking her heart. . . ."

"It seems like she made sure that Pete hated him too," I said.

"Yep."

"Why didn't she tell Pete the truth when she found out what Lou had done?"

"She was afraid that Pete would go to Sherman . . . you know, meet him to see what he was like." She finished pinning the tiny curls up onto my head and took down another section to work with. "See, by the time she learned what had really happened, Pete was all Lou Lou had. What if Pete blamed her for letting her daddy run Sherman off? What if he'd gotten to know Sherman and decided he could have a better life in Pulaski with Sherman and his family than with Lou Lou in Winter Garden?"

"I doubt that thought would've ever crossed his mind," I told her. "Pete adored his mother."

"But would he have if he'd found out the truth?" Sissy asked.

"Of course he would! He'd know that Lou Lou wasn't responsible for the actions of her father."

"Maybe and maybe not. Hon, losing Pete was Lou Lou Holman's biggest fear."

I could see that now. It was evident in everything she'd done.

I felt a pang of pity for Lou Lou. I could see now how she'd become the bitter woman I'd known.

Sissy handed me a mirror. "See what you think, gorgeous!"

"Wow." I hadn't seen hair this big since senior prom . . . photos of *Mom's* senior prom, to be exact.

Sissy was looking at me expectantly.

"Looks incredible!" I smiled, paid her for my enormous hair, gave her a tip, and left the salon.

It was a good thing Sissy had put enough pins in my hair to supply beauty pageants along the entire East Coast and had used half a can of spray to hold the updo in place, because it smushed against the top of the Beetle when I slid behind the wheel.

I called Ryan to ask him to give me some time before

heading to my house. I wanted to take my hair down and wash it before he saw me. But my call went to voice mail.

Oh well, when I got home, I could at least take a selfie—front and back—so that Jackie and I could laugh over the hair later. It wasn't that it was ugly. It was just big. Texas big. Sissy had done an excellent job of piling all of my hair up onto my head in a . . . well, an elaborate way.

W hen I pulled into my driveway, Ryan's red convertible was already there. And Ryan was sitting on my front porch. I groaned as I parked the car.

Dang.

He smirked as I maneuvered my head out of the car. "I knew you'd do it. I *knew* you'd do it!"

I raised my chin. "What did you expect? Like I told you, this is my life on the line."

He blew out a breath and shook his head. "You're impossible—you know that?"

I walked up the stairs and sat on the porch beside Ryan. "Have you been here long?"

"Only a few minutes. So did you learn anything valuable on your fishing expedition?"

"You mean, besides the answer to the question of how many bobby pins my head can hold without spraining my neck?" I smiled. "I found out that Lou Lou's mother confessed to her on her deathbed that her dad had been responsible for making Sherman Harding leave Winter Garden."

"After finding out, what did Lou Lou do with the information?"

"Apparently nothing. Sissy said that Lou Lou was afraid

to tell Pete the truth because she was scared that he'd want to meet his father and that, after meeting his father, Pete would want to go live with him."

"And then when Stan showed up, did she figure out the truth about his identity?" Ryan prompted.

"I don't know. Apparently, that was the one thing she didn't confide to her hairdresser. Incidentally, Lou Holman stabbed Sherman—he didn't pay him off. I think I should find out from Stan exactly what he knew before he came to Winter Garden and what he learned after he got here."

"I'll be the one talking with Stan."

I shook my head, which wasn't an easy feat, given its size and weight at this point. "He'd be more likely to talk with me. He said he'd been in jail before, so I imagine he'd be defensive around police officers."

"No dice. I'll tell him that we've learned that his father was once married to Lou Lou Holman and ask what his intentions were when he came to Winter Garden."

"Okay. I hope you find out something useful."

Chapter 22

§ After Ryan left, I went inside and fed the pets. I was getting ready to take the selfies for Jackie, and then wash my hair, when Stan Wheeler pulled into my driveway. I felt a chill run down my spine. I had no idea what this man was hiding, and I didn't want to be inside my house alone with him. I'd keep him out here on the porch, where all the neighbors could see us. I desperately hoped I could get my questions answered after all. I still thought the man would be more forthcoming with me than he would be with Ryan.

I stepped out onto the porch and pasted on a bright smile. "Hi, Stan!"

"Hey. I knocked off early because I wanted to talk with you. I heard about you calling my dad."

"I did. I . . . um . . . found out that Mr. Harding had been married to Lou Lou Holman, and I phoned to let him know she died last week."

"Why in the world would you do that?" he asked.

"Well . . ." I swallowed. "I thought maybe he'd like to know what happened to her."

"That was a long time ago," he said. "More than forty years, as a matter of fact. Why would he care? Why would *you*? Dad hadn't been in Lou Lou's life for nearly four decades."

"Um . . . yeah . . . looking back, it might not have been such a good idea. I learned he was your dad, though, because you two look so much alike. Or, at least, you know . . . you look like he looked when he was younger. I've obviously only seen the two photos . . . and those were grainy newspaper pictures . . . so what do I know?"

He shook his head. "What are you babbling on about?"

Stan was right. I *was* babbling. I needed to suck it up and to find out what I wanted to know. "Did Lou Lou know you were Sherman Harding's son?"

"Maybe. So what?"

"Did you know her history with your dad? And that Pete is your half brother?" I asked.

"Sure. Dad told me all of that before I left Pulaski."

"So, why did you come to Winter Garden? Did you want to meet your half brother . . . maybe make a connection with him?"

"I didn't give it a lot of thought." He put his hands on his hips. "I wanted to see them mainly . . . to just find out a little bit about who they were. I mean, they were important to Dad once . . . you know?"

"Of course. I can understand that. But you've been here for over a year. Why did you stay?"

"I don't see how any of this is your business," Stan said. "In fact, I'll call Roger tonight and tell him I'm quitting because I don't want to work anywhere near you anymore." He turned to go.

"Wait, Stan. I'm sorry. I just . . . Why haven't you told Pete you're his half brother?"

He shrugged.

"But now that his mother is dead, don't you think Pete would like to know he still has family? Maybe he'd like to go to Pulaski and meet your dad."

"He might." He studied the tops of his work boots.

"I heard just today that Lou stabbed your dad and threatened to kill him if he didn't leave Winter Garden and never come back."

Stan raised his eyes to mine. "You calling my daddy a coward?"

"No. I'd never say that. But he was young and knew he could have a life with you and your mom. . . . I think he made the right choice."

A muscle worked in his jaw. "Like I've done told you, none of this is any of your business. So stay out of it."

After Stan left, I went into the bedroom and sat down at the vanity. I took photos of myself from the front and from the back and texted them to Jackie. Then I began the difficult task of undoing what Sissy had done to my hair. I took out a few pins, and yet the hair stayed where it was. I took out more pins, and the hair on one side drooped a little. Finally, all of the bobby pins were in a pile on my vanity. I swept them into a drawer, secure in the knowledge that I'd never again have to buy bobby pins.

I looked in the mirror and laughed at the disarray. Nana would've said I looked like I'd stuck my finger in a light socket. I only hoped a shower, some shampoo, and conditioner would return my hair to normal. Before I went to the bathroom, however, I took another selfie and texted it to Jackie so she could see my mad-scientist hair.

I was chuckling as I went into the bathroom and turned on the shower. I retrieved a towel and washcloth from the closet.

I heard Rory's toenails click on the floor as he wandered into the hall to see what I was doing.

"What are you in the mood for this evening, Rory Borealis?" I asked him. "Wanna watch a movie when I get out?"

He turned and trotted toward the kitchen.

"Guess not. Maybe you'll change your mind."

I went into the bathroom and got into the shower. The weight of the water finally lost the battle with gravity and my hair once more fell to below my shoulders. I shampooed it twice and then one more time for good measure. Then I made sure to leave my conditioner on for a full minute while I sang a John Legend song to myself and thought about my nonexistent dating life.

I'd dated over the years, of course. I'd even had a steady relationship in college that had lasted for a few months. But then Nana had gotten sick, and I'd moved back to Winter Garden. The guy and I had planned to stay in touch, but the long-distance thing didn't really work out all that well for us. He finally called me and told me he was seeing someone else. It stung my pride, sure, but when I realized I didn't care as much as I should have, it underscored how little the relationship had meant to either of us.

And now here was Deputy Ryan Hall. I wondered what his story was . . . whether or not we could date once Lou Lou Holman's killer had been caught. Or should I say *if* Lou Lou's killer was caught? What if he . . . or she . . . wasn't caught? The murder would remain an open case, and there would be a cloud of suspicion over my head from now on.

I got out of the shower, slipped on a terry robe, and wrapped my hair in a towel.

I couldn't let myself think that Lou Lou's killer wouldn't be caught. If her murderer went free, my reputation here in Winter Garden—as well as the reputation of the Down South Café—would be ruined. I sighed. I had to believe that everything would work out fine.

Stan had gotten so defensive. I remembered his asking me, "Are you calling my daddy a coward?" He'd looked furious . . . like he could kill me. If Lou Lou had belittled Sherman to Stan, it might've been just enough reason to push him over the edge. He could very well have struck her out of anger without intending to kill her.

I took down the towel, spritzed a styling spray onto my hair, ran a wide-tooth comb through it, and began blowing it dry. Thank goodness, it was beginning to look normal.

On the other hand, that might've been the reason Stan came to Winter Garden in the first place, to get revenge on Lou Lou for allowing her father to run Sherman out of town. I decided to call Ryan and talk my theory over with him.

I thought I heard something in the hall and switched off the dryer. I listened for a second, didn't hear anything else, and finished drying my hair. I ran my hands through it. It felt smooth and soft and free of gunk.

I heard a crash. This time I was positive it wasn't my imagination. And judging from the chill that ran down my spine, I didn't think it was one of the animals either.

Chapter 23

I tightened the belt to my robe and stepped out of the bathroom. My bedroom looked as I'd left it. The bed was made, the decorative pillows were as I usually placed them, and there was only a slight indentation on the bedspread where I'd sat to take off my shoes.

I eased into the hallway and looked into the kitchen. I gasped. Stan Wheeler was sitting at my table drinking a bottle of water.

He looked up and smiled humorlessly. "Sorry if I scared you."

"W-well, you s-sure did. What . . . what're you doing here, Stan?" My eyes darted around the kitchen. I saw that Stan had placed a chair in front of the doggie door so Rory couldn't come inside.

He followed my gaze. "The dog was outside when I came in. I thought it best that he stay out there."

"I see." My mind scrambled for some means of escape. "You know, Ryan—the deputy—is on his way over. I have a date with him this evening."

"We'd better get this over with, then."

"G-get what over with?"

"You've already made your mind up that I'm the one who killed Lou Lou. I mean, you've been digging around in my past, asking me all these questions . . . even calling my dad up in Pulaski and getting him all bent out of shape."

"N-no, I don't have any idea who killed Lou Lou . . . b-but I'm leaning toward Pete."

He nodded toward the chair opposite him. "Sit down."

"I . . . need to get ready . . . for my date."

"We both know that's a load of bull. Sit down."

I slumped onto the chair across from Stan. At least, maybe I could figure out a way to get out of the house . . . run screaming to a neighbor's. The man had broken into my house and had all but practically confessed to killing Lou Lou. There was no way he was planning to let me leave.

"Why do you say I've made up my mind that you killed Lou Lou?" I said. "Did you?"

He nodded. "Didn't mean to. I was out in the rain trying to patch that stupid roof, and I flew mad and left to go see her. When I drove by the Joint, I saw her van still there. I went in to have it out with her. And I took my hammer with me because I felt like she had something that belonged to me."

A hammer. "And I guess you did have it out with her."

"I sure did." He lifted his bottle and took a drink, keeping his eyes on me while he did so. "I told that woman what I thought . . . about everything. She and her family had treated my daddy like dirt. Dad told me there was a secret compartment in the wall behind the desk. He'd heard that bank robbery story, and he'd seen Lou putting something in there once." He brought the hand that had been on his lap onto the table. In it, he clutched a claw hammer. "I took this hammer so I could get it."

I gulped. "Why didn't you get into the secret compartment, then?"

"We were arguing, and I told Lou Lou she wasn't going to treat me the way she'd done my daddy and that I intended to have what was coming to me. I raised up the hammer and started toward the wall behind the desk. Lou Lou said that was Pete's money. She was saving it for him. Well, I thought it should go to Daddy's other son."

"Why would she save the money for Pete?"

"Because the guy's lousy with money, and she knew it. When I shoved her out of the way so I could bust through the wall, she went to screaming and grabbed the phone. I knew she was going to call the police. So I hit her."

"Was the one blow all it took?" I asked.

"Yeah. I'm stronger than I look."

I clasped my hands together, desperately needing something to hold on to. "You could say it was self-defense, Stan. I'll back you up."

"How're you going to back me up?" he asked. "You weren't there."

"I know, but anyone could see how you . . . well, y-you had to defend yourself. Everybody in Winter Garden knows Lou Lou was a bully. They wouldn't be surprised if you told them she pulled a gun or a knife on you or something."

"I appreciate the thought, but I believe I'd be better off going with my own idea."

I gulped and dreaded for him to continue.

"After I left here a while ago, I knew it was only a matter of time before the police would come knocking," Stan said. "You'd found out too much about my past and my family's history with the Holmans. I thought a better story would be if you confessed to killing Lou Lou and then killed yourself."

"I had no reason to murder Lou Lou," I pointed out.

"Sure you did. You wanted the Joint, and she wouldn't sell it to you. You picked up the nearest thing you could find—this hammer—and struck out in a fit of rage. But, lately, your conscience has gotten the best of you, and you can't live with the guilt."

I shook my head. "Nobody'll buy that, Stan, and you . . . you'll go to prison for two murders. At least, you can try to pass off Lou Lou's death as something that happened in self-defense . . . or in the heat of the moment."

"You only want to *think* no one will buy that story, sweetie pie. Everyone knows you wanted Lou Lou to sell you the Joint and that she didn't want to. Pete was trying to talk her into it, but it's not likely he'd have been able to. Plus, you're the one who found her."

"Stan, I . . . I've told people about your connection to the Holmans and that you're Pete's half brother."

"It doesn't matter. You're getting ready to write a confession."

"No, I'm not."

"Yes, you are." He placed the hammer on the table, stood, and took a pistol from the waistband of his jeans.

"I'm not. I . . . I guess you'll have to shoot me without

the confession." The sound of my heartbeat was filling my ears.

Stan leveled the gun at me.

I made a whimpering sound, but I refused to break down or scream or beg. I was still thinking there might be a way I could get out of this.

Hedging my bets, I stood, pushing the table up and against Stan as hard as I could. He cursed as I spun around and ran back to my bedroom. I slammed the door, locked it, and climbed out the window. I heard him smashing through the door. I ran toward the street. I wondered how close Stan was to me, but I didn't dare look. I'd seen enough horror movies to know that when the girl looks back to see where her attacker is, she trips and falls and then gets cut to bits. Or, in my case, shot.

I'd just got to the road when headlights blinded me. I waved my arms to flag down the truck.

It was Roger and Jackie!

"Get me out of here!" I cried. "Stan's trying to kill me!"

As I leapt into the truck beside Jackie, Stan ran up beside the porch and began shooting at us.

Roger said a few choice words as we sped toward the police station.

The police apprehended Stan between my house and the trailer Stan had been renting from Lou Lou. I guessed he was going to grab whatever he could from his home and leave town.

Luckily for me, I'd sent that embarrassing selfie to Jackie. She saw a shadow at my bedroom window in the photo. She tried to call me right after that, but I was in the shower. She convinced Roger that they should leave their dinner in Bristol and come to check on me. Good thing she did.

Pete was devastated to learn the story behind Stan and his father. He refused to go talk with Stan, but he did drive up to Pulaski to meet Sherman Harding. Pete also bought his truck, and Chris Anne's brother became his partner.

Sheriff Billings traced the money that had been hidden in the wall and discovered that it was the money that had been stolen from the bank in North Carolina all those years ago. Grady might've wanted to paint himself as a hero to his family—or maybe that had all been Ms. Carter's doing—but he hadn't given the money back. Still, he and Bo had fallen out over the money and had never reconciled. That was a shame.

Epilogue

It was a beautiful day—the last day of June, in fact—when we had the ribbon-cutting ceremony for the Down South Café. Aunt Bess was there in a yellow dress and a big blue hat. I wasn't sure if she thought she was going to the café's grand opening or to the Kentucky Derby, but she'd said she wanted to match the decor.

Mom was there. She wore the same outfit that Jackie, Roger, Homer, the café staff, and I wore—blue jeans with a Down South Café T-shirt. The construction crew had taken their lunch break during the ceremony. Sarah's boyfriend had even skipped class so he could be at the grand opening with her. Billy brought his wife. Pete and Chris Anne stopped by. Dilly and several of the regulars from Lou's Joint had come by to help us celebrate.

We'd invited everyone we could think of, including the media. Ms. Peggy was there to personally do a front-page write-up on the café. Her photographer was snapping pictures left and right, and I was afraid we might all go blind from the flash. And there was a news crew from the local television station.

I was glad to see Sheriff Billings put in an appearance. And, of course, I was glad that Ryan was with him.

I gave a brief speech before cutting the yellow ribbon in front of the door of the café. I told guests about Nana and how much I appreciated her love, kindness, and generosity, and I got choked up. I thanked Mom, Aunt Bess, Roger, Jackie, and Sarah for their support, and I shed a tear or two. And I told Homer, the café staff, and the construction crew how grateful I was for their hard work. And then I welcomed everyone to the Down South Café before I really began crying in earnest.

Jackie, Mom, and I had set out a buffet along the counter so the guests could help themselves to lunch. I made sure the dishes were both familiar and diverse. We served potato salad, baked tomatoes with hazelnut bread crumbs, macaroni salad, roasted portobellos, beef and vegetable kebabs, fried chicken, biscuits, garlic herb bread twists, three-bean salad, mocha cake, and caramel apple pie. Our beverages were sweet tea, coffee, water, and pomegranate punch.

I proudly watched everyone go through the line. I felt someone beside me, and I turned to see Ryan there.

I smiled. "Hi."

"Hi," he said, returning my smile. "The place looks fantastic."

"Thank you. We—especially Roger and his crew—put a lot of work into it."

"Don't downplay your role. I was here on more than one occasion when you were covered in dust or paint or—"

"Panic." I laughed. "And you even saw me with giant hair. You're right. I did my part in making all this come together."

"And in crime solving."

I was glad he didn't say the actual words "solving Lou Lou's murder" out loud. I doubted anyone was paying attention to us, but I certainly didn't want to run the risk of reminding people of what was bound to be right beneath the surface anyway.

"Sheriff Billings would probably hire you on if you're interested," Ryan continued with a grin.

"I think I've got plenty to keep me busy right here."

He took a small clear bag out of his shirt pocket. Inside was the necklace Nana had given me and that I'd lost in Lou Lou's office so long ago. "As promised."

My eyes welled with tears for the umpteenth time. "Thank you."

Ryan took the necklace from the bag and held it up. "May I?"

I turned and held up my hair so he could fasten the necklace around my neck. I could practically feel Nana smiling down at me, proud of what I'd been able to accomplish.

Author's Note

When Amy shudders suddenly at the funeral home, she thinks, *Somebody just walked over my grave.* This saying originated in the eighteenth century from an English folk legend that stated an unexpected cold sensation was brought about when someone walked over the place where one was eventually to be buried.

*Recipes from
the Down South Café*

Grandmother's Meat Loaf

Yield: 8 servings

1½ pounds ground beef
2 eggs
2 cups bread crumbs
¾ cup diced onions
1 tablespoon salt
⅛ teaspoon pepper
½ cup cracker crumbs
1 cup tomato juice

Preheat oven to 325 degrees F. Mix all ingredients except tomato juice well. Add tomato juice gradually, making mixture solid enough to handle. Form into a loaf. Bake in a loaf pan for 45 minutes.

Granny's Oatmeal Pie

(Contributed by Suzie Welker)

Yield: 10–12 servings

1 pie crust (Directions for pie crust below.)
4 large brown eggs
1 cup sugar
2 tablespoons flour
1 teaspoon ground cinnamon (You can take
    cinnamon sticks and grind them yourself for
    a better-tasting pie.)
¼ teaspoon salt
1 cup light corn syrup (Do not use dark.)
¼ cup softened butter (I use only butter, never
    margarine. Soften by leaving out of fridge about
    an hour; do not put into mixture hot/boiling,
    as this will cook the eggs, creating a
    bad-tasting pie.)
1 teaspoon vanilla
1 cup quick-cooking oatmeal, uncooked

Preheat oven to 350 for metal pan or 325 for glass.

Beat eggs until frothy. Sift sugar, flour, cinnamon, and salt in a small bowl. The sifting mixes the dry ingredients together for a better blend. Add eggs to the dry mixture. Stir well. Mix corn syrup, butter, and vanilla in a separate bowl. Add to the first mixture. Slowly mix in oatmeal. Stir 2–3 minutes to ensure even distribution of oatmeal.

Pour into pie crust and bake for 45 minutes.

(Optional diced apples, raisins, or cranberries can be added for additional flavor. If adding apples, use 1 cup, diced very small; 1½ cups if using cranberries or raisins. I prefer the golden raisins but any can be used.)

PIE CRUST

1¼ cups all-purpose flour (Do not use self-rising.)
¼ teaspoon salt
½ cup butter cut into small squares (cold, not warm/softened)
¼ cup cold water

Mix flour and salt then sift. Using a pastry cutter (a pastry cutter is best, but you can use your hands), cut in the butter until the dough resembles coarse crumbles. Slowly add ¼ cup water, 1 tablespoon at a time.

Roll into a ball and chill in freezer for 1 hour. After 1 hour, take out and roll out using a heavy rolling pin. Place in metal or glass pie dish, then crimp edges with fingers or mash down with a small fork.

Baked Cinnamon and
Sugar Doughnuts

(Contributed by Jessica Potts of http://ahappyfooddance.com/)

*Yield: 12–15 regular-sized doughnuts
or about 30 minidoughnuts*

DOUGHNUTS

1 tablespoon baking powder
½ teaspoon salt
1½ cups all-purpose flour
1 egg
½ cup milk
1 teaspoon vanilla
5 tablespoons butter, softened
½ cup sugar

TOPPING

½ cup butter, melted
1 cup sugar
1 teaspoon cinnamon

Preheat oven to 350 degrees.

Lightly oil a doughnut pan.

In a medium bowl, combine baking powder, salt, and flour. Set aside.

In another bowl, add egg, milk, and vanilla and beat mixture lightly. Set aside.

In the bowl of a stand mixer, cream together the butter and sugar.

Add the wet ingredients in two parts, alternating with the dry ingredients, and finish by beating until everything is just combined.

Transfer the dough to a piping bag or a large plastic baggie with the tip cut off. Pipe into the doughnut pan, filling only halfway full.

Bake for 10–12 minutes, or until a toothpick inserted comes out clean.

Remove from the oven and transfer to a wire rack, allowing to cool just enough to handle.

While the doughnuts are baking, melt the ½ cup butter. In another bowl mix the cinnamon and sugar together for the topping,

To cover the doughnuts, dip each doughnut in the butter and then roll in the cinnamon-and-sugar mixture.

Country Ham with Redeye Gravy

(Contributed by Robin Coxon)

Yield: 2 servings

2 slices country ham (¼ inch thick)
2 tablespoons butter
½ cup strong brewed black coffee
⅓ cup water

In a large cast-iron skillet, fry the ham in butter over medium heat until lightly browned. Remove ham to a platter. Add the coffee and water to the skillet. Boil until reduced by about half, scraping up browned bits in the bottom of the pan. Pour gravy over the ham and serve with grits, biscuits, and eggs.

Preacher Cookies

Yield: 18–36 cookies, depending on size

2 cups sugar
1 stick butter
½ cup cream
2½ cups quick oatmeal
¾ cup peanut butter
1 teaspoon vanilla

For chocolate cookies, add one tablespoon of cocoa.

Mix and boil for 1½ minutes. Spread into greased pan.
Refrigerate.

Jeanne Robertson's
7-Up Pound Cake

*(Contributed by humorist Jeanne Robertson—
http://www.jeannerobertson.com)*

*Can be frozen until someone you know is sick . . . or
has "passed." Jeanne's secret notes in italics.*

2 sticks margarine
¼ cup shortening
3 cups sugar
1½ teaspoons lemon extract *(Give or take a little.)*
1½ teaspoons vanilla extract *(Sometimes Jeanne
    pours in more.)*
5 eggs
3 cups all-purpose flour—measure before sifting
7 ounces 7-Up *(Jeanne uses Diet 7-Up to cut
    calories.)*

Preheat oven to 300 degrees.

Cream margarine, shortening, and sugar. *(Put under
kitchen light until soft. Beat with a mixer.)*

Add lemon and vanilla extracts. *(Add now so you won't
forget. Cake tastes funny without 'em. Beat some more.)*

Add eggs one at a time. *(I throw all of them in at the
same time. First, take off shells.)*

Alternate adding flour and 7-Up, beating after each
addition. Finish with 7-Up. *(I don't alternate. Dump it all
in. Go for it! Turn mixer to highest level. Stand back. Add*

more 7-Up if it looks dry. Sprinkle in more flour if it looks too moist. This is not rocket science.)

Spray 10-inch tube pan with Baker's Joy. *(No need to flour. Important! Be generous. Trust me. Or split the batter and use two 8-inch tube pans. This will give you two cakes. Math.)*

Cook at 300 degrees for one hour or until it "tests done." *(To test, poke a knife or broom straw in and out of cake until nothing sticks. Note: It takes longer to cook one big cake than two smaller ones. Higher math. Think about it. Adapt.)*

Take whatever you cook out of the oven—let it sit for 30 minutes before flipping over on a plate. *(Flip the cake. Not you. Waiting a lot longer will require a chiseling step. It gets ugly.)*

Do you have a recipe you'd like to submit for an upcoming book? Email the author (gayle@gayletrent.com) for more information.

Love Gayle Leeson's Down South Café mysteries?
Read on for a sample of the first book in
Amanda Lee's Embroidery Mystery series!

The Quick and the Thread

is available from Obsidian wherever books are sold.

Just after crossing over . . . under . . . through . . . the covered bridge, I could see it. Barely. I could make out the top of it, and that was enough at the moment to make me set aside the troubling grammatical conundrum of whether one passes over, under, or through a covered bridge.

"There it is," I told Angus, an Irish wolfhound who was riding shotgun. "There's our sign!"

He woofed, which could mean anything from "I gotta pee" to "Yay!" I went with "Yay!"

"Me, too! I'm so excited."

I was closer to the store now and could really see the sign. I pointed. "See, Angus?" My voice was barely above a whisper. "Our sign."

THE SEVEN-YEAR STITCH.

I had named the shop the Seven-Year Stitch for three reasons. One, it's an embroidery specialty shop. Two, I'm a huge fan of classic movies. And three, it actually took me seven years to turn my dream of owning an embroidery shop into a reality.

Once upon a time, in a funky-cool land called San Francisco, I was an accountant. Not a funky-cool job, believe me, especially for a funky-cool girl like me, Marcy Singer. I had a corner cubicle near a window. You'd think the window would be a good thing, but it looked out upon a vacant building that grew more dilapidated by the day. Maybe by the hour. It was majorly depressing. One year, a coworker gave me a cactus for my birthday. I set it in that window, and it died. I told you it was depressing.

Still, my job wasn't that bad. I can't say I truly enjoyed it, but I am good with numbers and the work was tolerable. Then I got the call from Sadie. Not *a* call, mind you; *the* call.

"Hey, Marce. Are you sitting down?" Sadie had said.

"Sadie, I'm always sitting down. I keep a stationary bike frame and pedal it under my desk so my leg muscles won't atrophy."

"Good. The hardware store next to me just went out of business."

"And this is good because you hate the hardware guy?"

She'd given me an exasperated huff. "No, silly. It's good because the space is for lease. I've already called the landlord, and he's giving you the opportunity to snatch it up before anyone else does."

Sadie is an entrepreneur. She and her husband, Blake, own MacKenzies' Mochas, a charming coffee shop on the Oregon coast. She thinks everyone—or, at least,

Marcy Singer—should also own a charming shop on the Oregon coast.

"Wait, wait, wait," I'd said. "You expect me to come up there to Quaint City, Oregon—"

"Tallulah Falls, thank you very much."

"—and set up shop? Just like that?"

"Yes! It's not like you're happy there or like you're on some big five-year career plan."

"Thanks for reminding me."

"And you've not had a boyfriend or even a date for more than a year now. I could still strangle David when I think of how he broke your heart."

"Once again, thank you for the painful reminder."

"So what's keeping you there? This is your chance to open up the embroidery shop you used to talk about all the time in college."

"But what do I know about actually running a business?"

Sadie had huffed. "You can't tell me you've been keeping companies' books all these years without having picked up some pointers about how to—and how not to—run a business."

"You've got a point there. But what about Angus?"

"Marce, he will *love* it here! He can come to work with you every day, run up and down the beach. . . . Isn't that better than the situation he has now?"

I swallowed a lump of guilt the size of my fist.

"You're right, Sadie," I'd admitted. "A change will do us both good."

That had been three months ago. Now I was a resident of Tallulah Falls, Oregon, and today was the grand opening of the Seven-Year Stitch.

A cool, salty breeze off the ocean ruffled my hair as I hopped out of the bright red Jeep I'd bought to traipse up and down the coast.

Angus followed me out of the Jeep and trotted beside me up the river-rock steps to the walk that connected all the shops on this side of the street. The shops on the other side of the street were set up in a similar manner, with river-rock steps leading up to walks containing bits of shells and colorful rocks for aesthetic appeal. A narrow, two-lane road divided the shops, and black wrought-iron lampposts and benches added to the inviting community feel. A large clock tower sat in the middle of the town square, pulling everything together and somehow reminding us all of the preciousness of time. Tallulah Falls billed itself as the friendliest town on the Oregon coast, and so far, I had no reason to doubt that claim.

I unlocked the door and flipped the CLOSED sign to OPEN before turning to survey the shop. It was as if I were seeing it for the first time. And, in a way, I was. I'd been here until nearly midnight last night, putting the finishing touches on everything. This was my first look at the finished project. Like all my finished projects, I tried to view it objectively. But, like all my finished projects, I looked upon this one as a cherished child.

The floor was black-and-white tile, laid out like a gleaming chessboard. All my wood accents were maple. On the floor to my left, I had maple bins holding cross-stitch threads and yarns. When a customer first came in the door, she would see the cross-stitch threads. They started in white and went through shades of ecru, pink, red, orange, yellow, green, blue, purple, gray, and black. The yarns were organized the same way on the opposite side. Perle flosses, embroidery hoops, needles, and cross-stitch kits hung on maple-trimmed corkboard over the bins. On the other side of the corkboard—the side with the yarn—there were knitting needles, crochet hooks, tapestry needles, and needlepoint kits.

The walls were covered by shelves where I displayed pattern books, dolls with dresses I'd designed and embroidered, and framed samplers. I had some dolls for those who liked to sew and embroider outfits (like me), as well as for those who enjoy knitting and crocheting doll clothes.

Standing near the cash register was my life-size mannequin, who bore a striking resemblance to Marilyn Monroe, especially since I put a short curly blond wig on her and did her makeup. I even gave her a mole . . . er, beauty mark. I called her Jill. I was going to name her after Marilyn's character in *The Seven Year Itch*, but she didn't have a name. Can you believe that—a main character with no name? She was simply billed as "The Girl."

To the right of the door was the sitting area. As much as I loved to play with the amazing materials displayed all over the store, the sitting area was my favorite place in the shop. Two navy overstuffed sofas faced each other across an oval maple coffee table. The table sat on a navy, red, and white braided rug. There were red club chairs with matching ottomans near either end of the coffee table, and candlewick pillows with lace borders scattered over both the sofas. I made those, too—the pillows, not the sofas.

The bell over the door jingled, and I turned to see Sadie walking in with a travel coffee mug.

I smiled. "Is that what I think it is?"

"It is, if you think it's a nonfat vanilla latte with a hint of cinnamon." She handed me the mug. "Welcome to the neighborhood."

"Thanks. You're the best." The steaming mug felt good in my hands. I looked back over the store. "It looks good, doesn't it?"

"It looks fantastic. You've outdone yourself." She cocked her head. "Is that what you're wearing tonight?"

Happily married for the past five years, Sadie was always eager to play matchmaker for me. I hid a smile and held the hem of my vintage tee as if it were a dress. "You don't think Snoopy's Joe Cool is appropriate for the grand opening party?"

Sadie closed her eyes.

"I have a supercute dress for tonight," I said with a laugh, "and Mr. O'Ruff will be sporting a black tie for the momentous event."

Angus wagged his tail at the sound of his surname.

"Marce, you and that *pony*." Sadie scratched Angus behind the ears.

"He's a proud boy. Aren't you, Angus?"

Angus barked his agreement, and Sadie chuckled.

"I'm proud, too . . . of both of you." She grinned. "I'd better get back over to Blake. I'll be back to check on you again in a while."

Though we're the same age and had been roommates in college, Sadie clucked over me like a mother hen. It was sweet, but I could do without the fix-ups. Some of these guys she'd tried to foist on me . . . I have no idea where she got them—mainly because I was afraid to ask.

I went over to the counter and placed my big yellow

purse and floral tote bag on the bottom shelf before finally taking a sip of my latte.

"That's yummy, Angus. It's nice to have a friend who owns a coffee shop, isn't it?"

Angus lay down on the large bed I'd put behind the counter for him.

"That's a good idea," I told him. "Rest up. We've got a big day and an even bigger night ahead of us."

About the Author

Gayle Leeson lives in Virginia with her family, which includes a dog who adores her and a cat who can take her or leave her. She includes the meat loaf recipe in this book that her grandmother Marilyn Hicks taught her to make. For Gayle, a sandwich made with this meat loaf, fresh bread, and yellow mustard is a sentimental culinary delight.

Leeson, who is a native Virginian, also writes as Amanda Lee (the Embroidery Mystery series), Gayle Trent, and G. V. Trent. Please visit Leeson online at gayleleeson.com, gayletrent.com, on Facebook (facebook.com/gayletrentandamandalee), on Twitter (twitter.com/gayletrent), and on Pinterest (pinterest.com/gayletrent).